BOUND AND DECEASED

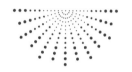

BOUND AND DECEASED

A TAYLOR QUINN QUILT SHOP MYSTERY

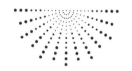

TESS ROTHERY

CHAPTER ONE

$\mathcal{N}$ovember rain battered the sides of the little house on Love Street. Taylor Quinn snuggled deep into her quilt. Her bedroom window was shut to the warring weather and her door was barred with the dresser she had dragged in front of it before turning out her light.

She'd managed to get her heart rate to settle down with the aid of her mother's soothing voice on the phone.

If there was one comfort left in life, it was that Laura Quinn had recorded so many episodes of her YouTube show before her death almost nine months ago.

Some nights were better than others.

Some nights Taylor didn't think of the murderer who had attacked her in the kitchen of her own home.

But most nights she did.

It was already midnight.

She needed to shut off her phone and go to sleep.

She missed sleeping.

She missed closing her eyes and the world turning off.

With her baby sister Belle living on campus now, Taylor's mind never turned off, and neither did her phone. What if Belle needed her? She was only sixteen and that school was full of older guys who liked to drink.

Taylor gave her phone screen a quick, embarrassed kiss and closed YouTube. It was a little painful to turn her mom's videos off, as though watching them would make up for all of the times she hadn't returned her calls or hadn't gone home for a visit.

The phone buzzed a text just as she was setting it on her side table.

Her heart twisted at the sound.

Had the worst happened? She grabbed it up and stared at the picture attached to the phone number.

It was a face she hadn't seen in months, though she still thought about him every day. A picture she didn't want to see. She froze, overwhelmed with anger and hope and dread all at once.

"*I drove all night. I'm here. Can I see you?*" Clay Seldon, the ex-boyfriend.

"*What?*" That single word response was all Taylor could muster. She sat up and hunched forward, not really trusting her senses.

After the initial shock of her mom's death had passed, Taylor had been left to face everything else she had lost when she moved back to her hometown to finish raising her teenage sister: her home in the city, her career, and her boyfriend of four years.

"*There aren't any hotels in this town and I'm in the cloth top Rabbit. Please let me in out of the cold.*"

It was a horribly wet night, but not all that cold, not hurts-you-cold. This was a mild November. Constantly damp, but not freezing. Clay could sleep in his car just fine or he could drive home again, the same way he had come. He could even warm up with a coffee from the twenty-four hour Arco to keep awake.

And yet, her heart nudged her to let him in, to help ease the fear and loneliness of this new life she lived, at least for a night.

She would have given anything for her mother's wisdom right now. She navigated away from the texts that stood there like little temptations and opened the Flour Sax Quilt Shop YouTube channel again.

The smiling, warm, and loving face of her mother was practically begging to be listened to. Not that she needed the video. Her mom's voice was in her head right now, telling her she needed to learn to be content with her own company.

Taylor turned to the video she had just watched.

Laura Quinn the famous quilter, teaching the audience how to pin the corners of their quilt blocks so they match.

Over and over she showed them dozens of wrong ways, and the one right way. As she worked, she said, "Spending time with practice squares will save you tons of heartache once you're working on a real quilt. It's soothing, too, in its own way. Contemplative, even. When my eldest daughter was little, I used to make her do this. She wasn't much for playing by herself and it drove her to distraction, but I made her do it. 'Taylor Rae Quinn...' I'd say..."

Taylor backed up the video and listened to her mom give this advice again. And again. Be comfortable with her own company.

Someday she'd be comfortable alone again.

She turned her phone off and set it on the bedside table.

She took a deep, cleansing breath and reached up to the ceiling, stretching the muscles of her shoulders and back.

Grandpa Ernie was just downstairs.

She wasn't alone.

The doorbell rang.

Taylor collapsed, shoulders curving forward, arms wrapping around her abdomen. She shivered.

It was just Clay.

It was just Clay.

It wasn't a maniac who had stolen his phone and used it to find her.

This wasn't a reasonable fear, but cold sweat broke out on her forehead.

She knew it was what they called traumatic stress response.

Because of the fight she'd had with the woman who'd killed her mother, she panicked at unexpected midnight visitors. And loud noises. And people who popped by in the daytime, or who said "Hi!" too loudly when she didn't see them coming.

Her phone buzzed, rattling on the old wooden nightstand.

She picked it up with a shaking hand, turned it over, and swiped it open.

The text was a photo of Clay's face, pouting. He stood on her front doorstep, the streetlight casting a gray-green haze on the road behind him.

She whacked the phone screen with her thumbs, angry texting as her heart raced. *"Did Lila kick you out?"*

"No. Please forgive me."

"Not by text"

"Then please let me in so I can drop to my knees and beg for your forgiveness."

She wondered if he had been drinking. This wasn't his usual style.

She wanted to slap his soft, goofy face till her hand stung.

She wanted to wrap her arms around him and kiss him and feel safe again. To not be alone.

"Lila was just a roommate. I swear."

She wanted him to quit texting.

She wanted the comfort of his presence because she was scared, and she was scared because she was the adult in the family now. The person responsible for an elderly grandfather and a teenage sister, and also because she had almost been killed in the room directly beneath her.

Taylor sat up and stiffened her spine. Now was not the time to be scared. Now was the time to be strong.

With a shaking finger, she sent one more text. *"Go home. If you really cared about me, you'd have called first and made a plan."*

"But I don't make plans, you know that."

She turned off her text alerts. Clay's bad planning was not her problem. She shoved her phone in the drawer of the side table, lay down, and pulled the comforting, well-worn, Dove-in-the-Window quilt back over her head. She would sleep tonight if it was the last thing she did.

☙

"Hey." Clay Seldon. The voice Taylor Quinn was most familiar with in the world, was right behind her. "I couldn't go home last night. Not without seeing you first. Please say you'll forgive me. I was wrong for not coming back to Comfort with you. So, so, so, wrong."

Taylor held her breath, counted to ten, then turned.

Clay's rusty-plaid button down was rumpled, and so was his light-brown hair. His face showed a bit of scruff, but Taylor knew it was on purpose. He couldn't grow that much beard in a week, much less overnight.

He scratched at his chin. "Let me buy you breakfast. Or coffee, or something, so we can talk."

"I have a busy day."

"Lunch then. Anything. I won't leave until I can convince you how sorry I am." Slowly he reached his hand to her, wrapped it around her waist, and pulled her to him. Their mouths met with ease, and he kissed her.

Taylor allowed it because it was familiar and because she wasn't sure she didn't want him.

She put her hand on his chest and pushed him away. "Breakfast. Now. My day is too busy after this." Maybe it was the kiss. Maybe it was those puppy dog eyes. Maybe it was both. Taylor just knew she wanted him at least for breakfast.

Maybe he was sorry. Maybe he could make it all right again.

You never know.

· · ·

Reuben's Diner was quiet at six in the morning. The kitchen was going strong, though, and the mingled aroma of bacon and coffee woke Taylor Quinn's appetite.

Belle's best buddy Cooper sat at a far booth with his mom Sissy and an older lady Taylor didn't recognize. She looked like Sissy, though, like they could be family. Same round, smiling face. Same gap in the two front teeth. But where Sissy was a tall, imposing woman, this lady was a sweet looking butterball.

Taylor was distracted. She hadn't expected the woman who judged her most harshly to be there for her reunion with Clay. Or the boy most likely to text Belle about what was happening.

Belle was firmly on #teamhudson even though Taylor swore up and down that wasn't a thing.

"Tay, where are you?" Clay nudged her gently in the side with his elbow. "Let's get a booth."

"What? Yes." They got a booth. Taylor sat with her back to the Dorney family.

The server came, one of the many Ruben's nieces and nephews, Aviva, a sporty brunette who worked before school. Aviva was another who might text Belle to tell her about the stranger Taylor was eating with this morning. And of course, showing up at this hour with a man implied they had spent the night together. Taylor dragged her hand through her hair in frustration and pulled it back into a ponytail. "You are terrible about making plans."

"I know. I know. But if I had called first, would it have helped? It's much harder to turn down a surprise."

"Like when you showed up homeless on my doorstep so many years ago?"

He grinned. "And look how well that turned out? Those were four happy years."

"But it didn't end well."

"I know you can't understand just yet, but you were asking too much of me. Leave my home, my work, my everything? It didn't make sense."

"It wasn't an ultimatum, though." Taylor stopped.

Aviva was back with their coffee and looked like she was very interested in their conversation. She set the mugs and little steel bowl filled with plastic containers of creamer on the table.

Taylor smiled at her stiffly, and she went away.

"How was it not an ultimatum? You didn't give me any time to find a place to live." Clay's crooked smile and big gray eyes were hard to argue with. He was as guileless as a puppy.

"You couldn't have just moved in with your parents while you were looking for somewhere to stay?"

His shoulders dropped. "Come on. You know I couldn't. With my parents? We aren't like you and your family. It's not comfortable there."

"I would hardly call my mom dying 'comfortable.'"

"Now you're misunderstanding on purpose."

"It took you nine months to change your mind." Taylor peeled open the little tub of creamer. For nine months Clay Seldon, who she had once hoped to marry, had been living with another woman instead of her.

"I never changed my mind about you. I have loved you since the day I met you. But yeah, it took me a long time to realize I couldn't live without you, and that whatever sacrifices I needed to make would be worth it."

"Please tell me you haven't quit your job." She wrapped her hands around the coffee, welcoming the warmth on the fall morning that was only getting colder.

He looked down at his mug and then back up with a sheepish grin. "No. But I did take two weeks off."

"Hedging your bets." Taylor cringed.

"Make up your mind. Which is it you want? I'll quit my job this second if you tell me to." He set his phone on the table. "I'll do it. Lila will ship my clothes and I'll never go back to Portland again."

"Calm down. Don't do anything stupid."

"Too late. I let you go. That was the stupidest thing I have ever done." His voice went deep and a little loud.

"Now you're putting on a show and I can promise you the Dorney family back there does not care." She didn't turn around, but she could feel Sissy's nosy eyes burning holes in the back of her head. How long would it take for the story of Taylor Quinn's new man to spread through the little town?

He lowered his voice again and reached his hand across the table. "In the years you've known me, I've done a lot of stupid stuff." He blushed. "You remember? How about when I walked out on my white-collar office job to help my buddy open his own computer repair shop?"

"Yes, that was stupid." If he was aiming for sympathy points, he was missing. That little act of compassion had cost their savings a good deal of money.

"And then I had the genius idea to take up mountain biking."

"Mountain biking isn't as dangerous as you managed to make it." She was determined not to laugh, but it was difficult.

"Both legs in casts. Two-story townhouse. I mean, that was stupid."

"Indeed. You're really selling me on you right now." Clay had been such a dope in his two casts, stuck in the townhouse. But he had been a good patient, not demanding. Entertaining. Fond memories flooded her of their life in that little townhouse.

"But the stupidest thing I ever did was let you go."

Taylor pushed her mug away, putting it between his outstretched hand and hers. "You didn't let me go away. I was needed here and you refused to stick with me."

"That's not how I remember it."

"Of course not. Gaslighting me, yet again."

Clay flexed his jaw. "Come on Tay, I'm not a bad guy. When have I ever tried to manipulate you, control you, or done anything other than support you?"

Taylor stared at him, her mouth slightly open.

"I mean besides this one really bad time that I made the worst decision of my life..." His voice trailed off.

A crash of plates jerked Taylor's attention to the group at the booth behind her. Aviva was waving a menu at the rosy faced lady who was eating with the Dorney's.

"Knock that off and call 911." Sissy Dorney's voice carried through the restaurant.

"Sorry! Yes! Sorry!" Aviva dropped the menu and scuttled back toward the kitchen.

"I've got it, Mom," Cooper out-spoke his mom, trying to get her attention. "I've already called. Let's lay her down."

"Are you crazy? You want her to choke on her vomit?" Sissy had the loudest voice Taylor had ever heard.

"This isn't exactly the atmosphere I was hoping for." Clay said.

"I think something a little more important is going on." Taylor stood to see if she could help, but the sound of sirens announced the ambulance had already arrived. Taylor sat back down to keep out of the way.

The few people eating at the café were eerily silent as the paramedics took the pale, unconscious woman out of the restaurant.

Sissy held her guest's hand as she was rushed into the ambulance.

Cooper was on his mom's heels but paused at Taylor's table and mouthed "help."

"I wonder what that was about." Clay's face lacked sincerity for the first time that morning. It shocked Taylor, yet again, to see how much he meant what he had been saying to her about his regret.

"I'd like to know as well, but I have to get back to work. Have a safe drive home." Taylor waved down the waitress.

"Woah, woah. Did you see that?" Aviva answered the summons to Taylor's booth and leaned heavily on the table.

"We couldn't have missed it." Clay didn't sound amused.

"She barfed. Right there." Aviva waved the folder with the check in it at the back table. "Not a lot, but still really gross." She locked her big brown eyes on Taylor's. "If she dies, will they say I poisoned her?"

Taylor shrugged and reached for the folder.

"Because I served her. And I don't think Uncle Gil would poison anyone and he's in the kitchen this morning."

"I doubt she was poisoned," Clay said.

Aviva turned to him, eyes narrowed. "You have a lot of experience with poison? Because I have a lot of experience with Reuben's and nobody has ever done that before."

"I'm sure no one will think you did it." Taylor tried for the folder again, but Aviva held it tight in her hand, and rested her hand on her hip.

"Then Sissy? Or Cooper? Someone's in big trouble if she dies."

Taylor slid a five onto the table for her coffee and a tip. "Cancel my order. I have to get back to work." She left Clay to handle Aviva.

Taylor was in no mood for a panicked teenager or a possible murder. She was totally over that phase of her life.

CHAPTER TWO

*R*oxy met Taylor at the worktable in the middle of the store. She stood in front of her big bin of hats, hoping that Taylor would wear a fun costume for the YouTube show. She wore a pincushion-like hat made of bright primary colored quilters cotton. It tilted at a jaunty angle, the long hat pins with pearlescent tips popping from it like real sewing pins. "Morning. Who ran off in that ambulance?"

Flour Sax Quilt Shop was on the same side of Main Street as Reuben's Diner and the ambulance, siren blaring, must have caught Roxy's eye as she came to work.

"A friend of Sissy Dorney's. They were eating breakfast when she fell ill or something." Taylor shrugged out of her puffy, charcoal colored, nylon winter coat and dropped her purse next to the worktable with a thump.

"And who was that man you were kissing?" Roxy managed to ask the loaded question with a calm and casual voice, though her eyes sparkled.

"You were up early." Taylor began to rifle through her purse, though she didn't really need anything it contained.

"A friend from out of town?"

"Clay." Taylor stared into her purse, not sure how to continue the subterfuge.

"This would be Clay you lived with in Portland?"

"Yes. That Clay." She snapped the purse shut and toted it to her desk behind the stairs. What was she supposed to do about Clay?

Roxy followed, her sensible sneakers silent on the rose-colored indoor-outdoor carpet. "Do you want to talk about it?"

"Yes." Taylor pressed both of her hands on the desk.

"Does your mom have any wisdom in her videos?"

Taylor chuckled. "I wouldn't be surprised, but you have wisdom too."

"Gosh." Roxy blushed lightly, just a touch of pink across her cheekbones. "I'm hardly a relationship expert." She was around ten years older than Taylor, maybe a little more. She had a teenage son. That son had a father who wasn't in the picture, but Taylor hadn't asked why. Maybe Roxy wasn't a relationship expert, but she sure seemed to have her head on her shoulders.

Taylor gave a surreptitious glance in Roxy's direction. The silly hat made her smile. Despite the issues of underemployment in a small town combined with raising a kid alone, Roxy had never lost her verve for life. She was small, hindered by a limp Taylor had also never asked about, and a consistent encourager. If not Roxy, then who could Taylor look to for help?

The door of the shop rattled before Taylor could answer her own question.

There, under the glowering clouds, clad in a woolen Burberry shawl and a crisp little hat stood Grandma Quinny. Taylor's father had passed away when she was only eleven, but Grandma and Grandpa Quinny had been a constant support in her life. Always there, always with a little more "help" than Taylor actually needed.

She was mouthing something dramatically, so Taylor let her in.

Before speaking, Grandma Quinny unwrapped herself, shook

her shawl, and hung it on a coat rack that stood to the right of the door. Then she gave Taylor a kiss on both cheeks, took her shoulders in her hands, and kissed her forehead too. "Darling."

Taylor gave her a quick squeeze. "We're just about to start filming, Grandma Quinny. Want to grab a seat and watch? I haven't made coffee yet."

"I have." Roxy piped up from where she was adjusting the camera on the tripod.

"Not right now. We need to have a discussion."

Taylor gave her wrist a dramatic look to show Grandma Quinny that time was of the essence, but she wasn't actually wearing a watch, so the point may have been lost.

"Sit down." Grandma Quinny pulled a slipper chair away from the wall where she was standing.

Taylor sat. It had been that kind of day already, and it was only eight in the morning.

"Your grandfather and I are going away."

"Good for you." Taylor smiled. A vacation, while nice, didn't seem like it needed such a dramatic announcement.

Grandma Quinny fluttered her hand as though to brush away Taylor's words.

"We'll be gone for six months and we need someone to stay at the farm and take care of things."

"I can ask around for you, but I still feel a little disconnected from the town." Taylor's gut knew what her grandmother was about to say, but she recoiled defensively.

"You, darling. We want you."

"What about...."

"You know we adore Ernie like our own brother."

"He wouldn't be comfortable staying somewhere different when he could be at home."

"That is why this is the perfect time for you to settle him in at the Bible Creek Care Home. And don't remind me that he's not Methodist. We know that."

Taylor scratched her forehead. "That's not why I've been

hesitating."

"We know that, as well, so don't forget we have the money for you. The little life insurance from your father."

Not so long ago, Taylor had learned her grandparents had taken a life insurance policy out on their son, because he had been a fire fighter. They had been holding on to the funds for her for around sixteen years, waiting for her to need it.

"It's not the money either."

Grandma Quinny pulled another chair to the middle of the store and sat on it. "It's not going to be easy, but it is the kindest thing to do. The sooner he moves, the sooner he gets accustomed to it."

Grandpa Ernie was struggling with his memory. Dementia. Though Taylor hadn't taken him to the doctor to find out what kind, or if it was something worse.

Roxy brought them two mugs of coffee.

"Thanks." Taylor accepted it with a smile.

Roxy stood behind the worktable spreading out production notes for their day's filming. "Your mom and I used to talk about this a lot."

Grandma Quinny lifted an eyebrow.

"She was scared," Roxy said. "You are too."

"True," Taylor agreed. It was easy to agree with Roxy.

Grandma reached for Taylor's hand and squeezed it. "Life is full of scary things Taylor, but they still need to be done. I'm taking Ernie and Ellery out for lunch today over at the Care Home. They have a lovely dining room and make all the old favorites. I plan on doing this once a week till we leave. It will help, I promise."

"But I like living with him." Taylor bit her lip.

Grandma squeezed her hand again. "I know. It's terrible to be alone, but you can't give him all the care he needs. And it's not your job."

"No, it's Ellery's job. That's what I pay her for." Taylor squared her shoulders. Getting her medical-minded cousin as day-help for Grandpa had been exactly the solution she had needed. Grandma Quinny had helped arrange it all and it was perfect. There was literally no need to change anything about their lives at home now.

Grandma Quinny smiled one of those knowing smiles.

Taylor sighed.

"Ellery has been working to improve her grades to get into nursing school."

"Yeah, I know. She passed her math class. But we've talked and I still have some time."

"You don't have forever, love. That's all I'm saying." Grandma Quinny stood. "I'll let you go, but I would like you to find some time to meet with me again. I need to give you instructions for farm-sitting and we need to talk to the sales office at Bible Creek Care Home." She wrapped herself back up in the soft woolen shawl and left.

Taylor lay her head on the table.

"A lot of life is like this." Roxy pulled several hats from her box. "Very few decisions end up being free will. Circumstances make them for us. Or sometimes rich grandparents with generous hearts do."

"I know I need to move Grandpa somewhere better for him, but I can't yet. I just want one Christmas with all of us at home."

Roxy passed her a camel trilby with a patchwork band. "How about this one?"

Taylor had agreed to try Roxy's cute hats again. She lacked some of her mom's natural on-camera sparkle. "This is good." The patchwork band matched the colors Taylor would be working with. If they were on their game today, which Taylor was definitely not, she'd be showing tricks for faking wedding ring blocks. She exhaled.

"It's a good lesson. It will get lots of hits. It's an iconic quilt," Roxy murmured encouragement while Taylor set out the tools and fabric she'd need.

"It's painfully ironic."

15

"Why?" Roxy shut her bin of hats and stowed it behind the register counter.

"Because this is the day Clay came home."

"How does that change anything?" Roxy asked. "The life you shared with Clay existed no matter what city he happens to be in at the moment."

Taylor tossed her hands up and gave her a slightly pained smile. "Okay, okay. Let's just film. I've had all I can take of heart stretching stuff today."

FILMING WAS ROCKY, but they made it. Interviews for part time help were rocky, too, but time passed anyway, and Taylor's mind was not completely obsessed with the fact that her ex was roaming the town at this very moment.

In fact, all three interviewees were highly qualified and motivated students from Comfort College of Art and Craft, the delightful little private school in town Taylor had graduated from. They had seemed smarter and more talented than she was, but at least worrying about which one would make her feel the least insufficient to run the store was a distraction from thinking about Clay Seldon. Having too many good candidates was a good problem to have.

The bad problem, the one Taylor wanted to face even less than she wanted to see Clay again, was what mood Grandpa Ernie might be in when she came home. Last time Taylor had suggested taking him to Bible Creek Care Home for lunch, he had refused in no uncertain terms and gotten quite angry about her interference in his life. He had gone so far as to say that Taylor couldn't kick him out of his home, but he could certainly kick her out of it.

But maybe with Grandma Quinny and Ellery along for the ride, it would be different.

She made her way slowly back to their little house on Love

Street, close enough to the shop to walk, even in the cold drizzle of a late November afternoon.

At home, Grandpa was asleep in his recliner.

"How'd it go?" Taylor whispered to Ellery as she put away her messenger bag full of work stuff.

"Good." Ellery gave Grandpa a fond look. "Lunch was good. He and Grandma are funny together. Lots of old memories."

"Yeah, they both grew up here." Taylor wandered slowly into the kitchen.

"Wasn't Grandpa Quinny from the city?" Ellery wrapped herself in a thick creamy alpaca wool cardigan that went to her knees.

"He was from Bend. It wasn't much of a city when he was a kid."

"Well, anyway. They're funny together. They get to telling stories and laughing. We sat with some other old guy at lunch that used to buy suits from Ernie." Many moons before the family ran Flour Sax Quilt Shop, Ernie Baker had been a tailor, and had run his business from that space on Main Street. He and his wife Delma had raised their daughter in the apartment above his shop.

"Buster Creedy?"

"Yeah, that was him."

"Good, he always liked Buster. Did Buster have good things to say about living there?"

Ellery shook her head. "I'm sure he thought he was just being funny, but he ran the place down pretty hard."

"Shoot."

"Grandma was fuming." Ellery chuckled, so Taylor did too.

"What are we going to do?" Taylor poured herself a glass of water and sat down.

"Don't let her make you rush. Ernie and I are doing fine. Your mom hasn't even been gone a year yet."

"And Belle's only been at school a couple of months." Taylor sipped the cold water, then drank the whole thing. Water. She needed more of it. Her mind seemed to clear when she was well hydrated.

Ellery glanced at her phone, like Taylor had done at her wrist when Grandma barged into the shop.

"See you tomorrow." Taylor sighed. She liked Ellery, but the poor girl had been there all day. She didn't need to sit around listening to Taylor moan all evening.

Ellery grinned. "Yup. See you tomorrow." Her trip home wasn't a long one either, and she would ride her e-scooter back, even in the rain. Taylor hadn't known her cousin Ellery all that well till she had become Grandpa's main caregiver, but she liked her. Calm and even tempered. Taylor wished she could keep Ellery forever, but the kid had dreams, and that was probably a good thing.

All of the Quinn girls had that spark of ambition. None of them really wanted to take the easiest route in life. Taylor was about to indulge in a little moment of self-pity regarding her own abandoned dreams when a knock on the kitchen door interrupted her.

The now familiar face of Belle's friend Cooper Dorney filled the kitchen window. Someone stood behind him, but she had a hood on obscuring her face.

Taylor let them in. "What's up?"

Cooper's face was white, and he had a jumpy nervous energy.

The person with him was Aviva, their waitress from this morning.

They skittered into the kitchen like someone was chasing them.

"She's dead." Cooper pulled out a chair.

Aviva fell into it, her lanky limbs limp like a rag doll.

Taylor filled the kettle with water. "Who's dead? The woman from this morning, I'm sure, but who exactly is she?"

"My mom's aunt Reynette."

"I'm so sorry. Your mom must be devastated." Taylor dug

through the cupboards looking for cookies or crackers. She managed to scrounge an unopened box of Ritz and a jar of Nutella. She put them on the table with a butter knife and a stack of napkins. "Is there something I can do to help?"

"You've got to find out who killed her." Aviva spoke in that breathless, frayed voice popular with young women who love drama.

The piercing whistle of the kettle gave Taylor time to process what she'd just heard. Find out who killed Cooper's mom's aunt?

That was crazy.

She wasn't a detective and trying to find out who had killed her mother had led to a show down in this kitchen that still kept her up at nights. And it had cost her a close relationship with her childhood best friend Maddie.

Maddie's wild idea to use amateur detective work as grief therapy had gone wrong right away, leaving ice between the two women. Why on earth would Taylor put herself through that again? Especially for someone like Sissy Dorney who she barely knew and who barely liked her?

Taylor brought the kettle and three mugs to the table. "This must be really hard for all of you right now."

"She was alive at the hospital and they took blood samples to see what was wrong. They came back positive for salicylate overdose," Cooper said.

"That's aspirin poisoning," Aviva clarified, then helped herself to a cracker and hazelnut spread.

"The results came back too late to save her. They were just telling us how they treat it when she died. It was all really fast and horrible."

"Your mom must be beside herself." Taylor felt like she was a record, skipping, but she didn't know what else to say. Death was horrid. Horrible. Awful. She didn't want to get any nearer to death than she needed to be.

"She's in shock," Aviva said. "It's going to be really hard

19

when it hits."

"What about the rest of Reynette's family? Are they in the area?"

"They're in shock," Aviva said.

"They just moved to town." Cooper held his mug in both hands, though it was still empty. "Her husband and her, anyway. She got a job teaching at Comfort College of Art and Craft."

"But aspirin overdose, I mean, that's hardly murder is it?" Taylor pictured the round-faced gentle looking woman she had seen so briefly. Reynette had seemed healthy, not like someone with a drug problem. And aspirin? That was hardly opioids or some other kind of heavy drug. "What has her husband said?"

"I told you, he's in shock." Aviva sounded impatient.

Taylor filled a mug for Aviva and shoved some tea bags her direction.

"They're talking to the doctors and to the funeral directors. Everyone takes aspirin. Her husband didn't know why she would have taken so much to make her sick like that, but she has something called sciatica, I think they said. So, the hospital assumes she was taking too much because of the pain."

"I think you have your answers." Taylor leaned back on the kitchen counter.

Murder was important and young people, these two were just high schoolers, liked to feel important even when it also felt awful. She remembered the feeling, and though she sympathized with them, she didn't want to play into it. She wanted to sort them out and send them on their way.

"No." Cooper's chin quivered. He looked so young, like he couldn't grow a mustache if they paid him, and so small for a junior in high school. "Her husband swears there's no aspirin in their whole house. Says she only ever used Tiger Balm. Only. Listen." He straightened up, an attempt to look like he wasn't about to start crying. "If she was poisoned, they are going to think my mom did it because we were the ones with her in the morning."

"That's…" Taylor was about to say crazy, but she couldn't. He was just a kid. He needed a safe adult to talk to and had picked her. Her heart warmed a little. "That's just not believable to anyone who knows your mom."

"You've got to help us find out what happened. Mom's going to try, but she doesn't know what she's doing. Please. Come home with us tonight and talk to her."

"I can't do that, Cooper. I have to be here to take care of Grandpa Ernie." His rough snoring could just be heard from the other room.

"Tomorrow then?"

Taylor wanted to bundle both of these half-grown people into quilts and set them in front of the TV with comfort food. She wanted to keep them there at the house till they felt all better, but that wasn't the same thing as being able to give them what they were asking for. "I've got work. I can't just skip a day."

"If they don't lay the blame on Sissy, they'll pin it on my Uncle Gil. They'll say he poisoned the food."

Gil Reuben, the head cook at the family diner, was even less likely to have killed Sissy's aunt than Sissy was. He couldn't even have known her. Taylor ran her hands through her hair and thought hard. Aviva and Cooper were feeding off each other's fear, but they were still scared. Someone ought to do something for them.

Aviva leaned in and whispered, "She didn't have any symptoms till she came to the restaurant. She drank one cup of coffee and then puked everywhere and then just…died." Had Aviva realized how much more dramatic the childlike whisper of fear was, she would never have turned to trendy vocal fray again.

Cooper was typing something on his phone, his eyebrows drawn together in concentration.

"Listen guys, I totally hear you. I can see why you're scared, but you can trust the police, okay?" Taylor's phone rang before she could say anything further. Belle's number was on the screen, so she answered it. "Yes?"

"And hello to you too." Belle's generally warm, well-loved voice was hard to hear. Cell service in Comfort wasn't fantastic. "Please help Cooper. He's terrified and you can do it."

"Did he just text you to make you call me?"

"Maybe he did. But what does it matter? You can help them. I know you can. You just need to meet people and ask questions. People tell you things."

"And they attack me with flashlight-guns." The woman who had killed her mother had attempted to kill her as well, with a unique and tricky weapon.

"You can stand up for yourself. Cooper and Aviva are just kids."

Taylor walked away from the table and dropped her voice. As much as she felt for the teens in her kitchen, she didn't want to relive what she had just gone through. "I don't have time for this. It's busy at the shop."

"You're hiring someone. Hire two someones and pay yourself less. You know you don't need the money right now. You've got free room and board with Grandpa."

"You are insane."

"I'm a genius, and you know it." This was true, but as far as Taylor was concerned, it didn't matter.

"What am I supposed to do?"

"Just go meet Sissy. Hang out with her. Help her. She's going to try and solve this herself and she's nowhere near as canny as you are."

"Belle…"

"Gotta go. Have study group tonight. Love you." Belle ended the call.

"Please?" Cooper asked. "For Belle."

Taylor stared at her baby sister's friends. Still at home finishing high school while Belle was off at college. She had never really had a choice. They knew she would help them. "I'll meet your mom tomorrow, but I'm not making any promises.

CHAPTER THREE

*W*hen Taylor arrived at the Dorney's house the next day at noon, she was met by a roomful of people. She wasn't usually shy, but it was a surprise to see so many faces. It knocked the little monologue she had been practicing right out of her mouth.

"Coffee?" Sissy was already laden with a mug of hot coffee when she opened the door. She wore a black smock, her name embroidered on the right-hand side. Her curly hair was tamed into waves and pinned back, something vintage about it pleased Taylor. She didn't have her sensible shoes on yet, but she looked like she was about to head out for a day's work at her salon rather than embark on an amateur detective scheme.

"Thank you." Taylor stepped in. She could see all the way into the great room from the entry, and it was crowded.

"Cooper told us you wanted to come over and offer some assistance." Sissy handed her the huge handmade ceramic mug and ushered her into the room with the crowd. "I wasn't sure what you thought you could offer, but he reminded me of how you single handedly caught your mother's killer, so I guess it won't hurt."

Taylor stood front and center in the room.

Sissy and four others waited with expectant looks on their faces. The nearest to her was an older man with a head full of thick gray hair and a pair of round, wire-rimmed glasses. He wore a ratty mustard colored cardigan sweater over a faded plaid shirt and had a slight hunch. He gave the impression of wisdom, but Taylor could have been reading too much into the glasses and sweater. Next to him, patting his leg, was a woman who looked about her age, but was possibly older. She had a head of dyed blonde hair styled in a shaggy lob. Her outfit looked expensive as did her diamond earrings. Taylor didn't know if they were real or not, but the well-fitted cut of her wool jacket made her think the diamonds could be real.

Another lady in her late twenties or early thirties sat in a recliner. Her face was blotchy from crying. Though she was slender, her round full face matched the glimpse Taylor'd had of the deceased. This could be a daughter. A man stood behind her, medium height, sandy hair. Nondescript in a way that made Taylor think she would have a hard time picking him out of a crowd, even if she had a picture. If she were an old-fashioned TV detective, those four would be her main suspects. But this was real life, and she had a feeling they were just the bereaved family.

"Well?" The rich looking lady next to the old man spoke with a firm voice. "Aren't you going to pitch your services?"

Taylor looked behind her for a chair. She was absolutely not going to stand there and "pitch her services."

Mercifully there was a small leather-like foot stool against the wall. She took a few stumbling steps backward and sat on it, being careful not to spill her coffee. "No, I'm not."

"I told Cooper you wouldn't be any help." Sissy sighed with disappointment and sat on a second foot stool.

"So did I," Taylor agreed. "He thought you'd need support, but it looks like you have plenty."

The round-faced woman dropped her face into her hands for a moment, shoulders shaking with silent sobs. Taylor remembered that kind of crying. She was definitely the daughter of the deceased.

"I'm really sorry for your loss, though. And I guess if there's something you need...maybe food for the funeral? I don't know. I'm happy to help if I can."

"Food? Cooper said you were a detective," the nondescript man said. "What kind of detective brings funeral food?"

"She's not a detective. She just works in a store," Sissy said.

The nondescript man just stared at Taylor.

"Flour Sax Quilt Shop." She sipped her coffee, growing more uncomfortable as the moments passed.

"Oh! Reynette loved Flour Sax." The expensive lady had removed her hand from the old man's knee and was leaning forward, chin resting on her fist. "Your mother was Laura Quinn then, wasn't she?"

"Yes."

"Reynette loved her YouTube channel as well. Your mom was a very talented lady."

"Thank you. Did Reynette quilt?" Taylor was fascinated by the rich lady and her interactions with the older man. They were close in a way that was not fatherly, but, at the same time, it seemed like he hardly noticed her or her affectionate touches.

"Sort of," the expensive lady said with a chuckle.

"Excuse me?" The crying lady interjected. "Gracie, you know very well my mother was an acclaimed quilter. That's why they hired her at the college."

"She was. I know. She was very talented. It's just not quilt shop quilting, you know? More like fiber arts, I guess."

"Yes, the college would like that," Taylor agreed. "I have a degree in fiber arts from Comfort College."

"Reynette was self-taught. Almost a quilting savant." Gracie smiled at the round-faced lady like she was giving in a little.

Taylor's own smile went a little tight. Not that there couldn't be quilting savants, but in her heart, Taylor knew this was an art form that was of women, for women, and by women. It belonged to the people, open to everyone. It wasn't ever meant to be an art that only special geniuses could participate in. She'd always hated the elitism that had developed in a craft form that came from need.

Taylor glanced at the round-faced woman and the little lecture died in her heart. This wasn't about her, her opinions on the art form, or even quilting.

"You see," the crackling voice of the elderly man started slowly, "Reynette was a dealer in vintage items and began to use these things to create her art. She was at the forefront of an important movement, which is why the school was so interested in her."

"It sounds wonderful." Taylor did not say that quilting with scrap fabric had long been the point of quilting. Or that recycling clothing was also a part of quilting's rich history. If this man wanted to think Reynette had invented it, what did it hurt?

"You all are talking like my mother has been dead forever." The round-faced woman shot an angry look from her wet eyes at the expensive young lady. "It's been less than twenty-four hours. She's not even at the funeral home yet."

"I'm sorry, Fawn," the old man spoke. "I'm in shock." His voice was tired. He was probably right about his shock, which would explain both the rich lady's hovering concern and the way he didn't seem to notice it.

The expensive young woman—Gracie. Taylor took a minute to try and pin her name on her—put her hand on his knee again and patted it. "And you were such newlyweds still."

Fawn, the round-faced woman's mouth puckered. "I still don't understand why you did that. We wanted to have a nice wedding for you."

"Oh, Fawn, what does it matter now? They got to be married, isn't that what's important?" Gracie scooted just a little closer to the older man.

Fawn's face crumpled.

The nondescript man patted Fawn's shoulder. "Hold up, if

you can. Just till we talk to the police."

Fawn reached for the hand on her shoulder and gripped it tightly. "Oh, Monty. If only I could trust them."

"There's no need for hysterics." Sissy had been silent through much of this. "Monty, why don't you and Fawn go for a walk and collect yourselves. You had a long drive down here. I'd like to talk to Taylor a little more before she goes." She turned to Taylor and lifted an eyebrow.

"I think I'd rather just lie down." Still holding Monty's hand, Fawn stood. Together they went upstairs.

After they were gone, Sissy turned a stern look to the expensive looking woman. "Gracie, you are not helping anything. I can't understand why you are here at all."

She sat up very straight. "Reynette was Una's stepmother. This loss affects our daughter." She squeezed the old man's hand. "Therefore, it affects me."

Taylor shuddered, but tried to hide it. So the old man and Gracie had a daughter together. That explained much, including the creepy feeling she was getting.

"You and me both." Sissy acknowledged Taylor's involuntary reaction. "I've never heard of such a thing, a trophy wife like you showing up when her ex is grieving. Unless you're just here to get him back." She looked the man up and down like a piece of meat she didn't find appetizing.

"I hardly think my husband would approve of that," Gracie smirked.

"Gracie introduced Reynette and I," the crackly voiced man in question spoke again. "Gracie and Fawn had been friends in college. She knew both of us."

"Oh Art, we don't need to get into all of this." Gracie's voice was soothing as though she were trying to comfort a sad child.

"If this was a murder," Taylor said softly, "we might need to discuss quite a few uncomfortable things." Yes, it was ugly curiosity that made her say it, but at this point Taylor was dying for the tea.

"Gracie was a student of mine almost fifteen years ago, at University of Oregon. I was a widower and she was a breath of fresh air. We married too quickly, though, and she was too young."

"Oh, I was too young. And I was a terrible wife back then. But you stuck by me, didn't you? I didn't deserve you, darling." She picked his hand up and kissed the back of it. "You think he's handsome now," she smiled softly at his pale, thin, lined face, "you should have seen him when he was forty-five. He took my breath away. It's not as bad as it sounds, I was twenty-one after all."

Taylor didn't dare catch Sissy's eye. From her perspective, that was exactly as bad as it sounded. "How long were you married?"

"Ten years," Art said. "We tried to make it work for our little one, but it didn't."

"And who broke it off?" Taylor asked again.

"It was mutual," Art sighed heavily as though it were an old story he was tired of telling.

"Please." Sissy rolled her eyes.

"Art, you don't have to take blame that isn't yours. I was an awful wife and ran off with my current husband."

"You say that Gracie introduced you to Reynette?" This was the dynamic that really interested Taylor.

"They have—had—such similar personalities," Gracie said. "She was gentle and wise and loved knowledge and learning. I'd met her several times in college. Fawn and I weren't best friends or anything, but we'd kept in touch. I went to their resale shop about a year ago to pick up this gorgeous vintage Givenchy I'd seen online. We got to talking and, before I knew it, I was telling her I knew someone she just had to meet.

At that, Art patted Gracie's knee. "Reynette was a special woman," he said. "I never thought I'd meet someone like her, not after my wife passed. Someone as brilliant, and passionate. A rare gem of a woman."

"It's okay." Gracie caught Taylor's eye. "I was a trophy wife. A hot little co-ed. I knew what I was when I married him. That's why I knew what he really longed for was a woman of substance, even if she was a bit more substantial than I am." She sat up a little, better showing off her tiny waist.

"That's unkind," Art said.

Gracie shrugged. "Everyone has their strengths, Art." Her words bit a little and Taylor thought maybe their split hadn't been as amicable as they were pretending.

"Did you see each other long before you married?" Taylor asked.

"It took a long time to finally get them together. The distance was a problem at first," Gracie said.

Art didn't seem to appreciate her telling his story and gave her knee a firmer sort of pat.

Sissy winced. She and Taylor exchanged another glance. Had that gentle looking man just slapped his ex-wife's leg?

"We met five months ago and married last week."

"Last week!" Taylor's shock was impossible to hide.

"Yes. We didn't want a fuss and wanted to move here for her job right away. I'm retired from the university and have been for quite some time. My son lives here as well, so it all seemed to fit together ."

"And your daughter?" Taylor asked.

A moment of confusion passed his face. Then recognition and a slight blush. "Yes, Gracie doesn't live far from here. She and Guy and Una are only about an hour away in Neskowin."

"At the coast then?"

"Yes, Guy owns a surf shop," Art said.

Sissy sniffed derisively.

Taylor wondered about Gracie's diamond earrings. A retired professor on the one hand and a surf shop owner on the chilly Oregon coast on the other didn't add up to well-cut suits and diamond earrings, at least not with her math.

"Art, we may have worn you out." Sissy got up and extended her hand. "Can I refill your coffee?"

He gave up his mug. "I think I need some lunch."

"The two coffee shops on main street both have nice sandwiches." Taylor didn't feel right suggesting the diner where his wife had died.

"Thanks." He stood and offered his arm to Gracie. She accepted.

He was less stooped as he walked. Standing, he looked less—old. Sixty wasn't that old, after all, but he had a thin pale face which ages a person. He and Gracie still made a strikingly handsome couple, even with his silver hair. Taylor expected their child, Una, was a beauty.

When they had left with a click of the front door, Sissy sighed heavily. "It's just a mess, isn't it?"

"Yes." Taylor leaned against the wall. "Cooper says Reynette was your aunt."

"She was, but she wasn't much older than me and we had always been close. When I was little and she was a teen, she'd sit me. I was so happy she accepted the job and moved here. I was the one who told her about the job and I was the one who told the school about her." Her own eyes filled with tears. "It's my fault she's dead."

"Oh! No. No, Sissy. It's not." Taylor meant it, but she didn't have smooth, convincing words.

Sissy patted her eyes with the heel of her hands and shrugged away the accidental grief that had escaped. "I told Cooper not to bother you, but I admit, I got my hopes up when you called. We've just got to catch whoever killed my best friend. And yes, I do think it had to be one of them." She stared at the couch where the widower and his ex-wife had been practically cuddling moments before. "Please, just help. I know you're not a professional, but it will be so much better than trying to do it alone."

CHAPTER FOUR

*CW*hile everything about Art's life seemed iffy to her at first glance, Taylor wasn't convinced Reynette's death was murder. The lab results were clear; she had died of aspirin poisoning, to use laymen's terms. With her diabetes, the stress of the overdose had destroyed her already compromised kidneys.

Taylor didn't make Sissy any promises, but she did think hard about the situation as she finished her day at the quilt shop. Reynette had rushed into marriage and uprooted her life for a new job. Maybe she'd realized she had made a huge mistake but was the kind of woman who couldn't accept failure. Suicide wasn't totally unreasonable.

The day dragged on and Taylor longed to be home with Grandpa Ernie, just hanging out. She missed his presence in the recliner at the back of the shop. She knew just sitting there all day, snoozing or watching TV, wasn't the best for him, but on midweek days like this when the shop was quiet and she was all alone, she just missed his company. No one truly loves chain retail work, but Taylor also missed the regular bustle of her job managing a Joann Fabric and Craft. She missed having employees to schedule and train and big shipments to handle and a class schedule to maintain. She drummed the end of her disappearing ink fabric pen on the worktable. She needed to get some classes going. Flour Sax had classroom space. She dreamed of seeing the other quilt shops make a big weekend event together. It had been done before and deemed too much work for the return on investment, but that was before they had someone with advertising experience. She hated that she sounded like she was tooting her own horn, but the other three quilt shops were run by quilters, not by MBAs. No, that sounded even worse. She'd have to work on her pitch for the guild. If they could tie the event in with something happening at the college, it would be even better. There was no reason besides being a bit off the beaten track that their town didn't go full Sisters (Oregon) and have a real presence in the quilt world. Taylor went back to stitching her sample block. The YouTube show was a demanding master and she was constantly planning content for it.

She had six sample blocks of a spool pattern layered and basted like miniature quilts. She would use it to teach tying a quilt, so the knots were little puffballs, how to hand quilt a design, and how to machine quilt, stitch in the ditch style. She was working on the finished blocks now and would do the samples for the camera. The work wasn't groundbreaking, but the data Belle had shared at their last meeting showed the channel was getting a lot of hits on basic instruction videos. The ad revenue was back up. Not as high as while her mom was living, but enough to show that Taylor needed to keep things going.

It was closing time when the door jangled open. Taylor wasn't surprised to hear it, but was very glad when she looked up and saw only Roxy and a woman she didn't recognize. "Good afternoon." Taylor trusted her friend not to keep her in the shop after hours.

"Taylor, meet Hannah."

Hannah was tall, slender, and young. Her face was sort of soft, and formless with round patches of not-quite-the-right-pink blush on them. She was blonde in the eyelash-less way that brought to mind summer days in Scandinavia and trips to Ikea. That said, she stood with confidence, her shoulders squared and her smile brave as she handed a piece of paper to Taylor. "I wanted to bring you my resume. Roxy said you were hiring."

"Thanks." Taylor accepted the paper with a tilt of her head. She hadn't discussed the other interviews with Roxy yet, but was nervous. Would she be expected to hire her friend? It had been hard enough to try and pick from the three other good candidates. Comfort College of Art and Craft wasn't cheap, and those students needed work.

"I'll look this over and give you a call tomorrow." Taylor turned the resume upside down and set it on the table.

"Of course. I don't want to bother you while you're closing." Hannah's smile was relaxed and confident. Her clothes were high end, if a little worn down at the edges. A cotton knit sweater with a Ralph Lauren logo and corduroy pants that looked a couple of years out of style, but still a step up from jeans when job hunting.

"I've been doing interviews in the morning, would tomorrow work?"

"Of course, what time?"

"How about nine?"

"Thanks very much. I look forward to it."

The whole exchange was normal, comfortable. Hannah felt like the kind of girl who wouldn't go off the deep end if she didn't get the job. They shook hands and she left.

At the door Roxy paused and gave her a thumbs up. This Hannah could probably handle it if Taylor didn't hire her, but could Roxy?

Taylor locked the door behind them and read Hannah's resume.

Hannah Warner was a twenty-five-year-old with plenty of retail experience, most of it in tourist towns on the beach. Some of it at a surf shop in Neskowin, contact Guy Sauvage.

Interesting timing.

Taylor owed it to Roxy to interview Hannah, even if Taylor didn't hire her, but it didn't matter who Taylor owed. She was dying to know what had brought Hannah to town at the same time her old boss's wife's ex-husband's new wife had died unexpectedly.

Taylor laughed out loud at the string of adjectives needed to describe the relationship between this Hannah and the deceased, and yet, it couldn't be a coincidence, could it?

HANNAH WARNER WAS right on time. She was dressed in khaki slacks and a cream silk button down. Her shoes were sturdy, comfortable, and clean. She definitely knew how to represent a store like this one, and survive a long day working at it.

Taylor offered her coffee then led her to a stool at the worktable. "So, Hannah, what brings you to Comfort?" This seemed like a good way to start a casual interview and satisfy her curiosity about the ex-employee of Art's ex-wife at the same time.

Hannah pressed her lips together and furrowed her brows for a moment. "I'm trying to think of how to describe the chain of events without making it sound like I'm lying." She shook her head. "Can I just say I came for a job that didn't work out?"

"What happened with that job?" Taylor had been inclined to like Roxy's recommendation, but she'd definitely have to hear whatever this unbelievable story was.

"I was assistant to a lady who ran a successful vintage clothing online resale business, but she died unexpectedly."

"I'm so sorry." Taylor had brought along the notebook she was using to keep track of things related to Reynette's death. She opened it and hovered her pen tip over the page. "What happened?"

"You probably heard about it already." Hannah folded her

hands and rested them on her knee. "She died of kidney failure, something about too much aspirin, but I know she'd been struggling to get her diabetes under control all summer. It was type 1, so a bit less responsive to the old diet and exercise routine."

Taylor itched to write that down, but she needed Hannah to think the notes were related to her interview. "What were your responsibilities in this job?"

"Reynette—my old boss—had her hands in a million pies so I ran quite a few aspects of her online shop. I spent some time sourcing clothes, but most of the time I priced items, handled the online listings, and shipped the items out."

"Have you talked to her family about continuing the job?" This time, she could write without looking weird.

"She just passed away yesterday," Hannah said. "I am going to fulfill outstanding orders but have paused the ability to take new ones for the time. I don't want the family to have to worry about that store right now."

Taylor scratched some thoughts on her page. Why wouldn't this employee not just keep working? The family surely wouldn't appreciate having their business shut down without their consent. "You'll want to discuss this with them as soon as possible."

"You're right. I know. I will but it just seemed like they needed some time first."

"They'll want to know you have found new work." Taylor gave Hannah another long assessing look. Hannah was unruffled and put together. You'd never know from looking that her life plans had just come crumbling apart.

"I told Roxy all about the problem—how I wasn't sure they'd want to run the online store with Reynette gone—and she strongly urged me to come by and talk to you. I can afford to work part time for a little while, and then, if they want to continue with the online store, I could easily do both."

"I see." Taylor made a note, though it was more about the future of her own business with Hannah than about Reynette.

She didn't want to hire someone who needed full time income and benefits. But she wanted someone who could easily get all of that somewhere else. Who didn't? The ideal employee is always someone who could make much more money in a better job but isn't interested in doing so. Hannah seemed to fit that bill. "And how do you know Roxy?"

"She's one of our best customers, actually. She has a good eye for a deal and has nabbed some stuff for her son over the last couple of years. Single moms are savvy shoppers."

"Your resume is impressive."

Hannah laughed. "Very few people would look at that resume and say it impresses. A string of tourist town gift shops and a thrift store."

Taylor joined her in a little laugh. "Yeah, but you can imagine a PhD in economics isn't useful to me here." Taylor pushed the resume to the side. "How did you end up working for Reynette? She wasn't based at the beach, was she?"

"The thrift store I worked at wasn't at the coast—Reynette owned it." Hannah tapped the resume. "We actually developed the online store together."

Taylor pressed her lips together for a moment. "You might want to talk to a lawyer. If you developed the store together, and can prove it, you might have some business ownership rights to consider."

Hannah nodded. "There are a lot of things I probably ought to do. To be honest, the first thing that came to mind was rent. I have savings, I can make it a little while but not forever."

Taylor stood. "Hannah, I like what I see, and I don't want to make you wait unnecessarily. I'm going to call a couple of your references and get back to you as soon as I can."

Hannah stood as well. "I understand. Thank you for your time." She offered another firm confident handshake that seemed a mismatch for her soft-featured face. "I look forward to hearing from you."

Taylor locked up behind them and wrote as much as she

could remember in her notebook. As for the references, she was going to call the only one she really wanted to talk to, Guy Sauvage at the surf shop. And she didn't care about his opinion of Hannah. She could have the job. She was clearly qualified and it would be handy to have someone around who had inside knowledge on Reynette Woods and company.

GRANDPA ERNIE WAS AGITATED when Taylor got home that night. She tried to catch a few minutes with Ellery to see what had happened during the day, but he wasn't about to give her space. He even followed her to the porch.

They gave up and Taylor let her go, thankful Ellery was willing to be paid via Venmo, so he didn't have to know anything about it.

Taylor and Grandpa went back to the living room. "Grandpa what's bothering you?" The sun had set about an hour ago, and that was usually a trigger for a mood shift, but it just seemed worse today.

"Where's Belle?" He stood in the middle of their small living room, leaning on a wooden cane. He didn't usually walk with a cane, though Taylor was glad to see it. His shuffling step had gotten shufflier in the months since she'd been home.

"She's at school." Taylor scooted past him and into the kitchen. He shuffled after her. Ellery had taken to having an early supper with grandpa, usually soup and half a sandwich. But Taylor was starving and needed to find some kind of dinner.

"At this hour? She should have been home long ago. Seems like she's been running around like her mother. She stays in bed all morning and then never comes home at night. I don't see her anymore."

"She's away at college, Grandpa. That's why you don't see her." Taylor found a box of macaroni and considered it. Empty carbs were so filling but wouldn't do anything to sharpen her focus tonight. She wanted to focus.

"How's she in college? She's just a girl."

"I know. I'm surprised, too, but she's super smart."

"Don't know how. Her mother was no kind of genius."

"Now Grandpa, be nice. Mom was very smart." Taylor didn't bother to engage in a nature vs nurture argument, and how being adopted might have given her little sister a head start.

He huffed into his mustache. "Not your mom. *Her* mom. That Colleen character was a real twit."

"Ah." It hadn't occurred to her that Grandpa Ernie remembered who Belle's bio mom was, much less that he remembered her from her rough teen years.

"I never wanted that girl hanging around. Always out with the boys, but Delma said we were a good influence on her." He slowly took a seat at the kitchen table and grunted as he settled into the wooden chair. "I don't see how, but we used to be able to keep Belle out of trouble. I told your mom she'd have to be careful. Blood will tell."

That did it. Taylor needed comfort food more than focus. She filled a little pot with water and put it on to boil. "Belle's not running around wild, Grandpa. She's off at college. Maybe we can visit her this weekend."

"What did she want to go to college for? Isn't she going to run the shop?"

"I don't know what she's going to do, but with a smart brain like hers she can do anything."

"You went away to college and then ran off to the city. Belle should stay here and run the shop."

"But I'm here running the shop now."

He grunted again and furrowed his brow.

"I'd like it if she came back and worked with me too." Taylor was doing her darndest not to argue with him in the evening. She had done some reading online and knew it was useless, but it was hard to remember, when hanging out with him. He was in his eighties, but it didn't feel like that was old enough for this. Even after all these months, she wasn't used to it yet.

"She coming home for Thanksgiving at least?"

As their plans were still up in the air, Taylor couldn't answer that one. "Do you want some macaroni?"

"No. I want a steak. Why can't I ever have steak anymore? That girl that comes here always makes me eat soup and I don't want soup."

"I'll get you some steak tomorrow, Grandpa. I have the afternoon off."

"That's another thing," he said. "You take too many days off. When I ran that place, I worked six days a week. It was my job and I did it."

Taylor bit her tongue. She started most days at seven in the morning and ended at seven in the evening. She did work six days a week, and sometimes seven.

She and Roxy each took an afternoon off a week. Or sometimes more, when business was slow. For their mental health. As far as Taylor knew, this wasn't a big priority in the seventies when Grandpa had been tailoring men's suits from the storefront that would become Flour Sax quilts. But even with those afternoons off, she worked far more than the forty-hour work week adults pretended was normal.

The chair scraped on the linoleum floor and Grandpa stood slowly. "I'm going to my room." He headed out, leaving his cane resting on the edge of the table. His steps were slow, and careful. She watched as he navigated the slight threshold between the kitchen and the living room with a lump in her throat. He did need the help during the day, but even their little house was becoming hard for him to manage. He needed something better. But was that really a room in a nursing home? There were quite a few single-story new construction homes on the other side of town. Maybe it was time to sell this old place with its unevenly settled foundation, narrow doors, and unmodified bathrooms. She'd certainly like living in a new construction home better than this one, even though she had grown up here.

Taylor traced a strawberry on the kitchen wallpaper. All of her mom's heart and energy had gone into Flour Sax. Keeping her Grandma Delma's quilt shop dream alive had meant taking what she could get in her own home, and not worrying about updating or style. When they had moved in here many years ago, Taylor had been horrified by the wallpaper. But it was old enough now it was almost back in style.

John Hancock, the handsome banker she had met when she moved home had been pushing her to do something with the equity from the sale of her condo in Portland. Taylor needed to. Between that home and this one she could buy something in that new neighborhood out right.

While Hancock had been impressed with how Taylor handled setting up a trust for her sister, he was about done with her and her slowness regarding her own funds. He hated to see it just sitting there, not earning her anything.

John Hancock was another one Taylor had gone out with a few times. She liked him. He was smart and funny. He didn't seem any more interested in a long-term relationship than she was either.

There had been times when Hudson and Taylor had gone out and all she could think of was how much more fun she would have had with John. There was an underlying vibe when Taylor was with Hudson, that idea that he was waiting to pounce. Waiting for her to come around and decide he was "the one." Taylor had done that "he's the one" thing already in life and wasn't impressed.

As she pondered the idea of selling, moving, and grabbing a bite next week with John, her phone rang.

"Yes?" Taylor poured the noodles into the boiling water as she answered.

"So, what did you think?" Roxy asked. "She's good, isn't she?"

"It's a funny coincidence that she used to work for Reynette, don't you think?" Taylor asked.

Roxy laughed. "Coincidence? But Taylor, that's why I brought her to you! When I spotted her at the Tillamook Cheese Outlet next door to us, I almost fell over. We talked for five minutes and I learned she'd need work, so I dragged her in."

"She had her resume with her?"

"Yup, that was why she was at Tillamook. She was going up and down Main Street looking for anything. I pulled her in because I knew you might close up before she got there. Donna was in the Cheese Shop and you know what she's like once she gets talking,"

"I have one question." Taylor stirred her noodles. "If I hire her to help myself find out what happened to Reynette, will I also get a good employee?"

"Totally. She's great. I'd have suggested her even if you weren't on the case, so to speak."

"Awesome. I'll call Guy right now and then get back to Hannah in the morning."

"Thanks, Taylor. Can I just say you are a pleasure to work for?"

"Sure, say it as often as you like."

Roxy laughed and rang off.

Taylor took a few minutes to think of questions while she finished fixing her quickie dinner, then she called the number Hannah had listed for the surf shop on her resume.

CHAPTER FIVE

*G*uy Sauvage of Savage Surf returned her call early the next morning. "Taylor Quinn? This is Guy. You called about Hannah Warner, I think."

"Yes, thank you for getting back to me so quickly." Taylor was shrouded against the damp, chilly morning with an over-sized acid-washed-denim jacket that had been her mom's in the eighties as she traveled the short blocks from her little house to the shop where she and Roxy would look over the edits of some video they had filmed the week before.

"What do you want to know?" Guy's voice was deep with a hint of California in the vowels.

Taylor pictured him as tall, tan, and muscled despite running their surf shop in Neskowin, a cloudy, rainy city on the Oregon Coast that would rent as many wet suits as it did boards. "She's applying for a job with me. What is she like as an employee?"

"Good worker, good worker. I liked her. Smiles for the customers, keeps busy. Keeps the shop clean."

"There's a lot of math here at a quilt shop, do you think she can handle that?"

"Sure. She's smart enough."

"Is she trustworthy?"

"Yeah, man. She is."

Taylor was used to calling on folks for jobs at Joann's, where previous employers were most likely to just say "I confirm she worked for us and legally that's all I can say." Big companies seem to be like that—distant, concerned about their own liability. "Cool, cool. So, Comfort is a small town. Old fashioned, kind of. If she makes people mad outside of work hours, they won't shop here. Any risk of that?"

He laughed, a deep, almost sexy sound. Lucky Gracie. "Hannah? No way. She teaches Sunday School. You got churches there in town? That's where you'll find her."

"We've got a church." Taylor pressed her lips together and tried to think of ways to turn the conversation to Reynette. "In the interview she mentioned coming out here to continue a job with a lady who has recently died." Might as well just jump in, right?

"Yeah. Pretty tragic."

"Did she work for both of you at the same time? And if so, did she handle juggling two jobs well?"

"She left us to work for Reynette, the gal who died. Hannah's solid, I swear. Now that Reynette's gone, I wish Hannah would come back. I like that kid." There was a wistfulness in his voice that made Taylor wonder exactly how much he liked her.

"Hmmm. You make me think. Am I going to hire her and have her run back to you?"

"Hey man." He sounded irritated now. "I don't know how many ways I have to say this. I recommend her. Hannah is a good employee."

"Sure, sure. I appreciate your time, but I really need someone I can rely on. Would you say without hesitation that if I hire her, I won't regret it? Like, she didn't kill her old boss, did she?" Taylor didn't know where that question came from. It just popped out, but she liked it. Good shock value.

"Kill Reynette? You've got to be crazy. Who would ever kill

her? She's like the Nana you always wished you had. She was awesome. Seriously."

"Just, one last time, and I'm sorry if I'm annoying you. If I hire her and spend the time training her, you think she'll stick around, even though she's not from here and doesn't know anyone? You believe she'd be loyal to us?"

He laughed. "You're hardcore, aren't you? What kind of shop did you say this was? Like pot or something?"

Taylor laughed too, to mimic his mood, though she herself was on the edge of her seat. "No, no. We're a just a quilt shop."

"Hannah knows Art, Reynette's husband. She'll probably want to stick around just to be there for his sake."

"Hmmm, really? Like maybe she might be some…comfort… to this Art guy?" Taylor put a little extra sugar on the word comfort. She had no idea how she was doing as a detective, but this was sort of like a game, and she was enjoying it.

"Art and Hannah? Woah." Guy paused. "You know, she's kind of an old soul, and he does have a thing for younger ladies. If she does hook up with him, will you call me? I'd love to hear that story."

"Will do. Thanks for all the answers. I know this was kind of a lot. I just have to be sure I can trust my new employee."

"Because the quilt world is fierce?" He laughed again. "Next time you're on the coast, come by and say hi."

"Will do, Guy. Thanks again." Taylor hung up and considered this Hannah. She sounded too good to be true, but she'd met Hannah and it was possible she was that good a catch. It's not like being hardworking and trustworthy were rare. But Taylor paused on the idea of Art hooking up with Hannah.

Hannah was young. Younger than Gracie by at least ten years, younger even than Taylor. Guy had indicated Art had dated other younger women in the past. Had his perfect wife Reynette proved to be a little older than he actually liked? If so, who better to poison her than the person who had all the access to her?

Taylor posed the idea to Roxy when they were settled in at the worktable with coffee and the video.

"But didn't you say he'd only been married a really short while? Surely he wouldn't have jumped in just to immediately kill her."

"Maybe he didn't jump in so much as get pushed." Taylor sipped her coffee. It was a bit strong and only had milk instead of cream. It made her feel tough, like a real detective.

"What would Reynette have gotten from this marriage if it had lasted?"

"Art's a pretty good-looking guy."

Roxy wrote that on the paper they were going to use to make notes about the video. "What else?"

"For some women that's enough. Maybe she was really lonely. I wonder how long she'd been single." Taylor realized she didn't know a thing about Reynette, not anything useful anyway.

"That's got to be easy to find out." Roxy pushed the laptop her way. "Google it."

Taylor did, but couldn't find much. "Searching Reynette Woods brings up news of her death in the county paper and her website, but only because her name is Reynette and that's pretty uncommon. Her previous name was Johnson and all I get Googling that is her business. She's an interesting one to be teaching at Comfort."

"Why?"

"She ran a large secondhand shop, nonprofit of course, funds going to the state foodbank. From there she, with Hannah, did their higher end resale stuff online. I kind of get why Gracie was a bit derisive about Reynette's quilting. She's not really a 'quilter' in the obsessive artist sense that you think of when you think of the College of Art and Craft."

"But she did quilt, didn't she?"

"Yeah, there's a blog on her store website that has a story about using donated clothes that weren't really resalable due to condition, cutting out the good bits, and turning them into quilts, but look." Taylor turned the screen. "Not to be rude, but the picture she posted is pretty simple. Just a four patch. And her corners...."

Roxy cringed. "She was going to be teaching? Is that quilt mixing acrylics and cotton?"

"I guess if it's old clothes it's at least done all the shrinking it will do."

Roxy stared at the screen in disbelief. "Was she super prolific or something?"

"Maybe so. There had to be something unique she had on offer. Every customer who comes in here every day seems more qualified to teach, based on their projects, than Reynette."

"Folk art," Roxy said dismally.

"Folk art can be really impressive."

"Real folk art can. But there is a market for 'primitives.' If she was putting out a huge number of these, then I bet they were going to market her as a primitive." Roxy glanced at the farthest wall of the shop, by the back door. One of her own quilts hung there, a masterpiece in triangles and curves and tiny delicate stitches. She had spent a year on it.

It had come in second at the state fair.

"I'll have to call and find out. Seems like that was what Gracie was implying, but wouldn't teaching at a college focused on art ruin her reputation as a primitive? I mean, you don't see old granddad who plays his spoons on his front porch getting a job at a music conservatory, do you?"

"If her job had something to do with her death, then you should definitely talk to the school about it. Maybe someone on staff really, really didn't want her teaching there." Roxy's jaw twitched. She at least didn't seem to want Reynette teaching at the college.

And Taylor didn't blame her. The college paid a good living wage plus benefits, if you could manage to get in on a full-time tenure track job. Those jobs were rare in little shops like Flour Sax.

"That seems as reasonable as her husband suddenly deciding he didn't want an old wife." Taylor appreciated Roxy's own frustration with the world they lived in, but she didn't buy the theory as a motive for murder.

Roxy narrowed her eyes in consideration as she wrapped her hands around her mug. "No. No it's not. Killing to get out of a bad marriage is more likely."

That thought didn't settle well with Taylor. It seemed so... murderous. A rivalry at the snooty art college full of eccentrics felt divorced from reality, like a costume drama TV show. But a man she'd just met killing a wife he decided he didn't like felt bad deep in her gut. If Taylor could prove that wasn't what happened, it would be a great relief.

Speaking of bad relationships, a familiar face appeared in the front door, with a lopsided grin.

"So that's Clay?" Roxy asked as they both watched him knock on the glass.

"Yup."

"I didn't get a good look at him last time."

"Yeah, yeah. Because I was kissing him."

"He's cute."

"That's a good word for him."

"But not as good looking as Hudson."

"Or as useful. If I took Clay back, I'd have to start fixing this building myself, and man, I'd hate to do that."

Clay frowned, tossed his hands to the side and mouthed, "Oh, come on."

"Will you let him in?"

"Nope," Taylor said. "We're not open." She turned her back on him and navigated to the videos they were supposed to approve.

Roxy's son Jonah was a good editor, and as always, Taylor approved the three fifteen-minute shows with no changes. It had been forty-five minutes, so obviously when they were done and Taylor looked back at the door, Clay was gone.

The feeling that enveloped Taylor wasn't one of relief though. He was gone from her door, but he was still out there, having his two weeks off from work, waiting patiently for her to take him back.

Or not so patiently.

He was at the back door knocking, just after opening. Roxy let him in.

"You can use the front door after eleven." They weren't flooded with customers, so Taylor didn't feel like saying it nicely.

"Sure, but then you'd have known it was me." That grin.

Of course, they had seen him through the window in the back door as well, but said with his cheeky grin it was, as Roxy had said earlier, "cute."

"Enjoying your vacation?" Taylor asked.

"I hiked the famous Bible Creek Falls in the rain. So that was fun. Then, since I was covered in mud, I ran down to the nearest laundromat. Did you know it was in Willamina? All the way in Willamina?"

"Yup. Nearest dentist is there too. And nearest TV repairman, though technically he's retired."

"Do you have plans for dinner tonight?"

"Yes." Not a lie. Taylor was eating with Grandpa Ernie like she did pretty much every night.

"Come on, Taylor, you've got to at least eat with me."

"What happened last time I tried that, Clay? Don't you remember? Someone died."

He laughed.

She pretended the sound of his laugh didn't make her happy. It had been nine months since their big dramatic break up and so much of the sting of it was gone already. She hadn't realized that until just this moment. She didn't want him back, but the sound of his laugh didn't make her angry either.

"How about after dinner? It's a Thursday, Tay. You're not going out on a hot date on a Thursday, are you?"

"No."

"Then can I please take you to that little wine bar down the block for a piece of cake and a glass of something you'd like?"

"No, Clay. You can't." Taylor swallowed. Besides not wanting to leave Grandpa Ernie home during the evening, that little wine bar was super romantic and the last time she had been there had been with Hudson.

He had almost won her over due to the atmosphere alone.

The bells on the door jangled and three lady quilters came in giggling in their matching "Stitch and Bitch" T-shirts.

It jangled again and again, and the little shop filled. The early drizzle had faded away leaving behind bright, if cold skies. The sun had drawn out the local crafters as well as folks from out of town.

Taylor was able to abandon Clay, but to her chagrin, he made himself at home in the corner of the store where they had her mom's old videos playing on a loop.

Grandma Quinny and her Aunt Carrie arrived pushing her youngest cousin in a stroller. The room was hard to navigate now, and Grandma Quinny seemed to fill it with her large presence even without the stroller. "Taylor, darling, Taylor!" She called out to her as though this was her home and Taylor ought to have answered the door for her.

"Back here Grandma!" Taylor hollered back. Why not? This was a small town.

From her spot by the hand dyed organic cotton they had just gotten, Taylor could see the bobbing heads of her aunt and Grandmother as they pushed through the crowd. It gave her a pretty good idea for reconfiguring the store, but she wasn't ready just yet. Her mom had laid this out...Taylor shook her head. She had to do what was best for the business, and as far as she could see, that involved slightly wider aisles from the door to the back.

"What's up?" Taylor gave Grandma Quinny a kiss, then dropped to give baby Hattie a little tickle. She was closing in on three, and not really a baby anymore, but who cared.

"Ellery invited us over for lunch with Ernie today and we wanted to see if you could get off in time to join us?"

Taylor assessed the crowd, "I'm sorry..."

"What has brought everyone in on a Thursday like this?" Grandma gave the customers a disapproving look. "Did you have a sale?"

"I think it's just the sun. Everyone was ready to get out of the house again."

"Interesting."

The door jangled open. This time it was Art's ex-wife Gracie, and Fawn, Reynette's daughter. They loitered by the cash register where Roxy was ringing up the ladies in the matching shirts.

"Not even an hour off for lunch?" Grandma Quinny pressed.

Taylor laughed at the idea of more than a half hour for lunch. "No, I'm sorry. I need to go help some customers as it is."

"We really were hoping...."

Taylor sighed. "Was today the day you were going to convince both Grandpa Ernie and me that it's time for a change in housing?"

"Oh Taylor, don't be so cynical. Your Aunt Carrie and I just had some time and we wanted to enjoy your company." Grandma Quinny pulled at the soft loose knit cotton scarf she had carefully wrapped around her neck.

"Sorry." A tap on her shoulder prevented her from elaborating. "Yes?" Taylor spun, only to find Clay, very close, and now with his hand on her lower back.

"Babe, I can help these ladies. You need a lunch break. You've been here since 6:30 this morning."

Carrie's brows flew up when he said babe. "Do you have someone to introduce us to?" she asked, her voice sweet like gummy bears.

"No."

"I'm Clay." He offered her his hand. "You might remember me as the fool who let Taylor get away."

Grandma Quinny frowned. "Yes, Clay. We do remember you." She tightened the scarf.

Taylor didn't know what folks had talked about behind her back, but she had been sure not to gossip about him around town.

He slipped his fingers from the small of her back to a grip around her waist, a move he had often done when he felt insecure.

Taylor wanted to shift out of his touch, but she was backed into a corner full of chicken wire baskets, stacked artistically, and full of spools of thread.

"Young man, why don't you come with me?" Grandma Quinny beckoned him to her.

He followed as most everyone would when she directed. "We need to have a bit of a talk. I think."

CHAPTER SIX

"*S*he's a terrifying woman." Despite ignoring his panicked texts, Clay had dropped by her house for dinner around seven. He sat at the table with Grandpa Ernie and Taylor and the frozen pizza she had lovingly cooked for twelve minutes at 400 degrees.

"She's not so bad." Taylor sheltered her plate with two slices of pizza protectively. Clay had already consumed two-thirds of the alfredo and spinach delight.

"She's a fine woman," Grandpa Ernie stated.

Taylor wasn't entirely sure he knew who they were talking about.

"I thought she was going to take me out to the woodshed for a whipping." Clay had been eking out the story one hint at a time for the last ten minutes, and Taylor still refused to ask him what had happened. She wouldn't have let him in, but he managed to be at the back door climbing the ramp Hudson had built them just exactly as Taylor was opening the door to let herself in.

"Is this how you let your friends speak of your folks?" Grandpa Ernie stared at Clay with disapproving eyes.

"No, Grandpa, it's not. Listen Clay, you need to move on."

Grandpa Ernie coughed.

"And show some respect." Taylor nibbled her pizza. Now that Clay was in her house, she wasn't sure how she could get him out again. And with both an empty bed in Belle's old room and a couch in the front room, Taylor wasn't sure she was justified in so doing. Except that he wasn't family, or friend, or even invited, so she didn't really have to let him stay. Her mind spun around on the issue.

"What happened to that good guy who killed all the raccoons?" Grandpa's memory of events surrounding the raccoon infestation in the apartment above Flour Sax Quilt Shop wasn't perfect, but Taylor didn't correct him. It wouldn't hurt Clay to think of her as hanging out with a guy that could take down a whole family of beasts.

"He's around still," Taylor said.

"Did he kill them with his bare hands?" Clay took the last piece of pizza and consumed it in two quick bites.

Grandpa still had the one on his plate. Taylor knew that Ellery and Grandpa had already had their soup and sandwiches, but Clay didn't.

"Yup," Grandpa Ernie said.

Taylor gave her grandpa a long, considering look. Was this a symptom of his slowly decaying memory or was he trolling Clay because Clay was acting like a jerk? She couldn't tell.

"I bet that Grandma Quinn could do it. She's a tough broad."

"Respect, young man, or get out of my house." Grandpa Ernie's face went red.

"Seriously, cool it, Clay. This is my family you're talking about."

"Sure, well, it explains you doesn't it?"

With a slow grind of chair legs on floor, Grandpa Ernie stood. "That is it." His words came out as slowly as the chair had moved. "You will leave this house immediately and not return."

Clay had the sense to blanche, but he didn't move. "Come on now, you know I'm just joking." He elbowed Taylor in the ribs.

"Do I?"

"You've met your grandma."

"Get out." Taylor too, stood and now only Clay was sitting.

Grandpa had shuffled into the front room, apparently heading for the door, to kick Clay out.

"She took me to that little prison museum and gave me a lecture on how to treat women. In a prison! You've got to know that makes her one bad..." He looked from Taylor to Grandpa Ernie, "Boss. It makes her one bad boss. An Iron Lady. It was a boss move."

"It didn't seem to make an impression on you though, did it?"

"Tay." He tipped his chair back on two legs. "We used to laugh about stuff like this together."

"I don't remember laughing when you made fun of my family. In fact, I don't remember you making fun of them. And, to top it off, I don't remember you coming down this way to meet them even." She smoothed the front of her white cotton button down shirt, her anxiety cooling at the sensation of the crisp professional fabric under her fingertips. Even after a long day's work. She stood up a little straighter.

"I did! I came for the Fourth of July."

"Five years ago."

"And? I still came."

"Go home, Clay. We're not getting back together."

Grandpa Ernie had picked up her phone and was staring at it with concentration. Taylor wondered if he was going to call 911, but after a moment, he was talking into it like smart phones were a part of his day to day life. "I recall you said we could call you when we had a pest problem..."

This time Taylor blanched. Was Grandpa calling Hudson to get rid of Clay? Some small part of her that was still a fourteen-year-old girl thrilled at the idea, but the majority of her was mortified.

"Let me take you out for ice cream and tell you the whole

prison lecture story." Clay didn't seem to hear what Grandpa Ernie was muttering in the other room. "It's pretty funny."

"I can't leave." Taylor crossed her arms. "I don't leave Grandpa home alone at night. He might not like the idea of needing a caregiver, but he needs one."

"Then let me run down to the market and buy some ice-cream."

"It closes at eight." Taylor hoped he wouldn't notice he still had time to get there.

"Awesome." He leapt to his feet, his happy grin back in place. "I'll be right back."

Taylor was too distracted by what she was hearing from Grandpa Ernie to give Clay's words the thought they deserved. He was leaving and that was enough for the moment.

She locked the kitchen door behind Clay and then joined her Grandpa in time to hear him say. "Good. We'll be here." He set the phone down.

"Didn't know you knew how to use one of those." Taylor sunk into the couch, glad to get off her feet and glad for the quiet of this room.

"Ellery taught me yesterday. She's a smart cookie, but she doesn't do much cleaning. I hope you don't pay her to clean."

"She's earning her keep."

"Babysitting." He huffed into his bushy mustache.

"You're hardly a baby." Taylor crossed her legs and yawned. "Did you just call Hudson?"

"Yup." He backed into his recliner slowly, a smile sneaking onto his face as he got comfortable.

"To kick Clay out?"

"I'm not the only one who needs someone to take care of me." He yanked on the bar that reclined his chair and sighed. "But I guess you got rid of him on your own."

"He claims he's coming back with ice cream."

"Good. We can have ice cream and then Hudson can kick him out."

Grandpa Ernie was so clear-headed tonight, and in such an entertaining mood. His pleased contented look might have been from knowing he could use a smart phone, or it might have been the thrill of being the man of the house.

Taylor thought for the hundredth time that Grandma Quinny was overreacting. And of course, Clay wasn't all together wrong. She could be an overwhelming woman.

"So that was the man you've been living with all these years?"

"Yup," Taylor echoed his own words.

"Bet you're glad you didn't marry him."

Her eyes were closed and head resting on the back of the couch. Was she? If they had been married, he'd have had to come here with her. She'd still have the Clay she had loved back then instead of this jerk-Clay she currently hated.

"You shouldn't have to think about it that long."

"Oh, marriage changes things," Taylor yawned. "If we had married years ago, we wouldn't be the people we are now. How would I know if I should have or shouldn't have? All I know is we didn't and so this is what it is."

"True." He nodded. "You should get married. You're not so young anymore."

"Nope. I'm not." By the time her mom had turned twenty-nine, Taylor had been nine, and her dad was two years away from dying. A whole lifetime lived in the years Taylor had just been doing her thing. And yet, she wasn't sorry that she didn't have a nine-year-old and she certainly wasn't sorry that she didn't have young widowhood to look forward to any time soon.

The soft sound of snoring was all Taylor got for a reply. It had been a long day for Grandpa.

She had almost joined him in a little evening snooze when a gentle and familiar knock on the door roused her. For being a big manly construction guy, Hudson didn't seem to feel obliged to draw notice to himself.

She let him in with a sleepy smile.

He leaned down and kissed her cheek. "It's been a while."

"It has. I've been meaning to call. Come in."

He ambled in and dropped onto the couch. "Looks like you took care of your pest problem." His grin was cheekier than Clay's ever was. Less self-deprecating too.

"I'm not too shabby when it's only one at a time."

"I'd make a joke about hordes of men surrounding you, but it's been a long day."

"I hear you. Can I get you something? A beer? Water?"

"Got a Coke or something?"

"Sure." Taylor went to the kitchen to scrounge a cold drink. She found a lone can of Pepsi at the back of the fridge. She turned to get herself a glass of water and spotted a face in the window of the kitchen door. That grin, definitely not as cheeky, but almost as cute.

Clay knew Taylor saw him but knocked anyway. Nice and loud.

"Want me to get it?" Hudson called from the other room.

Taylor exhaled loudly. "No, we can ignore him."

"Who is him?"

She returned to Hudson without her water. "Him is Clay Seldon the man I left behind in Portland."

"Ah yes. Good old Clay. The guy that didn't seem to care one bit about your family."

"I'd say he still doesn't seem to care."

The front doorbell rang.

"I wonder what he thinks of my truck in the driveway."

"I can't even imagine."

Hudson got up with an oof that sounded older than his twenty-five years and answered the door. "Yes?" He filled the doorway, his head with its thick dark hair almost touched the door frame, and his broad shoulders seemed to fill the width. He wore a dusty plaid flannel and jeans that were muddy from a day at some construction site.

"You must be the guy that killed a bear when he was only three." Clay stood at least three inches below Hudson and was narrow in the shoulders. The decided slump of a computer guy was another difference between the two, as was the rumpled T-shirt he had probably slept in and the very clean blue jeans that had cost an absurd amount of money. "Hope you like rocky road." He held up the box of ice-cream.

"Sure, thanks." Hudson pulled out his wallet, not moving from the doorway. "What do we owe you?" He handed Clay a five. "That about covers it, right?"

Clay laughed and accepted the money. He might be a slight man, but he was bold and walked in, pushing past Hudson with the strength of his big personality.

"Hey, Buddy." Hudson put a hand on Clay's shoulder. "Why don't you and I step outside for a minute?"

Clay stiffened. "Taylor's waiting for her ice-cream."

Taylor was about ready to go to bed and let these two duke it out for themselves. Technically she hadn't invited either of them there.

Hudson gripped Clay's shoulder hard and turned him toward the door. "Outside."

Clay twisted away, popping out of Hudson's hand.

Hudson looked shocked for a moment, then laughed. He grabbed the ice cream in a swift motion and tossed it to Taylor.

Taylor hadn't expected to catch it, but she did. "Whatever you do, don't wake up Grandpa Ernie," she muttered as she went to the kitchen. She almost started dishing the dessert but tossed it in the freezer instead.

"Everyone, outside." Taylor pushed past both of them and stood on the porch with her hands on her hips. They both followed.

"Hudson, it was very nice of you to come over just because Grandpa Ernie called you. Clay, you are being an ass. You know that, right?"

He laughed. "Come on, you love it. You like a confident guy who comes for what he wants."

"You're disgusting." Hudson curled his lip.

"Let me guess, you're letting her take her time."

The derision in the words 'take her time' was too much, Taylor was about to sock him right in the nose, but she wasn't fast enough.

Hudson's fist cracked Clay's face so hard it knocked him down the porch steps.

"Damn, I was right." Clay held his hand to his face as blood gushed down, but his eyes, though filled with tears, weren't cowed. "You're ledding her lead. Which is cude." His words were that of a man with a freshly broken nose. "But that's nod the way do win Daylor. The day she led me move indo her place, I made my move, didn't I?"

"Oh God, Clay, you make me sick. What is wrong with you?" For half a minute Taylor had considered getting him a towel or maybe ice for his nose, but she couldn't now.

Blood was still pouring down his face. He wobbled but grabbed for the rail. "I'm joking, Day," he said.

"Head back to wherever you're staying and clean yourself up, will you?" Taylor pleaded. The sight of him bleeding there worried her and she didn't want to worry about him.

"Sure, sure, but I'll be back domorrow. You love me sdill, I know id." He turned toward his car and fell over. Passed out. Loss of blood. Taylor stood, jaw dropped.

"Crap." Hudson stared too.

Taylor wondered if he was thinking what she was thinking— that he'd probably spend the night in jail over this one.

"Why don't you head out and I'll take care of him?" Taylor gave him a shove toward his truck.

But Hudson was already picking Clay up and carrying him in. "Running won't stop him from pressing charges if that's what he wants to do. Can you get some wet rags and ice?"

"Sure." Taylor followed Hudson and Clay inside. He lay Clay on the floor.

Grandpa Ernie was awake now. "That's a turn up isn't it?" He peered from his seat at the mess of Clay.

Hudson was already calling 911.

While he did, Taylor wiped Clay's face gently with a wet rag, and then pressed a dry towel under his nose. He was losing a lot of blood, but Taylor had a feeling he had passed out from a concussion. Not that she was a nurse.

"Don't you think Hudson should head out?" Taylor asked Grandpa.

"He'd never." Grandpa Ernie looked with approval at the tall man on the phone.

Hudson's cheeks were pink, and his face was drawn. Embarrassment, Taylor guessed.

But Grandpa Ernie wasn't embarrassed. He had gotten exactly what he had ordered.

CHAPTER SEVEN

*C*lay roused himself before the ambulance arrived. "Dang." He attempted to sit up.

"Maybe don't do that." Taylor pressed his shoulder gently.

He did anyway and leaned forward. "Now we know who'd win in a fight."

Hudson was seated on an uncomfortable straight-backed wooden chair by the front door. Her mom used to call it "The Boyfriend Chair." He looked exactly as uncomfortable as her mom liked to say it would make any potential boyfriends.

Hudson leaned forward, arms on his knees. "How's the head?"

"Busted," Clay said.

"I called the ambulance. Want to make sure I didn't break anything important." Hudson's words were quiet, deep and tinged with guilt.

Clay chuckled. "You pack a punch."

"You were way out of line."

"Yeah. I was." Blood started trickling out his nose again. He grabbed one of the towels that lay beside him and held it to his face. "Between you and that Grandma Quinn, I guess I know where I stand."

"The only opinion you need is mine." Taylor crossed her arms. "How hard is that to understand? Grandma Quinny might bully you. Hudson might beat you. What does any of that matter? I'm the one who says if you stay or go."

Clay moped at her with what might have been big puppy eyes, if one hadn't been almost swollen shut, the punch to the nose having been pretty effective. "And?"

"You're going to make me say it again?" She closed her eyes and prayed for patience. "You go."

He attempted a wobbly stand. "Fine."

The sirens from the ambulance halted his retreat.

The paramedics, Maria and Serge, gave him a thorough exam and then asked him if he wanted to go to the hospital.

"Nope."

"Is it okay if he stays here?" Maria asked Hudson.

Taylor seethed. Maria, who she'd known for at least twelve years, should have been asking her.

"Our concern is for a concussion. It would be nice if someone was around to check in on him now and again. That was one bad blow he got in your...sparring." Maria rolled her eyes. She hadn't bought the story Clay sold her.

"Yeah, he can stay with me." Hudson crossed his arms.

"All right, we check off on it then. But take care boys, fights aren't games." Maria and Serge left, shaking the dust off their sandals metaphorically.

"You're not fit to drive," Hudson said. "Grab your stuff and I'll take you to my place."

"Hold on," Clay interjected. "The nice lady said I should sleep here."

Taylor checked her watch. It was only nine. "Whatever. Stay here then. Belle's bed has clean sheets. Grandpa Ernie, are you good?"

He had been about to fall asleep again, so Taylor gave his shoulder a little shake. "Can I help you to your room?"

"Only if you kids quiet down."

She walked with him across the little living room to his bedroom while Hudson paced in front of the door.

When she returned, Hudson addressed her again. "Taylor..." He spoke slowly, his deep, resonant voice filled the room, though he wasn't being loud.

"It's fine. Clay won't die in the night. You can stay too. I give up. Everyone can stay the night."

"Don't give up." Hudson's eyes were proper puppy dog eyes. Emotional, expressive, winning.

She smiled at him softly. "That's not what I meant. This night has gotten out of hand. I'm getting the ice cream."

Hudson followed her into the kitchen. "Do you really want me to stay with you tonight too?"

She thought about it. She liked that he asked. She liked it a lot. He didn't presume he could stay. He didn't hint that he'd stay in her room. They hadn't slept together, and he wasn't going to press her about it.

And yet...part of her missed the kind of passionate pursuit that Clay brought to the game. His persistence could not overcome the injury of his abandoning her, but it was a stark contrast to Hudson.

Then again, he had been passionate enough to damage Clay's face.

She shrugged. "Is 'I don't know' a good enough answer?"

"No." There was laugh in Hudson's eyes despite his grim face.

Taylor passed him a bowl of ice cream. "It's early still. Go find something on TV."

He took the bowl and sat himself right next to Clay on the sofa. Clay shifted away. His swollen, broken face held a pouty little frown.

Taylor brought the other two bowls out and took her spot in Grandpa's chair. What was she supposed to do with these two men?

Eventually Clay fell asleep on the couch which was a huge

relief for Taylor. Not so much a relief for Hudson, who happened to be the shoulder Clay slumped down on when sleep came. "I guess I'm stuck here then."

"Why?" Taylor glanced up the stairs. She was tired. She was snuggly. She saw no reason, in this moment, that Hudson had to stay downstairs with Clay when he could come up and snuggle her.

"Paramedics wanted me to stay with him to make sure he didn't die in the night. If he sleeps here, then so do I. Unless you want to, I guess." He flexed his hand like his knuckles might hurt.

"We could both stay down here." Taylor yawned. It was only eleven, but she did keep early hours.

"Here, trade him spots." Hudson nudged Clay awake. "You'd better sleep in the recliner. For medical reasons."

Clay yawned but obeyed. He was out again in a matter of minutes.

"Definitely a concussion," Taylor said, nestling into Hudson's arms.

"What are you going to do about that guy?" Hudson asked, then laid a gentle kiss just below her ear.

"Get him back to wherever he's staying first thing in the morning."

Hudson responded with more kisses, but her phone rang interrupting them and waking Clay.

She would have ignored it, except for Clay hollering about the noise.

Caller ID said it was Sissy Dorney.

Taylor took the call to the kitchen.

"I hope it's not too late to call." Sissy didn't sound apologetic. It was just the kind of thing people say when they call late.

"It's fine. What's up?"

"I got us a chance to dig around in Aunt Reynette's place tomorrow morning. It's before your shop opens so it shouldn't be inconvenient." There was a bit of defensiveness in her words.

"To hunt for clues, you mean?"

"Yes. Art's overwhelmed. Gracie and Una went back home, and Fawn and Monty are making him go there too."

"To his ex-wife's house?"

"Yup. They said it would be good for him to be near his daughter right now, and that they'd take care of stuff. I offered to come in and clean in the morning while they drive him there." Sissy related the information like it was top secret knowledge.

"Clever, but why are they driving him?" Taylor rinsed the ice cream bowls while she talked. Her jaw hurt from clenching it in anger. Things had been going so well with Hudson just now.

"To make sure he actually goes to the coast."

"Fawn doesn't want to search it herself? I mean, it is her mom."

"She trusts me. Knows I know what's up."

"Well, okay. Just tell me what time and give me the address." Taylor found a pen and paper to take notes.

Sissy gave her the address of one of the gorgeous Queen Anne Victorians the town founders had built when the flour mill was making folks rich. Taylor agreed to be there at seven the next morning.

She stood in the kitchen door and looked at the scene in the living room. Clay slept under a bachelor buttons quilt Taylor had made in high school. Hudson was stretched out, arms on the back of the sofa, face turned to her, one eyebrow lifted.

What the heck? What did she have to lose? She really liked him a lot.

She joined him on the couch, but he didn't make a move.

She gave him a quick rundown of the call.

"Seven, huh? You'd better head to bed, then."

"Are you sure?" Taylor thought the words were going to come out in a husky, sexy kind of voice, but they didn't. Just matter of fact.

He sighed. "The thing is, you're not sure. And until you are, you get to sleep alone." He didn't seem aware of anything but

Taylor, his forehead touching hers, their eyes locked. "I don't know what kind of man that guy really is, or who you dated before him. I just know who I am. When I'm with a woman, it's because we're both sure."

Taylor leaned in and kissed him, a lot.

And then she went to bed alone.

"NICE PLACE." The words were inadequate to describe the scene Taylor had stepped into. The old Baily House was three-thousand square feet of architectural eye-candy. The last of the great, rich Baily family, Harrison, had only died in 2017. He had been a confirmed bachelor and had left no heirs when he passed away at ninety-seven years of age. Despite the age of the last resident, the house had not fallen into disrepair. The kitchen had been added to the house in the 1930s, but the old detached summer kitchen still stood on the property. Every inch of the woodwork was original and had been maintained with love and affection. The furniture was a mishmash collected through the hundred and fifty odd years of the house's existence, but it was high quality and just as clean and well-loved as the room Taylor stood in.

The belongings of the newest occupants, Art and Reynette Woods who were renting the house furnished on a six-month lease, were another story all together.

Boxes were stacked precariously on top of one another filling the front room. "Where do we start? Did you offer to unpack this place?"

"No way. Not this mess. Come back this way with me." Sissy had her hair wrapped in a silky pink head scarf. She wore serviceable jeans and a wildly patterned jersey tunic, a look that screamed "house cleaning day."

Taylor followed her to what would have been a butler's pantry—a smallish nook between the kitchen and dining room.

"Reynette liked cozy places so she was going to use this as her office."

"You've got to be kidding. In this house? It must have at least twelve better choices." Taylor turned around in the tiny nook. There was barely enough room for a chair to sit at much less the files for organizing a multifaceted business.

"Eleven, actually. They all had uses as well. A work room. A stock room. Art's study. Guest rooms. A library. But for the business finances and paperwork this was the one she liked."

"There's no telling with people, is there?"

"Nope. I told her she was crazy, but she laughed and said everything was in the cloud anyway. Let's get looking."

"The family's going to accept our digging through the business boxes as cleaning?" Taylor stared at the boxes that blocked the dining room doorway.

"We'll clean the kitchen and make some beds before we leave, don't worry. I'll take this side. You take that one." Sissy opened one of the glass fronted doors that ought to have held china or crystal or something like that.

"What are we looking for?"

"You're the detective." Sissy didn't sound like she believed it.

A wave of irritation rolled over Taylor. She was only here because Sissy had asked for help, and because she had developed a sort of mother-instinct for those stupid friends of Belle's. If Cooper and Aviva hadn't been so scared, she never would have stepped up. If Sissy didn't think she was useful, why bother? After a moment of seething she spoke up. "I'm not a detective. I'm a friend." Taylor paused at the word. "And I'm helping because I was asked to."

"Fine." Sissy was a large presence both literally and because of her 'big personality' for lack of a better phrase. She squared up her shoulders and for a moment Taylor wasn't sure there was room for the two of them. "We're looking for a motive. Seems like people get killed for sex or money and frankly, Reynette wasn't all that sexy, God bless her. Sweet, sure, but not sexy. I think it was about money.

Looks like the files in this cupboard have to do with her resale shops. Figure out what you've got and then see if anything looks fishy."

"Can do." Taylor thanked her lucky stars she had an MBA. She was fairly sure she'd be able to spot fishy financial dealings at least.

She dragged a stack of files off an open shelf and began her search. The first thing she came across was a record of all of the quilts Reynette had made, what contests she had entered them in, and how they had done. It was a tidy record, handwritten in a ledger book.

Reynette had been quilting quite a bit longer than her family had indicated. The first quilt had been entered in the Marion County Fair in 1999. It had placed third. The piece was a wall hanging, yellow brick road in cotton. It had sold three years later for $150. With a record like this Reynette must have kept photos too. But also, with a record like this Taylor had a hard time believing her as a primitive folk artist.

Taylor looked over each quilt on the list. In the twenty years Reynette had been quilting she had made around $100,000 on her quilts. Nice bit, but not all that impressive as a yearly sum. Nothing to kill over.

That said, her income had increased rapidly around 2016, and at least half of that $100,000 had been earned in the last few years.

Taylor set aside the log and hunted for a photo record of the quilts. Something major had changed for her in 2016, but it wasn't anything that showed up on the log. The quilts were being entered in the same old fairs and shows that everyone else entered. They were just suddenly selling for thousands of dollars instead of hundreds. And they were all selling instead of just some of them. While maybe not a reason to kill her, it was certainly irregular.

In a box on the top-most shelf Taylor found an old photo album with the pictures she was hoping for. She flipped through the pages, glancing at each quilt quickly. They were unremarkable. Good, but not exceptional. Nicely made, but not innovative. This album had quilts from 1999 to 2011. Taylor found no other record. "Sissy, you said Reynette said everything was stored on the cloud. Do you have any way for us to get into her computer?"

"What?" Sissy jerked her head up. "I almost forgot you were here. You're a quiet one."

"I found some interesting stuff regarding her work as a quilter, but the actual images of the quilts only go up to 2011."

"I don't see a computer in here, and if I did, I wouldn't know her passwords."

"Maybe her computer bag is somewhere..." Taylor scanned the floor to see if a satchel of some sort was hiding behind one of the many boxes but didn't see anything. "I can't think she'd box up the computer she was using to run a business. Or even if she did, I can't imagine it'd still be in a box. How long had they been in this house anyway?"

"They'd just gotten the keys a couple days before she passed." Sissy leaned heavily on the counter. "I can't find anything. She's my aunt though, and as far as I know, she's always been straight as an arrow."

"Of course, she was." Taylor shut the album and got it back on its shelf. "We'd better hit the kitchen."

"I can't think we've even scratched the surface," Sissy said as they skirted the many boxes in the kitchen.

"I agree. See if you can get us another day or two in here. I'd like to do more looking. Something seems off in her career as a quilter. It might have nothing to do with her death..."

"But if it did, we'd better find out."

There were only a handful of plates in the sink and they knocked it out fast, then went upstairs.

While Sissy made the bed, Taylor dug around in the bathroom. "I can't really believe it, but there isn't a single bottle of aspirin in here. No ibuprofen or acetaminophen either. No kind of pain relief except this little jar of Tiger Balm."

"Reynette didn't trust pain killers. So many people get addicted, you know. That's why I'm positive she did not accidentally overdose."

Taylor sat on a velvet wing back chair and admired the quilt on the bed. "I'd say that one is an early 2000s. Its store-bought fabric in a very traditional pattern."

"I don't know what Gracie was talking about," Sissy said. "The corners all meet up real nice."

"They do. It's a beautiful quilt. Is there a chance someone else made it?"

Sissy flipped back a corner. "It's got her signature. R with a little crown. Because Reynette means queen."

Taylor laughed. "Technically it would mean little girl king, wouldn't it?"

"And what's that but a queen?" Sissy glowered at Taylor.

She'd have to remember to treat Reynette like a beloved family member and not like a case study. Sissy cared about this woman as much as Taylor cared about anyone in her own family. Likely more if you were talking aunts and cousins. "Why don't you tell me a little bit about her?" Taylor asked softly.

"She was my best friend for a lot of years." Sissy crossed her arms. "And whoever did this to her is going to pay."

CHAPTER EIGHT

aylor should have expected Clay would turn up at Flour Sax as soon as it opened. He slid in quietly, his khaki pants and plaid button down looked like he'd been wearing them for weeks. His hair was tousled like he had done it on purpose. He took the seat by her mom's videos again. She tried to ignore him, but it wasn't easy. She had Hannah to train, though, so at least there was something important to keep her mind on.

Taylor ran through the register, the books, and inventory with Hannah in record time. Everything Guy Sauvage had said about her was true. She was bright and hardworking.

"It's been a good few hours," Taylor said at two. "Why don't you go take a lunch?"

"Ok." Hannah didn't sound interested in lunch, but she was agreeable. But as Flour Sax opened at eleven Monday through Friday during the off season, the lunch hour came a little late in the day. She had to be starving.

Hannah found her purse, logged out in the time book, and left via the back door.

Taylor didn't know where she'd take her lunch but was glad

to see she was heading out for a bit. Taylor needed some time with Clay. This stalking had to end.

They were alone in the shop, so she pulled a chair over to where he sat absorbed with her mom's quilt instructions.

"Man." His eyes were glued on the little screen. "I've been watching this for hours and it feels like I know her now."

"You could have known her."

One of Clay's eyes was purple and swollen shut, and his nose was red and purple, swollen and bent. A specific memory from their old life together flickered in her heart and made her want to kiss him better. They had been living together for two years and decided to take a week off to bike to the coast from their home in the suburbs. The trip was an easy two-day ride, and they decided to take it even slower, staying the night at a couple of Airbnb's on the way, just for kicks. It was going to be a great adventure, and Taylor had suspected he was going to propose on the beach.

But he got hit by a car in the coast range mountains instead.

A little Volkswagen had flung him right off the edge of the steeply inclined hill. Her mind still refused to call it a cliff, even today. Clay should have died, but he'd let go of the bike, like a genius, and while it had tumbled down the hill breaking into bits as it fell, he had landed in a patch of great big sword fern. His nose had broken, and two legs. But he hadn't died.

She had kissed his broken nose then.

He hadn't proposed.

Hadn't been planning on it either.

At this moment, he reached over to the little screen and pressed pause, then went back to the beginning. "Do you remember this video? It's a good one." He started it again.

"Fabric stashes are grown out of ideals and dreams and plentitude." Laura Quinn held up a skinny remnant of cotton printed all over in tiny blue bunnies. "We buy a little extra just in case. We know we might mess up. We usually do, right?" She laughed, then touched the fabric to her cheek. It was a bit left over from the baby quilt Taylor had made for Belle. "But then, days come when we no longer have plenty. When our needs exceed our means. That's when we dip into our stash and revel in our past glories." Taylor's mother was lost in some kind of happy dream. Maybe of those heady days with newborn Belle who had dragged both Laura and Taylor from under the shadow of grief that had been her father's passing. "But it's not just about fabric, is it? Are you keeping an emotional stash to get you through lean times? You should. You should store up in your heart the bounty from right now so that when times get tough you can call on it to comfort you. My mama had a heart full of old Bible verses. I bet your mama or your grandma did too. When she was fighting her cancer, my mama had that to call on, to comfort her. I have memories of my husband. Strong, hand-some, good." She blushed. "He was so good in so many ways. People ask me all the time why I never remarried, but as nice as all the other men I meet are, they don't live up to him." She paused, looked down at the assortment of mismatched fabrics on the table in front of her and ran her hand across them. "In the comments, tell me what you store up in your heart, like a fabric stash, to feed you in your time of need. I'd love to know. Songs maybe, verses, poems, memories. Photos even. Or…fabric." She smiled at the screen and the video ended. The brief pause before the next one would auto-play.

It had been nine months since Taylor and Clay had broken up.

Not even a year.

Her mom had always said you needed twelve full months after a significant loss to make any permanent decisions.

It had only been nine months since Taylor had lost her.

It was too soon to know if she never wanted to see Clay again or not.

Four years together…what was nine months compared to that?

He turned a little and caught her eye. "I store up your smile.

Memories of times you laughed with me, laughed at me, laughed near me. So many times, over the last few months when it's been the hardest, I've been able to pull up a memory of your smile to get me through."

Taylor scrunched her mouth like she'd eaten something sour. Clay and his little manipulations. Even when she was hours away, he held her responsible for something that shouldn't have been her job. "What's been so tough for you?" Her nose curled, like the idea that he might suffer smelled bad.

"Losing you. Starting over."

"You literally moved from one woman's furnished home to another, a mile away. I don't exactly consider that starting over."

"Won't you smile for me, just a little?"

"Clay, you've got to get out of here. Go back home."

"Where is home?" He spoke wistfully.

She sat and dropped her head to her hands. "She did kick you out, didn't she?"

He didn't say anything.

"Did you try something with her that she didn't want?"

He still didn't say anything.

"Oh, Clay, just get out of here, will you? I'm not your fallback plan. You can't just move in with me every time someone else kicks you out. Go back to Portland, be a man, and find a place to live." Taylor got up, walked straight to the register counter, and pulled out some paperwork. The words on the page in front of her were just a blur, but she pretended to work. After about a minute, Clay slunk out the front door

Just friends.

Yup. He and Lila, the girl he had moved in with, were totally just friends. Because she had rejected his moves for the last time and kicked him out.

Taylor thought back not to the day he had almost died, but to the day he had moved into her place, desperate because of a housing crisis. He'd made her laugh so hard while they moved his stuff in. He'd bought her dinner and wine. That night had been the first of what Taylor was sure was the rest of her life. He had been *the one*. Falling in love after years of friendship. Like in a movie.

The shop was so quiet she could just make out the sound of her mom's voice on the video across the store. "Life rarely turns out the way we plan, but quilts usually do. That's what's so nice about quilting. We can be in complete control so long as we're careful."

Quilts could even be perfect. Infinite do-overs. Rip it out till it's right. Taylor gazed at the walls that surrounded her with their sunny prints. Their bright, innocent, hopeful prints. Reprints of the colors and designs that had cheered a weary nation during the depression.

Quilting did have the ability to sooth an anxious soul, comfort a broken heart, or bring a sense of order into chaos. All you had to do was take it slow and careful.

There was no reason to be a sloppy quilter.

Which brought to mind Reynette.

A perfect distraction from the muddle Taylor found herself in.

Why was Reynette's reputation among her family that of a sloppy amateur when she'd been running a successful quilt side gig for twenty years—and had the records to prove it?

This was a question far more interesting than why Taylor had been such a sucker to fall for Clay Seldon in the first place.

Flour Sax had few customers that afternoon, so when Hannah returned from lunch, she and Taylor were able to chat for a while. As Guy had said, Hannah was a young woman of simple interests. Church, work, and a surprising passion for vintage clothes.

"The thing is," she was saying as Taylor locked up the front at the end of the day, "fast fashion has been around forever, so there is no shortage of vintage stuff to be found. You can make a killing as an online retailer if you know what a good example of the era is. It doesn't have to be a name brand so long as it exemplifies the style. Though obviously a quality designer brings in more money."

"I'd heard your boss was using some of the vintage stuff for quilts." Taylor tossed it out casually as though she wasn't eager for the answer.

"Reynette was kind of a genius. You've got to turn over your product pretty fast at a thrift store if you want to keep your customers coming back. They don't want to see the same stuff hanging there week after week. She realized the value in repurposing the fabric pretty early on."

"Seems like you wouldn't run into quality quilting cotton in clothing very often."

"Nope, that's why she switched up her style, and that too was an act of genius, don't you think?"

A flutter of excitement burst in Taylor's chest. Hannah was about to volunteer exactly the thing Taylor wanted to know.

"She was a really good quilter. No pattern or style was too hard for her. But when she tried to make a traditional quilt out of the wrong fabrics, no one wanted them. It made her look ignorant. So she switched it up and made what she called 'Sloppy Scrappies' instead. People died for them once she started in on it."

"I sort of find that hard to believe."

"It wouldn't have worked if they were honestly sloppy, of course." Hannah poked around on her phone for a minute. "Here, look at her old Instagram. We used it for a while and then realized we didn't need it. Our market was antique stores and flea markets."

Taylor scrolled through the feed that was a couple of years old. The quilts were definitely sloppy by her standards. Corners badly matched, surfaces not ironed. And yet, the artistry was impeccable.

Reynette had left behind the intricate patterns and embraced the crazy quilting of their grandparents with their silks, satins, velvets and heavy-handed embroidery. But instead of being dark and oppressive like those Victorian inspired pieces often were, Reynette's sloppy scrappies were magical rainbow creations. Where the formality of normal quilting had left her expressionless, this new thing she was doing seemed to have unchained her imagination. Unhinged it, even. The flow of color, the balance of color, was the stuff of genius. Everything was color and texture, and they told a story too. Not one of them was actually quilted. Instead they were tied with yarn—big clunky knots of yarn over every one of her quilts.

It was absurd, but at the same time, Taylor would have paid a pretty penny to have one to hang in her shop.

"You're speechless," Hannah spoke reverently.

"I am. My brain is filled entirely with superlatives and protestations. These shouldn't be beautiful. This shouldn't have worked." She was also remembering that terrible quilt Reynette had posted on her thrift shop website. If she was capable of this work, why had she not shared it there? Laziness probably. Too many things to update and that blog post had slipped through .

"But it did. She could piece a top in three days, and have it tied and bound by the end of day five. Just in the evenings after she was done running her shop and online resale empire during the day."

"And all of this was just to keep the stock fresh in the store?"

"It started that way, of course, but clearly she had a gift." Hannah pocketed her phone.

"What happened to them?"

"She sold them almost as fast as she could make them. But there are one or two left at her house, packed up somewhere. I'd like to talk to Art and see if I could sort through her online merchandise at least."

"What's happened to her store in the meantime?"

"Her son-in-law Montana has been running it. I assume it's work as usual."

"Your tone indicates running it into the ground." Taylor ran an old-fashioned sweeper over her rosy indoor-outdoor carpet while they talked. There had been too few people and too little fabric cut to need to haul out the big guns.

"He doesn't have any vision. I don't expect it will last long without her to guide him."

"What do you think of Art? Will he take the shop in hand or let it go?"

"Art is a mystery to me. I only met him twice before they married." Hannah glanced at her watch. "I'd better get going. I'm still getting settled at my new place."

"See you tomorrow." Taylor wished she had thought to invite her out to dinner. She could have talked about the thrift shop and those magical quilts forever.

Hannah had shared so much and yet she herself seemed a mystery. Could she really be as basic as she appeared? It would be good for her if she was. Taylor could use an uncomplicated hard worker at the shop. Roxy deserved help that would actually help.

Taylor called Hudson on her short walk home. "Just checking in on you. How's your hand?"

"That kid has a hard nose." Hudson was about four years younger than Taylor and a solid eight years younger than Clay. It was cute to hear him call Clay a kid. "Did he live through the day?"

"I think I finally got the fact of the thing through his equally hard head."

"And what is the fact of the thing, Taylor? There are a few of us who'd like to know."

"The fact is this: I am not in love with him and I hope I never see him again."

"That's a good start," Hudson said. "A very good start."

"How's dinner tomorrow night sound?" Taylor asked. "I owe you, of course, but I'd also like to eat with you because it's been too long, and I miss you."

"Long time since breakfast." He laughed.

"Long time since a real date."

"Sure, I'm free tomorrow."

"I'll pick you up at eight."

They ended the call with some polite compliments.

At her door, Taylor contemplated Hudson. He was a good guy. She was looking forward to seeing him. He sounded like he meant his compliments too. But how could a girl be sure he meant it when a guy said she was worth breaking a fist over? Either way, Taylor had a grin on her face when she paid Ellery and greeted Grandpa Ernie.

The grin left her face when she got a text from Carly about the Comfort Quilt Shop Guild.

She wanted to ignore the thing. What exactly constituted a quilt shop emergency anyway? However, she wasn't much hungry despite skipping lunch, and Grandpa Ernie seemed to be in a good mood, so they headed out to the town hall for the meeting.

CHAPTER NINE

$\mathcal{T}$his meeting of the Quilt Shop Guild was similar to all the others, including the table of snacks. Someone had planned the emergency well in advance, it seemed.

"My apologies." Carly, the owner of Bible Creek Quilt and Gift, stood in the center of the rustic town hall building, in front of a refreshments table. "This meeting is rushed, but I didn't want you to starve, and that was all I had at home."

It looked to be half a sheet cake with the remainder of an anniversary message, a bowl of pretzels, and a canister of cheese dip. "Please, fill your plates and then join us. This should be a quick meeting."

Taylor filled a plate for Grandpa Ernie and herself, and they sat at the empty table. They were soon joined by a couple of other quilt shop owners. June, the woman who owned Comfort Cozies teased him about the pretty young thing he takes out to lunch all the time now.

He beamed, bragged, and ate his pretzels.

"Shh." Carly stood before them with her finger to her lips. "I've spoken to a few of you already, but I couldn't call the meeting till I had final word from the college. They are obviously devastated at the loss of Reynette Woods, a true artist who had much to share, and are thrilled with the idea of a memorial event in her honor."

That seemed nice, but hardly an emergency.

"They want us to do it on Sunday."

"Sunday!" Shara from Dutch Hex almost shouted. "We can't be ready by Sunday. This is ridiculous."

"How hard can it be?" Taylor spun a thin crisp pretzel on her finger.

Shara shot her an angry look. "You've got all your best quilts just ready?"

"Why do we need our best quilts? What's going on and why haven't I been included?" Taylor dropped the pretzel and addressed Carly.

"Please, Taylor, relax. No one knows what's going on. Shara proposed a quilt sale for the Oregon Food Bank, since that's the charity Reynette was passionate about. The college will be hosting the memorial and some of the artists there will also have work for sale. As the backbone of the quilt community in this town, however, it is up to us to plan the event. Speakers, food, all of it." She turned from Taylor to the group at large. "I hope each of you will be willing to donate two quilts to auction."

Taylor whistled. "That is a lot in two days. I agree."

They hammered out some of the details, Carly, herself, humbly offering to speak, June from Comfort Cozies providing music, and Taylor and Shara seeking food donations from the town restaurants. It would be a mad dash, and Taylor wasn't excited about it. She stood to go as soon as she had her assignment, but Shara put her hand up. "Can we address the elephant in the room?"

"Who you calling an elephant?" Grandpa Ernie shouted with a laugh.

"Taylor. That's who." Shara's thin lip curled. "I know this meeting is technically about the memorial, but she crossed the line by ordering my proprietorial fabric."

"What are you talking about?" Taylor was too tired to argue, but not too tired to sound like she was arguing, apparently.

"I'm talking about the Lancaster Linens, all organic vintage print line. That's my line. We all know that. I've been carrying it exclusively for three years and yesterday one of my best customers popped by to say she liked your selection better."

There was a gasp from behind Taylor.

"You mean the organic *flour sack* reprints I ordered to sell at *Flour Sax Quilt Shop*? I find it impossible to believe that you are the only shop allowed to carry fabric that rightfully belongs in my store."

"Taylor..." the soft voice of June interrupted. "We have a mutual understanding among us that complementarianism is better than competition. If we each hold to our aesthetic, then we lift each other up."

"How is a flour sack reprint line not in the aesthetic of an entirely vintage fabric store literally named Flour Sax?" Taylor's face was hot. She wasn't sure if she was about to start yelling or crying, or maybe both. And she wasn't sure why she had let Shara set her off. Besides, of course, not having eaten anything but those pretzels all day and the drama Clay and Sissy had both brought into her life.

"You are talking about Lancaster Linens, right?" Shara repeated.

"Yes, they had a gorgeous new line of reprints, all organic, that are a lovely mark up for me."

"We all have lines that we carry exclusively," Carly of Bible Creek said. "I would never carry your Storybook line and I hope you would never carry my Lines of Truth."

"Why on earth would I want Bible themed fabric in my store? Shara cannot own flour sack reprints just because they come from a line with the name Lancaster in it."

Carly of Bible Creek looked at her watch. "This issue deserves its own meeting. Let's table it for now so we can focus on the memorial."

Shara was not pleased. "I'll table it so long as she takes that fabric off her shelves tonight."

"Get a life." Taylor walked slowly toward the door, dignified, and tall. Grandpa Ernie trailed behind her, slow, shaky, but with chin lifted high and mustache bristling.

Carly sidled up next to Taylor. "We have all been so patient, Taylor. We know we do things different down here and you come from the corporate world, but please do take that fabric down. We'll address this with equity at another meeting, I promise."

Grandpa Ernie scowled at Carly. "No one tells my daughter what to do with her fabric."

A tear burst out of Taylor's eye against her will. It had been a good few days, but there it was again. He couldn't quite remember who Taylor was.

Carly clucked gently.

Taylor helped Grandpa Ernie down the steps to the car and drove the few blocks home.

She had spent a lot of money on that organic fabric, and she was going to sell every inch of it if it was the last thing she did. Shara and her copy-cat store Dutch Hex would not dictate what sold at Flour Sax.

After Taylor got Grandpa Ernie settled into bed, she snuck back to her shop. She had five bolts of this Lancaster Linens organic feed sack reprints. She bit her tongue in annoyance when she looked at the name of the design line again. Feed sacks, of which flour sacks were just one style. But still, feed sack nostalgia was the point of their store.

Amish nostalgia was the point of Shara's.

This fabric still belonged with Taylor.

She selected a tiny overall daisy pattern, white flowers on deep-brown background, a polka dot and chicken pattern in yellow on dusty-green, a white background with blue, yellow, and brown daisy-like flowers, and a faded-blue background with brown and yellow paisley from her selection and set to work.

Four hours later she had a four-foot by four-foot, nine-patch wall hanging, machine quilted on the bias. Taylor hung it in the window, with a hand-written sign—she was a pro at hand drawn ads—letting the town know they had original organic reprints inside. Then she locked up and went home.

There were still a few hours left to sleep, and she could now that she had worked out her frustration and anger on a project. It was almost as good as shopping.

Roxy and Taylor began the next day by filming an impromptu history of feed and flour sack fabrics. It went so smoothly on the first try that Taylor let herself feel optimistic and hopeful about the day.

Unfortunately, Shara texted at nine saying she was coming over to discuss the food donations for the memorial event. She came around the back door, but it was obvious she had already seen the new window display. Moments later Carly from Bible Creek Quilt and Gift joined them, looking grim.

"Coffee?" Taylor gestured to the little coffee station she had set up with the Keurig and water cooler.

"Taylor, I can understand how you feel." Carly patted her shoulder. "But this is no time to escalate and antagonize."

"This shop has always wanted me out of business." Shara hissed her esses at Taylor.

Taylor and her mom *had* always wanted Dutch Hex to go out of business, but only because she had come in as a copy-cat, trying to steal the nostalgia-wholesome shoppers from Flour Sax. Shara could have opened any store she wanted, but even the name Dutch Hex, which referred to the painted quilt blocks on barns in Amish country, was similar to Flour Sax.

"Shara, let's try not to think catastrophically," Carly soothed.

"Who do you even think you are?" Shara responded. "You bought your shop. You didn't build it from the ground up. And anyway, since when did a 'Quilt and Gift Shop' start carrying books?"

Carly's cheeks reddened. "Our customers have been asking."

"Amish books?" Shara's face reddened, too, but out of anger.

"Christian fiction. Lots of kinds." Carly cleared her throat.

"Amish." Shara doubled down.

"And quilt mysteries." Carly took a long, slow breath.

"I carry Amish books." Shara leaned forward, like a cat ready to pounce.

"Shara, let's not argue about this right now. I came here to help Taylor see the need to take her fabric down."

Taylor was enjoying the show.

Carly was new to town. She had only owned her shop for the last five years, but she was one of those women who become the leader wherever she goes.

"Remove your Amish fiction books, and I'll believe you mean it."

"I don't carry the same titles you do," Carly said. "You carry some fairly racy Amish romance."

"How about you take your books down," Taylor said to Carly, then turned to Shara, "and you rename your shop, so it isn't a direct copy of mine." Taylor settled into a chair with her mug. She was the only one who had taken advantage of the offered caffeine. "And then I'll go shop to shop with my catalogue of original fabrics and make sure we all remove anything that could be easily confused with mine. That makes sense, right? Small repeated floral patterns were especially common to flour sacks."

Carly exhaled slowly. "You're trying to make a point that our issue with you carrying this fabric is absurd."

"Very good." Taylor sipped her coffee.

"But this is the way it has been done. We each have lines of fabric that the other stores won't carry."

"Bring me the list of fabrics you carry," Taylor said to Shara, "and I will show you all the ones I still don't have, how is that?"

Shara pressed her lips together and narrowed her eyes.

"Ladies…" Carly stood between them, hands up and out.

"I'll discuss food donations with Reuben's," Taylor said. "They can be counted on for some kind of hot comfort food. And I'll ask at Comfort Noir if they'd like to donate some wine. Who are you going to talk to?"

"I'll go to Country Market on the highway and see if they can provide some vegetarian options."

"How many people are we expecting?" Taylor asked Carly.

Carly's brows were drawn in confusion.

Taylor had flipped the switch to the memorial so suddenly, Carly had missed it. Taylor had, in a way, stolen her moment of glory.

It felt good, if petty. Like putting up the quilt.

"Strive for two hundred."

"Easy. If you ladies will excuse me, I'm still training my new employee." The polite ejection almost worked, but Taylor was greeted at the back door by Sissy. "I need to talk to you alone." She looked at Carly and Shara as though they were complete strangers.

"We were just leaving." Carly hooked her arm through Shara's. "We're going to my shop to talk about books."

Taylor felt the same thing that made Shara cringe. She had a feeling their discussion about books would end up with Shara being told that her Amish titles had to go…. She didn't want Shara to win, by any means, but she certainly didn't want her to lose to Carly.

What they needed was someone impartial to intervene in their troubles. Someone like June from Comfort Cozies. It had been the second shop to open in town, and Grandma Delma and June's mother had founded the guild together.

Shara, on the other hand, gave Taylor a triumphant look as she left with Carly. A look Taylor couldn't understand. In what way was going to Bible Creek Quilt and Gift to get a lecture a win for anyone?

"Want some coffee?" Again, Taylor directed her surprise guest to their little coffee set-up.

"When do you open today?" Sissy stood with her back to the Keurig.

"In an hour and a half."

"Good, then let's go."

"Hold up Sissy, I do have things to do before we unlock the doors."

"Can't Roxy do them for you? She's better at it anyway."

"Ouch! What was that about?"

"Everyone knows Roxy was running this place while your mom was trying to get internet famous."

"If you want me to help you, you can't come in here insulting me and mine and demanding I run at your whim." Taylor sat down and crossed her legs. "What on earth has happened since yesterday morning to make you so panicked?"

"Your new employee is heading over to the house right now to clean out the online shop stuff. Perhaps to eliminate anything that links her to the murder."

Taylor's interest was piqued. "And we can go too?"

"Yes. Fawn will be there. She called to say Hannah had texted Art and gotten permission. I don't like it one bit. Who knows what she'll be taking away?"

"What will our excuse for showing up be?"

"I don't need an excuse. I'm keeping a stranger from robbing my aunt's family."

"I need one. I'm Hannah's new employer. It would be a little odd for me to be afraid she's going to steal from them."

"Come up with whatever story you want, but come with me. I'll be in the office with the records. Fawn plans on following Hannah around. You can station yourself in the work room where all the quilting supplies are."

"Why not?" Taylor caught Roxy's eye. "You good if I go play detective for a while?"

Roxy shook her head in disbelief, but grinned.

There had been a lot of drama already this morning, and like always Roxy rolled with it like a pro.

CHAPTER TEN

*A*rt and Reynette Wood's Queen Anne Victorian was just as impressive the second day as it had been the first, and just as cluttered with boxes. Of course, it would be as no one had been in it since Sissy and Taylor were there last, but it was still a sort of shock to see the elegant wood paneling and built-ins and plaster work obscured by the stacks of cardboard cartons.

"Hello?" Hannah's voice, with a hint of curiosity, came from the kitchen. It was soon followed by her footsteps as Hannah met at the front door.

"Coming!" A voice from upstairs shouted down followed by the running feet of Fawn. "Aunt Sissy, I'm so glad you could come." She practically leapt to Sissy and gave her a big hug. "And you brought Taylor. That's great."

"I only have an hour or so before I have to open the shop," Taylor murmured. "Hi Hannah. Glad to see you."

Hannah frowned at Taylor. "I didn't realize you knew the family."

"It's a small town." Taylor shrugged. "Sissy's a family friend and asked me to help out in the sewing room. Sissy's not much of a quilter."

Sissy cleared her throat.

"I mean, she's a great quilter, but not like, for assessing the situation up there."

Sissy shook her head, still displeased with Taylor's representation of her. "I just can't be in two places at once, that's all. Art was really wanting some help with the bookkeeping for the business and so me and Taylor came to sort things out."

"I'm here to help with whatever." Taylor smiled, looking from face to face.

Fawn extended a hand her way. "Come upstairs with me, if you will. I need help in the work room."

"I'll head to the office if anyone needs me."

Hannah shrugged. "I'm just getting some water. I'll be in the stock room where the clothes for online sales are stored. I've got some questions for Art, so I'll be calling him."

"Cool, great," Fawn's voice was thin, but she led Taylor upstairs. "Listen, I don't want this Hannah lady digging around in Mom's stuff. I know that like, Art gets it all, but you and I know that's not really fair. They were married barely a month before she died."

"Have you spoken to the police lately?" Taylor looked around the work room. It was another room filled with unopened cartons. A folding worktable was open but empty and a large flat screen TV was leaning on the wall.

"I call them every day, but they think I'm crazy. We're making the funeral home store the body because we can't afford a private autopsy, and the cops say they don't need one."

"You do know the cause of death, right? Aspirin overdose."

"Salicylate poisoning," Fawn corrected. "Mom didn't overdose on a medicine she never takes."

"Forget the autopsy. You need to find the source of the salicylates. I'm pretty sure it's nothing in here."

"I don't know where to look."

"She had to eat it or drink it didn't she? Have you dug through the kitchen yet?"

Fawn looked confused. "Not really. Just kind of."

"What does kind of mean?"

"I looked around, but I didn't really see anything. It's not like I know what I'm looking for." Fawn looked down at her hands, her soft, moony eyes half closed.

"If you suspect Hannah, why are you up here while she's down in the kitchen getting water alone? Also, what makes you suspect her?"

Fawn's face went sort of green. "Because the day after Hannah moved here, Mom died. Doesn't get any more suspicious than that, does it?"

"Have you done any reading up on aspirin, I mean Salicylate poisoning? Can it be done in a day like that?"

Fawn shrugged and picked at the sleeve of her sweater.

"Listen. Go downstairs and follow Hannah's every move. I'll look around in here and see if I can turn up something. Maybe she has snacks she keeps in her sewing room and they got tampered with." Taylor's mama-instinct kicked in. She knew the utter panic from your mom dying and not knowing why. She was glad, suddenly, that she'd had Belle to focus her energies on nine months ago.

Fawn needed someone to give her specific instructions and then tell her she had done a good job. Taylor could do that much at least, and maybe make her morning's efforts worthwhile.

Fawn nodded and then ran back downstairs.

For her part in today's charade Taylor had to keep busy for an hour. With the memorial just around the corner it occurred to her that she might as well look for some works in progress to display.

The boxes weren't taped shut, just overlapped, so it was easy to snoop. She opened the box on top of the nearest stack. It was full of T-shirts in the red color family. The box under it were T's in the blue color family. She guessed at what was in the one beneath it and found she was correct: Yellows. The yellows also had greens, the blues had purples and the reds had oranges. Very organized.

Another stack of boxes was also color organized, but the clothing items were more varied. They seemed to have been selected by the weight of the weave—that rayon Sunday-dress blend. She checked boxes across the room and found one with precut squares. It was quite a mish mash of colors, so Taylor suspected it was for specific quilt. The one beneath it, however, had two finished quilt tops, and one complete quilt. She pulled them out and spread them on the floor to see if she could discover their magic.

The completed quilt was pleasing, but it wasn't the wow that the quilts on Instagram had been.

There is something about a quilt in real life that dazzles the eye. The precision is part of that, from the tiny pieces creating a fabric mosaic to the intricate stitching, whether hand or machine, that holds it together. Part of the magic of the quilt exists when the eye is mesmerized, and you find yourself lost in the work that went into the creation.

These sloppy scrappies just didn't have that kind of power. Reynette didn't iron the seams flat before putting the rows of blocks together so the rows were bunched and lumpy in ways they shouldn't have been. The corner matching showed she wasn't careful about her pinning, either, some corners being more than half an inch off the mark. Having seen her other work, her careful traditional work, Taylor suspected this sloppiness was on purpose.

But Reynette's color work was pleasing. These were a vast improvement over the one picture Taylor had first seen on the website.

The top Taylor was looking at had been made up of three-inch squares of blues, creams, grays, and whites pieced together like a sky filled with clouds. Reynette had mixed denims, cotton T-shirt material, and polyester blends shot through with metallic threads. A blue cotton crepe with deep wrinkles and tiny white flowers gave the impression of rainfall toward the bottom seam. But as nice as this was, the work looked better online. Captured in the right light in a field of wheat and that kind thing. Maybe even photoshop.

Taylor rocked back on her heels.

And yet, Hannah had said Instagram was useless for them. Their real success came from flea markets and antique sales. That meant people bought them more when seen in person.

Either way, unless one of the artists at the school found this kind of false primitivism as offensive as Shara found Taylor selling Lancaster Linens, Taylor couldn't see it having anything to do with Reynette's death. That said, the memorial would be a good chance to talk to her future co-workers at the college. Whatever the local quilt store owners thought about her, Taylor's old friends at the college still liked her.

Weekends ought to be busy at Flour Sax, but the weather was terrible, and it was getting closer to Thanksgiving. At three, Taylor left Roxy in charge of the shop and their new hire so she could run down to Reuben's to solicit a food donation for Reynette's memorial. There, she spotted Ellie, the owner's daughter, who had been running the diner for years, leaning on the counter talking to one of her cooks. "Hey there." Taylor joined her.

"What can we get you?" Ellie asked with a tired smile. The dining room was empty.

Taylor didn't know if they'd had a lunch rush or not, but considering the driving rain, she expected it hadn't been a mad rush. "Just a coffee, if you don't mind."

The cook, who Taylor could swear she knew, but whose name wasn't coming to mind, filled a thick ceramic diner mug with hot black coffee. It was late for caffeine, a thought that made her feel older than she wanted to feel, but the hot mug and rich aroma was a great comfort on such a damp day. "So, have you been following the Reynette Woods story?" Taylor took a satisfying sip.

"Yeah. She practically died in our booth. It's been on my mind." Ellie rubbed her eyes with the heel of her hand.

"The Quilt Shop Guild is hosting a memorial for her at Comfort College of Art and Craft."

"You're putting on the funeral?"

"No, the family will have a quiet event for a funeral. This is more a memorial of her art, a kind of retrospective."

"To each his own."

Ellie's attitude wasn't the kind that made Taylor think she'd get free food.

"I was wondering if...."

Ellie reached across the counter and grabbed a half a sheet of paper. "This is our catering menu."

Taylor didn't look at it. "The event is tomorrow."

Ellie laughed. "You want me to give you free food tomorrow?"

"Yes." Taylor figured honesty was the best policy. "Each shop is donating two quilts to auction for the Oregon Food Bank. Reynette ran a thrift shop that supported the cause."

"From everything I've heard about the Woods family, they can afford to buy food for the event."

"I'm sure they could. But the family isn't putting the event on, the shops are."

"Are you all bankrupt?"

Taylor stiffened. Ellie's chilly attitude was worse than the rain outside.

Aviva, the waitress who had been serving the day Reynette died spotted Taylor as she came out of a cleaning closet. Her eyebrows flew up and she shook her head softly. Then she motioned outside.

"Got it. I'll look for donations elsewhere. It's no big deal." Taylor slipped off her stool.

"Good."

She left her full mug on the counter with a five, which was more than a cup of coffee at the diner cost. She left out the front door but went around back, the way Aviva had directed.

Aviva was waiting under the awning over the back door. "The police have been at my heels. I know everyone is saying it was some kind of overdose, but Aunt Ellie is a mess. She's pretty much had to talk to the cops every single day. And I know you must be thinking the rain is keeping people away, but rain used to bring people here on weekends. They'd get all cold and wet from shopping or they'd get cabin fever and have to come out. But we had literally no one for breakfast and only two tables at lunch. She's sick to death with worry and sick to death of Reynette."

"Got it. Wish I had known earlier though...." Taylor picked at her thumbnail. "You haven't overheard any of the conversations your aunt has been having with the cops, have you?"

"Just one. They came in here and sat at a booth together while I was mopping last night."

"Anything you can share with me?"

Aviva narrowed her eyes. "How is your investigation going?"

"I want to tell you everything, I swear, but I'm not ready."

Aviva seemed to be deciding if she was 'ready' to share with Taylor or not, but her youthful taste for drama won out. "Okay, listen, it wasn't much. I think they'd worn her down a lot. Aunt Ellie had already given them her first aid box and said they'd already been to her house. They'd asked for the food and drink Reynette had when she was here, but we'd already cleaned it all up. Besides, she'd literally only had like, half a cup of coffee. It would have all had to have been aspirin and that would have tasted disgusting, right? They believed Aunt Ellie, but only because Cooper and Sissy vouched for how much Reynette had eaten."

"If they really believed she hadn't eaten anything here, why do they keep coming back?"

"That's what Aunt Ellie asked, and then she refused to answer anything else without a lawyer. They got real defensive then, the whole hands up 'Woah, woah, woah' kind of defensive."

"What question made her finally snap?"

"They were asking her about the other times Reynette had been in."

"And?"

"She and Sissy had eaten here about five times in the last week before she died. I Googled it, and that seemed like enough meals to hide enough aspirin to kill her." Aviva's wide-eyed-wonder at the tragedy of it all was almost too much. She was Belle's age, but Belle, despite her dyed black hair and over-lined eyes seemed decades older in many ways.

"If it was a slow poisoning kind of thing, her getting really sick here that morning would have been some coincidence."

"That's exactly what Aunt Ellie said, and that's why she wouldn't talk to them anymore without a lawyer. But after she left, Grandpa got real mad and said it made her look guilty and she shouldn't get messed up with lawyers."

"I disagree with your grandpa on this one. I think Ellie definitely needs a lawyer." Despite the cover above them, the wind was driving the rain sideways and had started to soak through Taylor's jean jacket. "I've got my eye on some issues with her work as a quilter. If you've talked to Ellie about what I'm doing at all, you can let her know we're working hard to get her out of this mess."

Aviva wrapped her arms around her and shivered. "Thanks, but I think I'll keep this a secret. If there's a killer out there, we don't need them knowing you're on their tail."

"Thanks for thinking of me."

Aviva headed in, but Taylor stayed on the stoop for a moment.

Why would the cops be so focused on the restaurant, and

why would the family keep that a secret? The corners on this one didn't match, that was for sure.

The rain pounded the ground, in huge, fat bullets of water. Taylor considered camping under the awning rather than hustling down the wet sidewalk back to her shop. While considering her options, a car honk startled her.

In the blurry distance Taylor spotted a familiar two door. She wasn't the type to be scared away by a little rain, but she wasn't usually the type to turn down a free ride either. The car pulled up and a door popped open.

She braved the few feet of watery punishment and hopped into the familiar sanctuary of Clay's old car.

"Glad I didn't run back to Portland now, aren't you?" He said with a grin.

The car smelled like stinky man. At least he hadn't tried to cover it with body spray. Taylor glanced in the backseat, being a curious person generally, and noted a pillow, blanket, and duffel bag. She didn't say anything about it. There was no way she was letting him guilt her into a spot in her bed. "I'm due back at the shop."

He started the car. "This vacation isn't exactly my best ever. Remember the Thanksgiving we spent in Cabo?"

"Yeah…" It had only been a year ago. Instead of coming home and spending the last Thanksgiving ever with her mom, she had angered her coworkers by taking vacation during the busiest shopping holiday of the year and gone to Mexico with this guy. Taylor had, as usual, suspected he was going to propose.

He hadn't.

"We were warm and dry and happy."

"And fielding calls all week from family who were very disappointed in us for not being with them."

"But it was magical because despite your job as a retail manager you had Thanksgiving off!"

"I believe Grandma Quinny called that insult to injury."

"Awe, don't blacken a great memory like that. We had a blast."

He was right. It had been a blast. She'd begged, bartered, and bribed her boss and all her assistant managers to get Black Friday off, but she hadn't gotten it. Clay didn't seem to remember that they had flown down on a Sunday, enjoyed three days of sunshine and then flown back on Thanksgiving Day so she could be at work again bright and early that Friday.

Technically, yes, she had been on vacation on Thanksgiving. But she hadn't magically managed to miss the most important retail shopping day of the year. And to get that much off she'd had to work boxing day. She had been too tired to drive down to Comfort and back on Christmas, so she'd also missed the last Christmas her mom would ever have.

Her hand was on the car door handle. "I've got to get to work. It's okay if you don't drive me."

He pulled out of the diner parking lot. "I've got you, Tay. That's the whole reason I'm here, after all. You can count on me." It took less than three minutes to get them to the little parking area behind her own shop. He followed her in, which wasn't welcome, but didn't seem to be something she could escape.

CHAPTER ELEVEN

*R*euben's Diner had been a bust, but the Tillamook Cheese factory outlet that was next door to her shop generously donated several cheese and cracker trays, and Berry Noir, the fancy restaurant at the vineyard just down the road from town had come through with several bottles of wine and a couple of trays of *amuse bouche*.

Shara had managed to get a couple of trays of finger sandwiches from the deli at the grocery store as well as a large selection of soft drinks. All in all, for one day's notice they had done well on the food.

Art hadn't responded to her request to auction the quilts and quilt tops she'd found at his house, but she'd still display them. He couldn't possibly object to that.

Roxy had helped her pull down two display quilts from Flour Sax, one she had made a few years back and one that she had led a class in making just that summer. Taylor also donated her Lancaster Linen's nine patch window display in a guilt-driven moment.

The other shops came through as well. All together quilt shop row had gathered ten quilts to auction off for the food bank, and actually, that felt rather good. Taylor hadn't done anything truly sacrificial in ages. Sure, this little murder investigation didn't really serve her in any way, but it also wasn't real. She was doing it, but what was she doing exactly? Nothing tangible, that was for sure.

At the moment, Taylor was standing with Sissy next to the quilts from her shop, sipping a smooth house red.

Carly from Bible Creek Quilt and Gift had given her memorial message and invited the surprisingly large crowd to mingle, eat, and take part in the silent auction. They met in the chapel at the college.

The college of Art and Craft wasn't a religious institution by any means, but this building had been the pioneer church for their little town. A beautiful old building built with bricks from Willamina Clay Products at Willamina Oregon. It was a drafty, vaulty, spooky, and beautiful space. Though it was called the chapel, the only religious events it ever held were the rare memorial or wedding. Instead, its long walls and open spaces were the favorite gallery on campus.

The whole student body had turned out for the event, a given considering there was free food involved. The faculty and staff all seemed to be present as well. But the crowd had to have at least forty fans—quilters from out of town who knew Reynette for her art and had come to pay tribute.

That was Hannah's doing. She had sent out an invite to Reynette's email list. The list, Hannah said, was over 20,000 emails strong so maybe forty people wasn't that impressive, but still, they'd only had a day's notice to make their plans. Taylor was impressed.

"That one looks shifty." Sissy's whisper was a classic example of how whispers can be a lot easier to hear than just a low, quiet voice.

Taylor turned the direction Sissy was looking, as did several of the ladies standing nearby.

The "shifty" looking woman was a tall, slender, serious-faced instructor from the college. Taylor had met her in the shop before, though she didn't seem impressed with Flour Sax's reprint fabric, or light, colorful atmosphere. Taylor wouldn't have called the woman shifty, rather morose, and maybe a little snobbish. Fiber Arts, which was Taylor's degree focus, was just one of the art forms at Comfort College. This lady taught part-time in the small but growing glass department. Taylor watched her carefully fold a napkin around a stack of cheese and slip it into her pocket. Apparently, the students weren't the only folks starving at the school. "I'll go chat with her."

Taylor escaped the shadow of Sissy, who had stuck by her like glue for the whole memorial. She meandered over to where the snobby instructor was standing and sipped her wine. She admired the quilt hanging behind the instructor. "Wish we had been able to display more of Reynette's work."

"Indeed." The tall lady frowned. "I hadn't seen any of it in person myself."

"I find it's a real conversation starter." Taylor's comment was purposefully open ended. She'd agree with whatever the instructor had to say so she could build a connection with her.

The instructor shook her head. "It's not my place to say."

"Nor mine. I'm just a friend of the family."

"Are you not the owner of Flour Sax now that your mother has died?" The instructor turned a piercing look her direction. "I was under the impression you were one of the hosts of the event."

"Well, yes. There is that. But I didn't know Reynette. And I am a friend of the family."

"I see."

"And you are?" Taylor gave her a mild, friendly smile, though it irked her that the instructor had seen through her ruse.

"Gilly. From the glass department. I'm here to support my coworkers."

"Glass department...." Taylor murmured. "Like glass pipes and what have you?" She needled the instructor out of frustration.

105

"Excuse me?"

"When I was getting my degree here, before I went to grad school, the college didn't have a glass department."

Gilly seemed unmoved by the news Taylor was an alumna. "We have one now."

The conversation stalled out. Before Taylor could drum up more chit chat Betty Harris, one of her favorite fibers instructors, joined them. She was dressed in a caftan she had woven herself, muted earth tones in a soft, loose, tactile weave.

"Oh Taylor, it's been too long." Betty came straight in for a welcome hug.

Gilly from the glass department stepped away.

Betty reached a long arm to Gilly and gave her elbow a squeeze. "It's always hard when school is disrupted like this, isn't it?" She addressed her colleague.

"You don't have classes on Sundays, do you?" Taylor asked.

"No, but the students were given the week off after the death."

"I can't imagine why," Gilly said. "Not to be cruel, but Reynette hadn't even started yet. She hadn't even been on campus, had she?"

"She'd come in to set up her office, yes, but she wasn't going to begin teaching till winter quarter began."

"Such a waste. I had students with projects in progress. I've allowed them to continue to work but of course it causes trouble with the grading. Those who didn't choose to come in can't be marked accordingly even though the projects will suffer from the delay."

"It's the same for all of us. I suppose not my class. I still teach spinning and weaving, and of course, there's nothing time sensitive about that. But many of the classes were hindered as yours was."

"And with the holiday next week," Gilly shook her head, "a whole week off was excessive."

"Can you think of any reason why they did that?" Taylor

asked.

"The administration said it was for the mental health of the students and so they could go home if they were afraid. The woman died of a drug overdose, what was there to be afraid of? It's not like there's a killer on the loose or anything so gothic as that."

Taylor appreciated Gilly's use of the word gothic in their surroundings. Surrounded by quilts that were at least American Gothic. "More of that young millennial, old generation z snowflake-ishness?" Taylor asked. Gilly was clearly older than Taylor, but Taylor didn't dare guess how much so. If she was faithful in her skin care, she could be in her mid forties, if not.... no. Taylor didn't dare guess.

"I suspect so. You'd know more than I do, Betty." Gilly shrugged and maneuvered away to greet someone dressed in a sleek wool pants suit.

"Were you excited about Reynette joining the school?" Taylor asked. Betty was a far better resource for this conversation than Gilly had been. If anyone would have known about professional rivalry amongst the quilters, it was the head of the fibers department.

"Oh!" Betty's face lit up as a tall, somewhat familiar looking man approached. "Let me introduce you to Jason—Jason, a moment?"

The man stopped and smiled sadly at Betty. He walked much more slowly than his unlined face suggested he should walk. He stood with a slight stoop and wore a pair of wire-rim glasses on his narrow nose. Taylor would have guessed him to be about forty-five, but it was hard to say with the very skinny. Low body fat could be terribly aging.

"Taylor, this is Jason Woods, Art's son. I'm so glad you could join us."

He nodded at her, so serious and studious.

"I'm sorry for your loss," Taylor offered.

He sighed. "Yes. This is quite a blow to my father."

"He was very much in love, I assume." Taylor tilted her head and frowned sadly. Jason looked just like his father.

"I assume as well. Otherwise how do you explain the speed of their romance?"

"I've heard it was a whirlwind."

"Indeed. They seemed to have just met, to me, and suddenly they were married. They announced their engagement just two weeks ago, and the next thing we knew, they were married and had moved to town."

"How long have you been in Comfort?"

"Just over six years."

It was almost exactly the length of time Taylor had been away, which explained why she didn't know him.

"What brought you here?"

"Me?" He seemed surprised to be asked about himself. "I like the atmosphere. Small college towns make nice homes. I commute to McMinnville to teach at the community college."

"That's a bit of a drive every day, isn't it?"

"I don't need to go in every day. Just three times a week and rarely in the summers."

"Nice work if you can get it." The platitude fell from Taylor's mouth with sincerity.

"Yes. It is."

"What field are you in?"

"History, like my father." His eyes were fixed on a spot on the ground, near Taylor's feet for the whole conversation.

She couldn't help but look. She saw nothing but the well cared for oak floors. "It must be wonderful to have him in town."

He furrowed his brow. "He seems to like his house."

"He seems young to retire..."

"Retire? No. Sabbatical."

"I see. He seems to have fully supported his new wife's new job."

"Yes. He is a firm believer in education. This would have

been good for them."

"The job?" Taylor asked.

"They had little else in common."

"I hadn't realized. Gracie seemed to think they were a perfect match."

"Did she? Interesting."

"I'm sorry he wasn't able to make it to the memorial. He must be enjoying time with his daughter."

Jason still stared at the ground.

"Is your father close with Una?"

"Excuse me?"

"Is your father close with your sister?"

"Oh. Yes. I suppose. Avuncular really, but that's to be expected with a late in life child, isn't it?"

"I wouldn't know." Jason was a cold fish. He seemed bothered to be here, and bothered that his father had moved to town, and completely unbothered that he had a half-sister less than an hour away.

"It was nice of you to come on behalf of your father."

"I came for Gilly." He looked around the room. His eye stopped on the tall snobbish woman, and his whole person seemed to relax. "I try to support her in her workplace as much as possible."

"I didn't realize. Have you been together long?"

"Yes."

Taylor glanced at Betty who had engaged another instructor in conversation. Taylor knew the woman from the language arts department. In fact, she was the entire language arts department. As an unaccredited school, the college of arts and crafts could skimp on some of the more traditional classes.

As Taylor watched the language arts instructor and Betty, a blur of deep red wool and silver hair swooped in—Grandma Quinny. "Oh Betty, Betty. Can you imagine? Married for only two weeks I hear?" Her warm, rich voice rose over the quiet murmuring of the crowd.

Jason seemed to shrink at the presence of Taylor's overwhelming grandmother.

Taylor opened her mouth to ask him how he and Gilly from the glass program had met, but he managed to escape before she could.

"Taylor, this was very good of you." Grandma Quinny leaned in to kiss her forehead. "I hadn't yet met Reynette but was so looking forward to it. I enjoy anyone who is doing something new in a traditional field."

Grandma Quinny had taught business classes on and off at the college for years. Taylor fully supported that branch and had hoped they'd make Grandma Quinny's courses required for graduation. Of her graduating class of fifty-seven only four were working artists these six years later. They could make beautiful things, but most of them didn't have a sweet clue about how to turn their passion into an income.

Betty and Grandma Quinny began a fast-paced talk about the tragedy of widowhood, though neither of them was a widow. They were intense and loud and didn't notice Taylor walk away. Taylor wanted another moment with Jason and Gilly, if possible, but they were gone.

Sissy was engaged with Shara in a heated argument. Taylor didn't want to know, so she left as well. Roxy wouldn't mind a hand at the shop, and Taylor had a big favor to ask her.

Roxy agreed to cover for her all day on Monday. The weather report was no good and running out to the coast to talk to Art sounded useful.

Grandpa Ernie was not convinced. "Why would I want to go to the coast? It's cold."

"We wouldn't be going to the beach itself. We'd just go to Neskowin for the day. Have a change of scenery. Eat at a different restaurant."

"Why would I want to go to Neskowin? It's not oyster season."

"Don't you get tired of staying around here all day?" Taylor made a face at their cozy living room. Taylor loved it, of course, but she pretended she didn't.

"No, I don't. It's much better than sitting around that old quilt shop all day. I told your mother I was sick and tired of it."

"I know." Taylor was pretending again. It was easier. Maybe he had told her mom that before she'd passed. Maybe he thought he had. "A trip to the beach won't hurt you."

"Makes my rheumatism act up."

"You'd rather stay here with Ellery then? That's fine. I don't mind." Taylor had actually hoped for his company. Someone to bounce ideas off, someone to be her reason for the trip.

"No, I wouldn't. I don't need a babysitter."

"Then what do you want to do tomorrow, Grandpa? Whatever you want, you've got it."

"I'm supposed to make Quinn a suit."

Taylor wasn't sure if he was referring to her other grandpa or her deceased father. He called them both Quinn at times. But Taylor did know that he was gone for the night. He hadn't made suits for anyone for at least thirty years.

"I'll call him," Taylor said.

"Good." Grandpa Ernie let the electric recliner lift him to his feet and then shuffled off to his room.

Taylor didn't call her other grandfather, but she did call her cousin Ellery.

"Hey Elle," Taylor said when she answered.

"Tay, what's up?"

"Grandpa Ernie's getting pretty bad."

"Mostly in the evening though. Well, early morning can be rough, but for the daytime and afternoon he's really with it."

"That's good to hear. I tried to get him to go to the coast with me tomorrow."

"He doesn't like big changes like that."

"I guess not. I was just thinking you could probably use a break."

"True. It's been a long week."

"Can you take him to the day center at Bible Creek Care Home? I'm afraid we need to start getting him used to that place." Taylor tried to sound bright, but her stomach twisted at the thought.

"I'm sorry. I know this must be really hard for you." Ellery was quite a few years younger than Taylor, and Taylor was used to thinking of her as a kid. But she had a very soothing way of speaking. Ellery was going to be a great nurse once she got into the nursing school. Having her from dawn till dusk with Grandpa Ernie wasn't helping that goal.

"Life is full of hard things, isn't it?"

"Yup. Listen, I'll take him there for lunch tomorrow and then we can go from lunch to the day center. And Tuesday, I'll take him in the morning. We can make the transition easier if we're consistent."

"Ellery, honest to gosh, I don't know what I'd do without you." Her mind went to the YouTube money that she was about ready to launch into a massive ad campaign for Flour Sax. Taylor had been doing a little here and there to test the local market-places but hadn't bit the bullet on a major campaign yet. She wished she could pay for Ellery's nursing school instead. She'd have to talk to Grandma Quinny. She of the big heart and love of family, and generous spirit could help her figure out the best way to help. "That sounds like a great plan. When I get back tomorrow night, we can look over the schedule and make sure you have two days off in a row, asap."

"Thanks Taylor, I appreciate it."

Taylor ended the call feeling more secure than she had expected. It wasn't that she wanted to cart her grandfather off to an old folks' home, but...she wasn't a stay at home mom with a live-in grandparent. She was a single working woman, and she just couldn't give him what he needed.

CHAPTER TWELVE

$\mathcal{T}$he mountains were blanketed in thick wooly fog as Taylor drove to the coast. On the other side of the coast range mountains, she was met with aggressive, unwelcoming rain. If she had been the kind of person to shy away from hardship, she would have turned around and gone back home where the days' rain was merely a silken mist. Without Grandpa Ernie there as an excuse for taking a day trip, she had begged Sissy to come with her.

To her welcome surprise Sissy was not a bossy navigator. "Art," Sissy had called him on their drive out, "my friend and I are coming by to see you. We just want to make sure you're okay." Sissy had him on speaker phone.

He responded slowly and with a quavering voice. You would have thought he was at least eighty. "That is thoughtful of you."

"Where can we find you this morning?"

"I can meet you at The Morning Mug for a little breakfast."

"Sure, sure but we'd also love to meet that little girl of yours. Would Una like breakfast out? My treat?"

"That's not necessary, Sissy," he said. "And she has school today."

"Oh, of course she does, silly me. How about Gracie? We'd welcome her company."

"She's working."

"At a surf shop in weather like this?"

"There's always something to do when you own a business."

"There sure is. Okay, Art, we'll meet you at Morning Mug. Thanks."

Taylor knew where the café was and went straight to it. Art was seated in the window at a bar height table, stooped over a paper cup of coffee.

Sissy and Taylor ordered muffins and coffee and joined him. The Morning Mug was a coast themed café, like most of them are on the coast, with classic yellow slicker clad fishermen statues by the front door and all things commercial fishing inside. They served any number of salmon-based breakfasts including the kedgeree and the cream cheese and lox muffin Taylor had ordered. It was good, but a traditional bagel would have been better.

"Nice of you ladies to come out." Art had deep shadows under his eyes.

"Have you been sleeping?" Sissy asked. "You don't look like it. You should come home."

"I agree with you. Coastal living doesn't suit me. Never has. It's so dismal out here."

"Only in the winter." Taylor felt the need to represent a little love for the coast, though she herself was more of a lakes and rivers kind of girl.

"Indeed. I do enjoy a day at the beach with Una in the summer."

"Has she enjoyed having you around?" Taylor asked.

"I suppose so, but it can be so challenging for a child to have a disruption in their normal schedule. Her life here with her mother and Guy is very good. I don't like to discommode her."

"You're her father. You don't bother her." Sissy clucked.

"In my own place and time, we get along very well, but I can tell she finds this a bit of a stretch. To have both Guy and me in the same home must bother her little mind somewhat."

"You know better than I do, but I have raised a child or two myself." Sissy defended her stance.

"Change does affect children, but I'm sure even if it is a bit of a stress, it's the positive kind, not distress." Taylor hadn't raised any kids but wanted to say something to lift Art's spirits, if only a little. To be widowed was one thing, but to be widowed and also feel like a burden to your own child sounded heartbreaking.

He smiled, though not with those watery, deeply shadowed eyes that hid behind his wire rimmed glasses.

"How has she handled the news about Reynette? I had a loss at her age, so I understand a bit what she might be feeling." As always, even alluding to the loss of her father brought a little smart to Taylor's eyes. She sipped her coffee so she could look away.

He tilted his head sympathetically. "I'm sorry to hear that."

"Thank you. Perhaps losing her stepmother has more to do with her being out of sorts than your visit does."

"I don't believe she had formed any lasting attachment to Reynette."

"Had they spent much time together?" Taylor nibbled the muffin. The streaks of cream cheese were rich and the bits of lox a lovely savory treat. She was changing her mind about a bagel being better.

"No." He sipped his coffee and seemed to look past her, to the other side of the street—the buildings that hid the ocean view.

"Art, I know you were delivered here and dumped by your family, but if you want to escape, you can. We'd be happy to take you back." Sissy's offer was out of the blue, but Taylor nodded enthusiastically.

He brightened quite a bit. "I hate being a third wheel. It's not a comfortable position for a man."

"I would think especially so if he is third wheel to his ex-wife."

Art laughed. "All is not how it seems." He looked around the room, then satisfied that the empty room was truly empty, he said, "Gracie was a mistake that I truly regret. Guy Sauvage was the best thing that ever happened to me."

"Apart from Una, of course." Sissy's mama bear came out.

"Someday we'll know…"

"What will you know?"

"Una is a lovely child, but she looks more like Guy every day. Perhaps she is my daughter. But perhaps she's his and they enjoy having the child support checks more than they would enjoy her having his name."

Taylor gritted her teeth. That old biological chestnut. Biology didn't make family, and this man had been little Una's father since her birth.

But Sissy nodded in understanding. "One would keep one's distance in such a case."

Taylor bit her tongue. Hard.

"Can we take you home to pack?" Sissy asked. "I'd like to say hi to Gracie before we leave though, would you mind?"

"Not at all." He pointed to a yellow slicker like the famous fisherman statues wore. "I'm prepare to walk. It's good for my health."

"Then if you give us your address, we'll meet you back at the house after we visit with Gracie at the shop for a bit. Just to see how she's doing. She was friends with Reynette longer than you were, if I recall." Sissy's smile was all innocence.

"Yes, that would be kind of you. Reynette was almost a second mother to her."

Sissy and Taylor sipped their coffees in silence as he wrapped himself in his protective outerwear and ventured into the weather.

"He just gives me the creeps," Sissy said as soon as he was outside their line of vision.

"That's exactly it, isn't it? The more time I spend with him, the creepier he is. His son's creepiness sort of hit me right off though."

"Yes, Jason. He was on the library committee with me last year. Creepy is a great word for those Woods men."

"But is it killed-my-wife creepy or just that normal creepy you run across now and then?" Taylor finished the last crumbs of her muffin and wished she had a second to take home for later.

"Even if he didn't kill her, he somehow managed to make a perfectly lovely woman like my aunt Reynette think he was someone to hitch her wagon to. Can you imagine? She had money and freedom. Her daughter was grown. She had her passion for sewing. What did she need him for?"

"Was she lonely?" Taylor crumpled her muffin paper in her fist and stood.

"I'd have to be real lonely to hook up with him."

"How long had she been…alone?" Taylor gathered her things and led Sissy to the door. She dropped her muffin paper in the garbage on her way out. The rain outside came down in steely sheets. She barely wanted to walk to the car, much less get out of it again before they made it all the way home, but she had brought this on herself.

"She'd divorced that loser she used to be married to at least twenty years ago."

"Ten years is a long time to be alone." Taylor had not gone ten months yet, but she could already feel the overwhelming longing to not be alone. Why else would she be holding on to Grandpa Ernie's company so tight? The quiet house all to herself every night was not appealing.

"Wanna know what I'd like to wrap my mind around?" Sissy managed to push Taylor out into the rain.

"Sure, what?"

"Why on earth would that man stay at the home of a man he thinks stole his wife?"

"He said he was glad to see her go." Taylor pulled her hood over her head and scuttled to the car.

"That's what he said, but he doesn't seem to care for Una, so why maintain a relationship with the three of them at all?"

"I wonder that, too." They were safely in the car, dripping on the fabric seats of Taylor's mom's old Audi.

"Let's see if Guy and Gracie can clear that up for us." Sissy buckled up and gave directions to Guy and Gracie's surf shop.

Savage Surf was one block closer to the ocean than Morning Mug, and they felt foolish pulling over again just as they turned the corner. Despite the weather and it being almost Thanksgiving, the shop was open.

A young woman probably in her late teens sat at the counter next to the register, her nose in a book. She looked up as they entered and nodded slightly. "Get in here out of the rain." She gave her attention back to her book before they could respond.

The shop was small and packed. One wall sported a variety of swimming suits, the other was covered in various body boards for sale. A handful of spinning displays in the middle of the room sold sun block, rain hats, sunglasses, bandanas, aloe vera, and buckets of sand toys. Surfboards hung from the ceiling and a menu board on the back wall showed the prices for renting wet suits, boards and other equipment. "Are Guy or Gracie around?" Taylor asked.

"In the back. Doing inventory," the helpful young person said.

"Can we see them?" Sissy asked.

The girl shrugged then hollered over her shoulder. "Guy, someone's here to see you."

"Just a sec!" A female voice responded.

A moment later both of them popped out. "Oh! Hello." Gracie's face was one of innocent confusion. Guy was immediately taken by the wall of swimming suits. Without saying even hello, he began to organize them.

"We had a memorial for Reynette yesterday," Sissy said. "Missed Art at it."

"Hannah told us." Gracie tilted her head and smiled sadly. "But we thought it was best that Art just be with Una for a while. In fact, Guy and I are staying at the cabin while the two of them have some time alone."

"The cabin?"

"Sure, even folks who live at the coast want to get away." She laughed lightly. "We have a cabin in the mountains on a nice little stream. Close enough we can come in to work without any trouble, but away from town for when we just can't take the tourists anymore."

"Funny to want to escape your bread and butter," Sissy said.

"It's for me and Una more than Guy." Gracie's smile never wavered. "She deserves some quiet down time too."

Guy still hadn't spoken. He was a tall handsome man, like you'd expect at a surf shop. He looked to be the same age as Gracie. Virile with a square and scruffy jaw. He wore board shorts and a surf branded T-shirt despite the weather.

"Have you talked to Fawn lately?" Taylor ventured. Gracie and Fawn were supposed to be old friends after all.

Guy snorted. "Every five minutes." He shoved a stack of kids' sun-blocking swim shirts on a hook in the middle of the wall. "I swear those two are the worst."

Taylor could feel Sissy bristle all the way across the shop.

"How's she holding up?"

"Not well." Gracie boosted herself onto the counter for a seat. Her employee had to scoot back to make room for her. "She and her mom were super close."

"Did she work for her mom?"

"Yeah, with Montana. They both ran the thrift store."

"I guess it's closed right now then?" Taylor was holding up her end of the conversation okay, but Sissy was fuming. She seemed to have grown a foot taller, and her shoulders were thrown back, chin out.

"Of course not. Montana has been there every day, plus they have a staff."

"Is she still thinking someone killed her mom?" Taylor asked.

Gracie looked past her to where Sissy stood staring at Guy. "I don't know that she ever thought that. I was under the impression you two were the ones who suspected foul play."

"My aunt didn't die of a drug overdose." Sissy had to hold herself back from hollering.

"No, just of having taken a bit too much over the counter." Guy didn't sound sympathetic.

"She didn't." Sissy stepped forward, almost like she was ready to fight.

"It's a hard time for everyone," Taylor soothed. "That's why we came out here, really. Sissy...You know, we're old friends Sissy and I, and she needs more closure."

Sissy gritted her teeth.

"I can see why. You know I loved her, too, don't you? Why else would I want her as my daughter's stepmom?"

"Still claiming Art's the dad, huh?" Sissy spit.

Taylor moved back to Sissy and put a hand on her shoulder. "Don't say anything you'll regret."

Guy stiffened. "Una is my girl. I've been raising her since the day she was born. Before even. I'm the one who went to all the doctor's appointments with Gracie. I'm her dad."

"That's what I hear," Sissy's voice oozed with sarcasm.

"Shut up." Gracie's face was red.

"Belle, my sister, she was adopted," Taylor said this to Guy. "But she's my sister and damn anyone who claims biology trumps."

"Exactly." Guy calmed down. "Art's a good guy, but he has that 'I already raised my kids' thing going."

"I met Guy shortly after I found out I was pregnant. Guy didn't suggest I terminate."

"Art did?" Taylor's stomach went sour.

"I guess when we married, he wasn't looking for a whole second family."

"Disgusting," Sissy said. "How dare he marry a young girl like you and not realize you'd want your own family?"

"I don't know that I did before I got pregnant. We hadn't talked about it. We'd talked about research trips and books we could co-author and what I'd do my PhD Thesis in."

"Do you ever wish you had done all that?" This was a new side to Gracie, one Taylor hadn't expected.

"No way. The minute the stick turned pink I knew what I wanted. I wanted my one and only—my Una. Not that I don't love working, or study, but Art seemed to think it was one or the other."

"If you hadn't met Guy would you have stayed with Art?"

"Nope. I was done. I was already living with my mother when I met Guy. Mom and I came here for a weekend just to cry and mope and stuff in the rain. Ran into this shop to dry off and there he was."

"And there *she* was." Guy smiled at his wife, his face glowing. "I knew instantly that she was my person, my family for the rest of my life. It did take a while for the divorce to finalize, but from the day I first laid eyes on Gracie, I never stopped loving her."

"Awe." It came out on accident, and Taylor blushed. Guy just loved Gracie so much that Taylor's awe was a literal involuntary reaction to the emotion pouring out of him.

"And Art?" Sissy hadn't softened to the man who had not had nice things to say about Fawn.

"He's always wondered if he was really Una's father, but I have been perfectly happy to get him a DNA test, so he just goes along with it now."

"Does Jason have much of a relationship with Una?"

"God no," Guy said. "I keep that one away from my family as much as possible."

"Is he dangerous?" Taylor asked, quivering. She could feel it in her bones that Jason couldn't be trusted, and Guy was confirming it.

"He's a racist reactionary jerk. If you ever see him, ask him about his area of study. He's practically a Nazi apologist."

"He's not that bad." Gracie's voice sounded weary like she was tired of this same argument. "But his focus of study is colonization with an emphasis on worldwide growth and development."

"So not literally Nazis." Taylor echoed.

"No, not literally."

Taylor drummed her fingers on the wire edge of a basket full of sunglasses, not sure what else she should ask. She was personally ready to pin the whole mess on Jason. She took a deep breath and gave it one more try. "Gracie, I've been told Reynette was like a second mother to you…Are you sure you're doing okay?"

"Fawn and I have been friends for a long time, but I wouldn't say Reynette was a second mother to me, not really, but I did care for her."

"Sissy is sure her aunt never took any kind of pain pills. What do you think?"

"She must have, right? Because how else would she have taken too many? It's not like aspirin is something you could hide in someone's food. You'd be able to taste that bitterness. I mean, if it was enough to kill you, you would."

"It builds up over time," Guy said. "I'm with Reynette on pain pills. Keep that stuff away from me."

Something about that made Gracie blush and look down with a little smile. Maybe it was the overt manliness of the statement.

With his muscly broad shoulders and square jaw, Taylor's heart fluttered a little too.

"If someone tried to kill her, they'd have had to have access to her normal food, so they could add it in small enough doses that she couldn't notice for a long, long time."

"So, Art then," Sissy said. "The creepy old man you've left alone with your daughter." Sissy framed that sentence as one last jab at Guy.

His eyes narrowed and jaw flexed. He looked at Gracie.

She looked up at him and shook her head. "He's not a creepy old man, and I was truly in love with him. This is an argument we have all the time. Guy thinks there was a power imbalance in my relationship that invalidates my decision making. But I loved him. I chose him as much as he chose me. I wasn't groomed by him. I was an adult." She recited it like a mantra that she'd learned to make sense of her life. Maybe it was because Guy had undermined Gracie's own memories with his doubts.

"Listen, Art wants to get out of here as badly as Guy wants him gone," Taylor said. "In fact, we're headed over to your place next to collect him and bring him back to Comfort. Una has school, right? You should know that when she gets back, he won't be there."

Gracie huffed in annoyance. "How like him, to disappear on her. I guess I'll have to be there to explain it."

"Let me," Guy offered.

They locked eyes, another moment fraught with love, passion, emotion, all the stuff of the soap operas their life together seemed to mirror. "Okay. But don't let her have candy for snack."

That moment of motherly common sense broke the tension and Sissy laughed out loud. "Dads will do what dads do. Come on, let's get the creepy old man and bring him home."

"Thanks." Guy held out a hand to Sissy. She gave him a firm handshake and they left.

CHAPTER THIRTEEN

*W*hen they got to her car, Taylor didn't immediately drive away. "What do you think? Did he do it?"

Sissy sat stiff shouldered and furrow browed. "Seems likely. He had access to her food. They make a strong case for him being a real jerk. Even Gracie's vow that he's not so bad feels like she's crying for help."

Taylor mulled this thought. "They've almost overplayed it, haven't they? Did Gracie and Guy kill Reynette and plan to pin it on Jason?"

"But why would any of those three kill her?" Sissy sighed heavily, the weight of her grief showing through her anger.

"Can we follow the money to a logical motive? Gracie claims she has money, but what if that's to divert our suspicions. Art inheriting his wife's riches could conceivably increase Gracie's child support check, right?"

"I paid close attention in that surf shop." Sissy's nostril curled like the shop smelled bad. "Everything there was expensive. And new. Nothing dusty, no old stock sitting around. They seem to have plenty."

"They could be up to their eyebrows in debt," Taylor offered.

"Art wouldn't have wanted her dead. A steady high income

is better than inheriting some cash and a business you don't want to run. I don't think it was him." Her words grew in anger as she spoke.

Taylor knew the anger, knew it well. The anger at losing someone you love sometimes flew out, injuring an innocent bystander. Taylor took a deep breath to calm her defensive instincts. She was just an innocent bystander. "Maybe it wasn't the money. Maybe Gracie wanted to hurt him for the way he treats their daughter." Taylor wrapped her hands around the steering wheel, gripping it for security.

Sissy nodded slowly, her face shifting from stiff with anger to soft sadness. The family motive seemed to hit home with her in a way money hadn't. "And maybe Guy wanted Art out of Una's life?"

"But would killing Reynette have kept Art away from Una? Having a new wife might have distracted him better."

Sissy inhaled sharply, but didn't disagree.

"When we pick him up, let's ask him what his plans are. That will fill in a lot of the blanks for us, I suspect."

Sissy grunted an agreement and Taylor headed out.

Gracie and Guy lived in a tidy two-story cedar beach house. It had a rope fence with faded red and white buoys set at the end of the driveway. The yard was green and lush and the landscaping an almost magazine-worthy example of what grows well in the sandy coastal soil. In a different season it could have been the cover of Sunset Magazine.

"Why don't you collect him?" Taylor said as she parked.

Sissy marched to the door, determined.

The stubborn insistence of everyone who knew Reynette that she just wouldn't have taken aspirin, combined with the discomfort Taylor got from considering the Woods family structure too closely made the whole thing feel like murder, even without any strong evidence. Taylor had plenty of time to think about it as Sissy waited in the driving rain for someone to answer the door.

Sissy stood under a pergola at the front door for five full

minutes. When Taylor couldn't take the waiting any longer, she texted her to get back in the car.

Sissy came, her anger on the surface again. "I knocked. I rang the doorbell. I texted him. No answer."

"He's old. Call him instead of texting." Taylor said it with a laugh, but a shiver traced her arms.

Where was Art?

Sissy called him.

No answer.

"I don't like this. What if he didn't make it home?" Taylor rubbed the tip of her finger and thumb together anxiously. This was not a day for anyone to be lost, much less an older, grief-stricken man.

"Drive the path from the coffee shop to the house. Any way he could have walked, lets visit it."

Taylor did. There weren't many different roads to and from, but she drove each one. There was no sign of him. "Maybe he went out to the beach for a minute?"

"And what, got swept away? We should be so lucky."

"No, don't say that. Even if he did kill her, we don't want him dead. Not yet anyway. Justice first, right?"

Sissy huffed but didn't argue.

"Let's have Gracie call him. Maybe he just didn't recognize your number."

They returned to Savage Surf.

Gracie was on a ladder dusting the decorative surfboards.

"Gracie, get down from there. We need to talk." Sissy stood, feet apart, arms crossed. She looked like she was ready to take a rebellious teenager to task.

Gracie looked down. "Hold on a second. Is something wrong?"

"We can't get a hold of Art. He's not answering the door or his phone."

Gracie climbed down the ladder and dusted her hands off on her knees. "What do you want me to do? Drive around and look for him?" She rolled her eyes. "I know I took him home like a hurt puppy, but he is a grown man."

"We were just hoping you'd call him for us. I thought maybe he didn't recognize our number." Taylor used a friendlier tone than Sissy, it seemed to help.

"Fine." Gracie seemed put off, a strange switch for someone who had acted so strongly concerned not so long ago.

"Where's Guy?" Taylor asked.

"He had to run back to the cabin for some files."

Gracie had her phone out and was tapping at it. She didn't seem pleased that Guy was gone, which may have explained her change in mood.

"That is weird." She stared at the screen. "He's not answering texts and he always does. He's text obsessed."

"We wanted you to call him," Sissy demanded.

Taylor put a hand on Sissy's elbow hoping it would calm her, but Sissy only flexed her arm slightly.

"Okay. Relax. I will." Gracie dialed and held the phone to her ear. After a moment, she shook her head. "Not there. Let me call Guy."

They didn't argue.

"Guy…" Gracie's voice was strained. "Guy, the ladies can't find Art. I want to run out with them and make sure he's okay. Umm hmm…" She paused for a while, first her face reddened, but then her brow smoothed out and she smiled a little. "Peyton can close up if neither of us are back in time." Another pause. A giggle. "You, too." She ended the call and pocketed her phone. "Peyton!"

The indifferent employee popped out from behind the corner. "What?"

"I've got to run an errand. Close up if I'm not here in time."

"Cool."

They went straight back to Gracie's house. She let them in the front door. "Art! Are you sleeping?" They followed Gracie upstairs. She stopped at a door and knocked. "Art? You in there?" She pressed it open, but the room was empty. "Maybe he's down in the game room…"

Gracie went down the stairs slowly, listening as she went. She poked her head into the kitchen and the hall bath, but the main floor was empty. They continued down to a basement that was mostly unfinished. It, too, was empty.

"Sorry about this goose chase." Taylor was a little embarrassed, not sure what she had expected to find in the house. His body maybe?

"I guess he just forgot you were coming." Gracie stood in the middle of what looked like a rather fun kid hangout. An old sofa, a beanbag chair, and a big fluffy rug brought some comfort to the concrete floored space. A huge TV hung on one wall with a game system of some kind under it. It didn't look like the kind of room Art would have wanted to spend time in, young daughter or not.

"I'll call some of our friends and see if he's just out. Maybe hit up the library. But he probably just forgot." She shrugged. "He's certainly not here, anyway." She walked them to the door and ushered them out, then shut the door on them. A very final end to her short hunt for Art.

The rain was beginning to let up. "That's that?" Sissy's eyebrows were pulled tightly together. "I thought she was going to hunt the town with us."

"Apparently not." Taylor huddled under the awning over the front door. "But the rain is starting to let up. Why don't we check the beach?"

They drove to the nearest beach access, parked, and walked toward the wintery ocean. The sky was a blanket of heavy, wet wool that created a seamless cold horizon, sky and ocean blending together.

"Great view. Thanks." Sissy kicked the sand with her booted foot. "What a waste this drive was."

Taylor didn't respond. There wasn't much to say.

"I swear to you, someone killed my aunt and they are out there right now, thinking they can get away with it."

"It sure does look like that." The tide was coming in, inching its way up the sand as the waves lashed out over and over again. It was the Pacific Ocean, calm, soothing. But frigid and remorseless all the same. "Let's go home. The secret doesn't lie at the coast. Just text Art and tell him we were sorry to miss him."

Those freezing ocean waves, promising nothing good as they overtook the sandy beach made Taylor want nothing more than a cozy fire, a warm quilt, and a killer locked up in jail, far from the people she loved.

After dropping Sissy off, Taylor went straight back to Flour Sax. Technically, she had the day off, but she wanted some alone time upstairs in the newly repaired apartment. If she was going to figure out what had happened to Reynette Woods, she needed time to think. It was noon, and they'd only been open an hour, but Roxy was cutting yardage for customers. It was the kind of positive sign Taylor needed after a rough start to the day.

Hannah was ringing folks up like she had been in the quilt biz her whole life. A great contrast to the not-so-wonder-child the Sauvage family had working at their surf shop.

Taylor slipped past both of them and ran upstairs.

The apartment was a homey place. For a brief time, when she was little and finances were tight, she had lived in it. And before that, her grandparents had lived there. Since those long-ago days it had become a sort of lumber room and shop storage. The trouble with the raccoons had been sorted by the very helpful Hudson East, and the apartment was useful again.

The stock for the shop was organized in the largest bedroom, and the random detritus of life none of them had been able to part with was stored in the other. The main room was empty, except for a surplus of large wall mirrors Taylor had picked up on sale, plus some excess chicken wire baskets, and a large assortment of pastel polo shirts Taylor had scored online. One day she'd have them embroidered with the Flour Sax logo, she just hadn't gotten around to it yet.

The floors had been stripped of the old carpet to reveal the seventy-year-old parquet floor and the walls were freshly painted. The space was a good pallet cleanser and a handy place to think.

The 1950s folding table her Grandma Delma used to piece quilts on was set in a corner of the main room with the matching chair. Taylor had recovered it in light-blue gingham oilcloth last summer. She grabbed a notebook from the kitchen, sat at the table, took a deep breath, and opened Google on her phone.

Roxy popped her head in the door with an apologetic smile. "Taylor, sorry to bother you. I know you're not on the clock."

"What's up?" Taylor set the phone down.

"I went over the YouTube schedule with Belle last night."

"You talked to Belle? I'm jealous. I can't get her to return a call."

"Didn't really talk to her. It was all via Instagram message."

Taylor just shook her head. She didn't get the way teens communicated and maybe she never would. Her only hope lay in that Belle would grow out of it. "What do I need to know?"

"We announced the compilation of your mom's advice quite a while ago, but we're pretty far behind scheduling it."

Taylor flipped her phone over, so she wasn't looking at the screen anymore. Or so it wasn't looking at her. "Yeah…"

"The clips have to be chosen by you. They just have to be. You know that."

"I do."

"But Jonah is more than happy to edit it into one video."

Jonah, Roxy's son, was their film editing genius. With every episode they uploaded, Taylor got more excited about his future life after high school.

"So…"

"How much longer do we have?"

"You promised your viewers it would be ready by Christmas."

"Ah."

Roxy nodded.

"So I have a month?"

Roxy shook her head.

"Jonah has finals. And a band concert. He needs the list of clips ASAP so he can compile them and make it awesome in time. You don't have a month."

Taylor sighed. "I'll work on it now."

"Thank you. And sorry. I know you're the boss, but Belle is the boss of the schedule and she kind of let me have it last night."

Taylor laughed. "Via Instagram messages?"

Roxy laughed too. "Yes. Not a single emoji in any of them. She was serious and firm."

"Okay...I'll finalize the list. You tell her I'll send it to Jonah as soon as she calls me."

"No way. I'm not messing with her. She's one too many for me." Roxy disappeared behind the door.

Taylor had to agree with her though. The genius sister who landed at Oregon State University after only two years of high school, and with a full two years of college under her belt already, could out talk any of them on anything, so long as she was in the mood to talk. Which, Taylor was happy to report, was becoming more common. Though she didn't hear from Belle often, when she did, the kid seemed willing to make eye contact and answer people with full sentences. Taylor couldn't wait for Thanksgiving.

Like a punch in the gut, Taylor realized that was just three days away. But that was one crisis too many. She penciled a list just to make her head stop spinning.

1. Watch three of mom's videos for advice clips. That would be forty-five minutes.

2. Call the Kirbys and ask her sister's bio-family what she

could bring to dinner. It was nonsense to think Taylor could host the holiday herself.

And 3. Brainstorm about the murder...

She scratched that off and wrote: Prep the store for Black Friday.

Taylor could brainstorm about the murder after the biggest shopping day of the year.

The card table and folding chair were not the most comfortable way to watch YouTube videos, but at least it made her focus. No snuggling down and getting lost in memories like usual.

In the first video she selected, her mom was showing how to cut old button-down shirts into strips so you could make a father's quilt. She was using Grandpa Ernie's old shirts, but she was likely thinking about Todd, Taylor's father.

Taylor still had his shirts folded and boxed in that room full of old stuff just on the other side of the door. She was supposed to tackle the project, but she couldn't yet. It had been seventeen years since he had died, but still she waited. Cutting up his clothes was so permanent. She knew he was never coming back. Just like her mom. And there it was, the flood of emotion overwhelming her even though she'd promised herself to focus.

"And that's the thing about remarriage..." Her mom was still working and still talking on the small screen. "You're marrying a family with a history. Not just a man. Those adult kids end the thing almost as often as fights over money do. I know you'll tell me why I'm wrong in the comments, please do because maybe someday I'll finally meet someone ..." Her face had brightened, like maybe she was thinking of someone specific. She was so young—not yet fifty. Her skin was smooth the way only a lifetime of wearing sunblock and living in the Northwest can achieve. Her hair was glossy with only a hint of gray. She and Taylor had reached that age where folks sometimes wondered if they were sisters.

Laura Quinn could have won the heart of any man in the world.

But she'd never remarry now.

Taylor scribbled notes while her mom talked. This wasn't a good clip for the compilation video. It wasn't encouraging to hear her say that remarriage is a bad idea. No one wanted to think there was no hope for love after loss.

But her thoughts about adult children caught Taylor's imagination. Adult children, so claimed her mother, destroyed more second marriages than fights over money. Combine the two? Maybe you get murder.

Taylor made a list of adult children that included Gracie the ex-wife. She was the adult proxy for a child, after all.

Fawn seemed to be deeply grieving, and her husband had a lot of work on his hands now that the genius behind the store was gone. With Art inheriting everything, those two didn't gain by the loss of Reynette.

What about Jason? A snob as far as Taylor could tell. Someone who surely felt his father was better than Reynette. Who was she, after all? A thrift shop owner who made money online. Not a highly educated academic. He struck her as someone with an anti-social personality disorder. If it was severe enough, he might have decided getting rid of Reynette altogether was the simplest solution to the problem.

And living in town he must have had some access to her food. If Art would just answer their calls, Taylor could ask how often he and Reynette saw Jason.

She supposed she could go to the horse's mouth and see what Jason had to say for himself, but if he had slowly poisoned his new stepmom, he certainly wasn't going to tell her about how often he popped by their house to see them.

His girlfriend Gilly from the glass department was another story though.

Taylor shut her phone off, ran down the stairs, and kept running till she was at Comfort College of Art and Craft, her alma mater.

CHAPTER FOURTEEN

*T*aylor barged through the front doors and just kept going. She ran like she was escaping whatever it was that had been haunting her up in the apartment.

"Whoa!" The soft gentle voice of Isaiah who ran the school office stopped her in her tracks. "Taylor, love, you need to check in at the office."

Taylor turned on her heel and faced her friend. Small of stature, but big of heart, she had known him for many years, since her time as a student, and it hadn't occurred to her in the almost year she had been home to check in with him. "Sorry. I was just...well, when inspiration strikes!"

He laughed deep in his throat. "Hold on to your vision but sign in at the office."

Taylor followed him to his domain, an expansive room of glowing golden oak where the accessories had been handmade and gifted to him over the many years of his service. From ceramic lamps and vases to the very desk he worked from. She spotted a new stained-glass lampshade hanging from the ceiling. "Is that from the new department?"

"Yes, isn't it wonderful? We're so lucky to have been able to add a department like this. So much beautiful work being done in glass. Chihuly came and spoke last year. He's an old friend of Gilly Framell."

"That's amazing." Taylor wasn't kidding. Chihuly was an international superstar as far as glass art went. "I came to see Gilly, actually. Is she in?"

"Yes, I'll tell her you're on the way over." He buzzed an intercom that had been ancient when Taylor was a student.

If Gilly was surprised Taylor Quinn from Flour Sax would come by, she didn't sound like it.

"Just head out back. She's in the glass blowing studio which is behind the pottery."

"Thanks." Taylor paused, wanting to invite him to lunch, but she didn't know when she'd have time. She waved awkwardly and left.

She tried not to run down the hallowed halls of art. They were hung with donated pieces from the faculty. Paintings both abstract and realism lined the first hall. When she turned the corner to head to the east side outbuildings, the art on display reflected the fiber arts that had become what the school was known for. Taylor paused in front of a quilt made of scraps left over from wool Grandpa Ernie had used for making suits. Grandma Delma taught at the college one semester when Taylor was very young and donated this piece. It seemed to move, the wool suiting soft and supple like silk. The thin stripes almost invisible but shimmering at the same time. Taylor closed her eyes. She missed Grandma Delma dearly. But she had something to do, so she hustled to the new glass works building.

If she could make herself seem friendly and chatty and welcoming, Gilly would surely tell her all about how her boyfriend Jason was constantly over at his dad's new place helping out. That's all Taylor would need to confirm her fears.

Out back Taylor knocked on the door of the new studio. In her day it had been a general studio where students could come work on just about anything. She hardly recognized it now. Massive equipment she had no names for filled the space and brightly colored translucent miracles glowed from every corner. Yes, Isaiah was right, this was a good addition to a good school. "Gilly?"

Gilly was behind a very traditional wood teacher's desk. She stood, her long lean frame draped in a suit that reminded Taylor of her Grandma Delma's quilt. Gilly looked up from her phone but didn't seem to register Taylor's presence.

Taylor was about to introduce herself when her own phone pinged a text alert. She checked it to give herself time to figure out what to say.

It was from Sissy. "*Urgent. Art's been found. Dead. In the Ocean. Let's get back there.*"

Taylor looked up again and locked eyes with Gilly. Her gut had fallen to her knees and she was frozen. What now? What next? *Who* next?

"You'll have to excuse me," Gilly said. "There's been a family emergency."

"Is there anything I can do to help?"

Gilly frowned at Taylor. "No. Why would there be?" Then she turned to a student who was working in a corner. "Please close down everything when you are finished."

"Of course, Gilly!" The student smiled brightly.

Taylor had left her car parked at Flour Sax. She went there first, then headed to Sissy's. She didn't agree it was time for another trip to the coast today, but she needed details and Sissy seemed to have them.

Sissy was waiting on the front step of her house. Taylor had barely got the car in park when Sissy jumped in.

"The ER at Tillamook."

"Slow down. What's going on?"

"We need to go to the ER in Tillamook. That's where Art is." Sissy spoke breathlessly and wrestled with the seat buckle.

"If he's at the ER, are you sure he's dead?" Taylor's own heart started to calm. Not dead was very good right now.

"I only know what Gracie told me. Let's get out there."

Taylor didn't have any good reason not to go, so she rushed to Tillamook, another town on the other side of the coast range mountains, but about an hour and a half away.

THE HOSPITAL WAS small like the one nearer to home and they found Gracie pacing the emergency room waiting area.

Sissy was in no condition to talk—her features contorting back and forth between rage and confusion, with just a hint that she was about to break down in tears—but that didn't stop her. "What's going on? You said Art had been killed."

Gracie was pale, ashen even. "No, not killed. I said they'd found him, and it was awful."

Taylor doubted that was exactly the way Gracie had put it. "What's going on?"

"He was wandering the beach, soaked head to toe, in a daze when a lady found him. He had a big bloody bash in his head. She called 911 immediately and they brought him here."

"How did they know to call you?"

"He had my card in his wallet, so they called it."

"Didn't check his phone?" Taylor asked.

"It was soaked. Just destroyed, I think."

"When he was found he was walking, walking, but with a head injury. Is this for sure?" While she spoke, Taylor led Sissy to the chairs. She couldn't make her sit, but she tried.

The three women stood in a tight triangle, facing off, the tension palpable.

"That's how they found him, but nobody knows what happened. His skull is cracked. He's confused. They're treating him for that, and shock, and hypothermia and everything."

"But he'll live?"

She shook her head. "I don't know! I don't know."

Taylor didn't know how they had beat Jason and Gilly to the hospital, but Art's son and his girlfriend pushed through the door that moment. They had both lost their reserved polish somewhere on the drive to the coast and rushed the desk full of questions.

"Excuse me." Gracie held up a hand as though Taylor had been in the middle of something, and went to Jason.

She put the same hand on his back. "Jason, I'm so glad you made it. It's just awful."

He turned to her, his eyes blazing, and shook her off. "What did you do to him?"

"You're mistaken." Gracie took a step back. "The hospital called. There's been some kind of accident."

"I don't believe you. Dad doesn't have accidents." Jason flexed his jaw. His eyes flamed.

"He was on the beach. I don't know. He fell maybe and hit his head on a rock. He seems to have fallen in the ocean at some point because he was soaked and close to hypothermia when he was found."

"Then he didn't hit his head on a rock, did he? This beach is sand as far as the eye can see."

"He wasn't out here. He was back home in Neskowin. Plenty of rocks there."

"Not in the ocean."

"High tide, Jason. It must have happened during high tide." Gracie reached for him, then pulled her hand away as though he were hot.

Taylor swallowed. Had Art been in that encroaching surf as Sissy and Taylor stood there watching or had those ominous waves just been hungry for him?

"You're in shock, you need to sit," Gracie said.

"We're hardly in shock." Gilly had managed to calm herself down and spoke to Gracie with scorn in her voice. "And we're not fools either. Someone killed this man's wife and now he's in the hospital."

Sissy stormed to Jason and Gilly. "How dare you speak of my aunt!"

"Calm down. I'm only here to help Jason." Gilly stretched out her long arm and placed a rather elegant hand on Sissy's sleeve.

Sissy jerked away.

"Why don't we all sit down, take a breath. We need to calm down and focus on what really matters." Gracie stepped between Sissy and Gilly.

"Excuse me?" Gilly raised an eyebrow at her.

"Stay out of this. This is a family matter," Gracie's voice cracked.

"A family matter, is it *Mother?*" The scorn in Jason's voice as he said that word was palpable.

"That's enough, Jason. Let's discuss this like adults. We all need something, maybe a cup of coffee." Gracie's face had reddened, but Taylor was impressed with her resolve.

"Where's Guy? Why aren't you letting him fight your battles for you?" Jason asked.

"This is not a battle. We're all here for the same reason—for your father."

"You mean my father's money?"

Taylor caught Sissy's eye. This was the first time she'd heard that Art might have means.

"You're speaking of your mother's money. Your father has never had two dimes to rub together," Gracie spoke quietly, her eyes tired.

Jason smirked. "And that's why you left him. If he didn't have money, you didn't need him. I'm right, aren't I?"

She swallowed roughly and tears sprung to her eyes. "This is not the time."

"That's always your answer, isn't it? It's never a good time for you."

She threw her hands up in the air. "No, Jason. It will never be a good time for me to run away with you."

The room seemed to freeze at her words. Silence, even from the front desk.

"I never wanted you. I loved your father, but it didn't work out."

Jason slowly opened his mouth as though to refute her claim, but she stopped him.

"You never could take a hint. Or a gentle rejection. 'It's not the right time for us' was the nicest thing I could think to say to my husband's disgusting son who was trying to have an affair with me. But is this really what you want us to discuss right now, at the hospital while he might be dying?"

Gilly's lip curled subtly in disgust. Her eye was on Jason.

Taylor could picture the scene so clearly, the twenty-year-old bride of the middle-aged professor. His son, meeting stepmom for the first time. The envy, the frustration. Jason was a cold intellectual, but he was still a man. How could his father fall for someone like that? An empty-headed beauty after a life with Jason's mom, who Taylor was sure he only remembered as perfection herself. And if his dad could have her, why couldn't he?

The scene in her head made her gag.

Jason's face was red, but his mouth was clamped shut. The light was gone from his eyes. He had disassociated from the scene in front of him, or at least it looked like he had. He wasn't going to acknowledge her accusations.

Sissy was at the desk talking to the medical assistant. After a moment she sidled up to Taylor. "Let's get out of here. Art won't be able to see anyone for quite a while and, when he's ready, who knows what he'll remember. If we're lucky, our call will be the last one on his phone records and the cops will want to talk to us."

Taylor exhaled through tight lips. How was she supposed to help Sissy untie a knot like this? "I don't know if that's luck or not. It would certainly be lucky if we could get more out of the cops than they want to give."

Sissy shook her head and her jaw flexed stubbornly. She wasn't any happier with their long drive to Tillamook for nothing than Taylor was.

They returned to the car for one last trek over the mountains for that day.

"I'm not saying you're bad at detective work," Sissy said, "but you don't seem to be getting anywhere, and I'm going to get everything out of those cops that I can."

Taylor could only agree with the condemnation of her detective skills. She wasn't one. She was a shop owner who really needed to implement the huge marketing scheme she'd been dreaming up.

Taylor was lost in these thoughts as they drove back and almost didn't notice her phone ringing.

"Can I get that?" Sissy held the phone out.

"What, yes. Sorry."

"Yes?" Sissy put the phone on speaker.

"Taylor? This is Gracie. I can't get a hold of Fawn and Art is asking for her."

"I'll see what I can do." Sissy didn't correct the mistake. She hung up and grabbed her own phone. "Head to Reynette's. I'll text Fawn that we're coming."

Taylor did as she was told and exactly twenty-seven minutes later, they were at the door of the grand Victorian place Art had planned on sharing with Reynette.

"Is Fawn staying here now?" Taylor asked as they got out.

"Art asked her and Montana to stay for a while. He didn't want to be alone."

Sissy let herself in.

Interesting that Art hadn't just gone to stay with his own son who lived in town. Maybe he knew Jason had tried to seduce Gracie all those years ago.

"Fawn? Fawn?" Sissy hollered her way through the house.

"Up here!" The voice of her niece came from the second story.

They found her in the work room surrounded by secondhand clothes.

"What are you doing?" Taylor asked as she stared at the mess.

"I'm not going to quilt any of this stuff, so I'm making bundles to donate to the shelter in Portland. Lots of homeless right now."

"True." Taylor sat on a folding chair and watched her sort the clothes that had been boxed by color and texture into piles by size and season, or at least that's what the new piles looked like.

"Fawn, why would Art be asking for you from the hospital?" Sissy stood in the doorway with her hands on her hips.

That arrested her attention. "What? Art's in the hospital?"

"Has no one told you?"

"Who would tell me?" Fawn scrunched her mouth up. "I'm just the one doing all the practical work now that Mom is gone."

"You don't have time to feel sorry for yourself," Sissy reprimanded. "Art has been in some kind of accident. He was found battered and wandering the beach half-drowned. He's in the ER in Tillamook and he's asking for you."

Fawn picked up a lightweight windbreaker, then let it fall again. "Maybe he wants me to bring him something to wear." There was a hopelessness in her voice.

"Did you and Art get along?" Taylor asked.

"We hardly had time. Mom had barely met him before they became inseparable and then suddenly married."

"Were you and your mom close before that? I don't mean emotionally, I mean did you speak often, get together often, that sort of thing?"

"We used to, but she got so busy when her online sales took off."

"The quilts?" Taylor asked.

"Mostly the clothes. She'd always been a quilter. We used to do that together." Fawn picked at the cuff of a frayed corduroy jacket.

"She grew distant before she met Art?"

Fawn nodded. "She loved business. Making money. New

ideas. She was always full of new ideas. I don't think I was fast enough for her. I couldn't keep up."

"So, she sort of went her own way?" As Taylor asked questions of Fawn, Sissy was flipping through the pages of a three-ring binder. Taylor wished she had the binder. Like the deceased Reynette, Taylor also preferred business.

"She wasn't really on her own. She had Hannah." Fawn's voice got softer and younger and sadder as she spoke.

"And you were left out?"

"Me and Monty had the shop, and she'd call to check in on us, or to come take the best stuff out to sell, or to let Hannah come take the best stuff out."

"Hold on, your mom and Hannah took your best stuff to sell online?"

"Yeah, she said it was all the same business, but it wasn't really. The online shop cut our profits pretty badly." Fawn tossed the jacket to her feet. "We've been trying to save for a house."

"I hear you." But did she? Ideas of Monty and Fawn helping themselves to the till to stash money and Hannah catching them swirled around her brain.

"She wasn't paying you enough." Sissy slammed the binder shut. "Minimum wage? Did she really think that was okay?"

"Thrift shops are non-profit." Fawn's voice was resigned. "But we could have had a raise if we'd been able to make more."

"Hannah made more than you," Sissy charged.

"I know." Fawn kicked the jacket away. "I made minimum wage, but Monty was on salary."

"Why Monty and not you?" Sissy asked. "Why would your mom pick him over you?"

"I don't know."

"Don't give me that." Sissy rolled her eyes.

"Sissy…" Taylor didn't see how bullying her cousin was going to help.

"I'm not as smart as him."

"Don't give me that either. You've always been very bright."

"I don't know then, okay? I'm not great with numbers and I couldn't keep the books. I tried for a long time, but I always made a mess of it. So, I handled the inside, the store stuff, and he handled the finances. He never made mistakes, so she made him the manager. I don't know why I make mistakes and he doesn't. I just do."

"Did you fight with your mom about that?" Taylor asked.

"A long time ago, but we got over it."

"Why does she pay Hannah more than you?" Sissy asked. "That's not right."

"Hannah brings in more money than me. And she doesn't make as much as me and Monty make together."

"Is that what your mom said?"

"No."

"It's really stupid. Who told you that?"

"I said I wasn't smart." Fat tears filled Fawn's eyes.

"Stop with that. I say you are smart. Who told you that it was okay to pay Hannah more than you because you and Monty made more together than she did? You should make more together, you're two people. You should make more than twice what she makes because you're family."

Taylor didn't correct this common business misconception. She could see why Hannah made more. Hannah was sharp and hardworking. Fawn seemed to be a mess. Taylor certainly wouldn't have offered her top dollar to work at Flour Sax.

"I guess because I was going to inherit…" She scrunched her mouth up in consternation and looked at her aunt. "Maybe she thought we didn't need much money now because we'd get all the businesses when she died."

"Do you?" Sissy demanded.

"Monty says we won't get anything now that she's married. Husband's get it all."

"Is Monty a lawyer?" Sissy made her opinion of Monty clear in her tone of voice.

"He knows. His dad died."

"You need to talk to a lawyer. Second marriages might be different than first marriages. Businesses are definitely different than regular bank accounts, and anyway, Art and Reynette were hardly married any time at all. Surely he doesn't get everything."

She shrugged. "What does it matter? Mom is gone. I'd rather have her than any business on Earth."

Taylor choked a little. She knew exactly how Fawn felt.

CHAPTER FIFTEEN

"**C**ome over for dinner tonight. Bring Ernie." Grandma Quinny's call was a command, not an invitation, but her voice was cheerful. "We're having duck. Not one of ours though, don't worry. Grandpa Quinny's always wanted to roast a duck." After a long day of driving back and forth to the coast, of dealing with a traumatized, broken family, and of being treated like Sissy Dorney's personal detective, the last thing Taylor wanted was this.

Taylor had finally made it home, and was holed up in her bedroom, listening to the half dozen calls she had ignored through the day. She let the rest of her grandmother's voicemail play and considered it against her other offer.

John Hancock, the handsome banker Taylor had seen a few times over the last nine months had texted an impromptu dinner invite.

John Hancock was smart and uncomplicated. He liked to go to movies on opening nights and to eat at nice restaurants. He wasn't looking for a girlfriend, but when they were out, he treated her like she was the best girl in the world.

A new restaurant had opened in Sheridan, and he was in the mood to try it, if Taylor was.

She was. For sure.

A night out with someone who wasn't overly concerned about her family or her housing or murder sounded like a million dollars. She wondered if she could send Grandpa Ernie over to the Quinn Grandparent's house for dinner without her… Another call came through and interrupted her reverie.

"Taylor…" Belle's voice had a surprisingly mature sound. "I've been talking to Cooper. What's going on with his aunt's murder investigation?"

"That is the last thing I want to talk about. I just spent the whole day driving to the coast and back trying to make head or tail of the thing."

"I hear that man she married is dead."

"No, he's not." Actually, Taylor hadn't heard the latest. Maybe he was.

"Hurt, then."

"Yeah, something bad happened to him. What's up, Belle, what do you need?"

"I need you to help my friend. He's a wreck."

"Why's Cooper a wreck?" Not that death was easy for anyone, but Taylor had a hard time imagining this boy doubled over in grief because of the death of a great aunt. Didn't seem natural.

"He's had to talk to the police three times and Aviva has had to talk to them five. He's scared."

"He exaggerates."

"Do you not realize he spent several days helping Art and Reynette move in?"

"I didn't know that, but even so, what does it matter?"

"This is a case of poisoning that couldn't have happened at the café, right? But Cooper had access to her food and drink for long enough. Or that's how the police are making him feel. Please help him."

"I'm doing my best, Belle. I promise. But hey, since you're on the phone, let's talk Thanksgiving."

"You'll pick me up on the way to the Kirby's, right?" Belle said it like it was a given.

Taylor wanted to discuss the matter and their feelings over it, but Belle was just on it, like it made perfect sense for Belle, Taylor, and their Grandpa to eat at Belle's bio-parent's house. "Yeah…what should we bring?"

"I'm in the middle of a couple of huge projects over here, can you just call Colleen and work that out?"

"Of course."

"Thanks. See you Thursday morning."

"Sure, of course. Hey, Belle…"

"Mm hmmm?"

"Love you."

"You too." Belle hung up.

Taylor'd have to tell Grandma Quinny they weren't going to her place for Thanksgiving. She didn't want to do that in person. She didn't think she could pull it off.

She texted John that she'd love to try the new place out in Sheridan, then called Grandma Quinny.

Voicemail seemed an even worse way to tell her they wouldn't be at the family holiday dinner, so she just said she had plans for tonight.

Ellery had left for the evening, but Sheridan wasn't far away. Grandpa Ernie would surely be fine for the length of one dinner out.

GRANDPA ERNIE GRUMPED a bit but claimed he didn't need a sitter and Taylor had better go on dates or she'd never get married.

Taylor set him up with a tray of snacks and the remote control and promised she'd only be three hours.

John arrived promptly at seven. Shorter than Hudson, but taller than Clay, he made a nice impression on Grandpa Ernie in his well-cut suit.

"Banker, right?" Grandpa Ernie said after huffing a few times into his full mustache.

"Yessir. Investments and planning." He offered Grandpa a firm handshake. "Good to see you again."

"Always good to see a man who knows how to dress for a lady."

Taylor was also holding a small bouquet of rusty colored mums John Hancock had brought for her. "Let me put these in some water and we can go."

John H sat on the sofa and chatted with Grandpa Ernie while Taylor found a small vase.

He offered her his arm when she rejoined them in the living room, and they walked out to his vintage Mercedes. "I like that Ernie Baker." John was calm and chatty as he opened the car door for Taylor. "In full disclosure, my brother owns this restaurant, so you have to pretend you like it no matter what."

"Younger brother, right?"

"How'd you guess?"

"Your parents wouldn't have named their second son John Hancock. That's the kind of stuff you pull on a first and first only."

"Unless you're George Foreman."

"Good point!" Rain fell on them in a soaking heavy mist. She ducked into his car and he shut the door against the weather with a satisfying click.

Sheridan, Oregon was a nice enough town about the same size as Comfort, right between Willamina and McMinnville. The kind of place Taylor drove through often enough, but rarely stopped at.

Hancock's was a pub in the British style, in the middle of the downtown strip, sandwiched between two rival pizza shops. The comforting warm aroma of roasting beef enveloped them as they entered.

The room was filled with round pub tables and private booths. Settles lined one wall and what could only be called an inglenook flanked the other side of the room. The bar felt like a movie set and it was a movie she'd love to be in. Stairs led up to what must have been rooms for rent. An honest and true "public house."

They got comfortable in one of the high-backed private booths and a waitress in a disappointingly American uniform of polo shirt and khakis brought them menus and took their drink orders. A whisky-ginger for her and a Coke for John since he was driving.

"This weather, right?" Taylor ran her fingers through hair that had gotten soaked in their short walk from car to Hancock's.

"Good night to pretend we're in England. Bad night to go out for Hawaiian food." When John Hancock smiled, his eyes always seemed to be laughing.

"Good night for German food, bad night for Mediterranean," Taylor agreed. The menu had several heavy, beef-based dishes that sounded like they would fix all her problems. The steak and kidney pie tempted her, but she wasn't sure about eating kidneys.

"Good night for smorgasbord, bad night for barbeque."

"Ooh. I don't know. Is it ever a bad night for barbeque?" Taylor looked up at him, batting her eyelids. It was so easy with John.

The waiter came back with their drinks. Taylor was brave and ordered the steak and kidney pie. John went with toad-in-the-hole.

"What prompted your brother to do this?" Taylor gazed around the pub that almost felt real.

"We're trust fund babies." He spoke apologetically, though there was a twinkle in his eye. "I don't usually advertise that, but you seem like the kind of woman who can take the news without going crazy."

"Obviously." Taylor waved her hand as though she and luxury were old friends.

"Henry aged into his money and wanted to invest it in a business and the community."

"Does he have a restaurant background?"

"Management side, but yes. He's been in hospitality for the last ten years."

"And when you came into your money, you chose banking?"

"These trust funds of ours aren't all that much. Kind of like Belle's, actually. Enough that you have to make some tough decisions, but not enough to get your own reality show." He referred to the trust fund he had helped Taylor establish for her sister with the money from a very generous life insurance policy. Half a million was set aside for Belle which she could access for school and school alone till she graduated. Then, there were other restrictions on it till she came of age. It had been a relatively painless way to split their mom's assets equally after she had learned Belle had never been legally adopted and wouldn't inherit anything.

"What inspired him to go all out English on it?"

"Many, many, trips back to mother England. He met a girl online a few years ago and went back to see her a lot. Ended up falling for the country, but not the girl."

"So, trust fund. As your parents are both alive, there must have been some old money somewhere along the line, if that's not a wildly nosey thing to say."

"It is, but that's okay. I'm the one who brought it up. We're old money in the pioneer sense. A wagon train ancestor bought lots of land in the Portland area and the family managed to hold onto it till the 1990s."

"Imagine the trust funds if they'd held onto it another twenty years."

He gave a mock sigh. "If only."

"So, did you have to share it with like a million cousins?"

"Nope just my brother and sister. We're the last of this line."

"That's good. No one to try and murder you for the money then...." Taylor had murder on the brain of course, but the weather outside and atmosphere inside was very Poirot. Adding a trust fund inheritance to the mix just made it worse.

"We're very lucky we like each other. Well, not my sister. She thinks we're both a waste of space. She's an Instagram influencer."

"Gosh."

"That's about right." He laughed. "She gets lots of free diet food. She doesn't need to diet, which is why they send it to her. If they sent it to someone who needed it, the world would know it doesn't work."

Taylor didn't like the sound of a skinny young girl with lots of free laxatives and appetite suppressants. "Do you worry about her?"

"I try not to. She's dating a college basketball player—he's a few years younger than her. I like to think he can handle her."

"Better your sister than mine." Taylor held her hands up in surrender. "I worry enough about Belle and she's just at college. Plus, she'll be seventeen any day now which isn't even all that young for college."

"But it is young for being half-way done."

"True. Ug. Sorry. Little sisters don't make good date conversation." Taylor sipped her drink, sweet, but not too sweet. Strong, but not knock her out. "Murder doesn't make good date conversation either, but it's on my mind. A friend asked me to help her figure out what happened to her aunt." Taylor took a moment to give John the details of Reynette's death.

"I'd heard of that. I'm sorry for your friend Sissy. Must be hard."

"Yeah. I keep thinking it can't really have been murder. I mean…aspirin overdose…No one thinks she took any, but who doesn't take aspirin? And if you never take it, maybe it's easier to overdose on."

"I'm no chemist, don't ask me. I'm just a money guy, so I'd say follow the money."

"There's a lot of it to follow. A lot of dollar trails with her different businesses. And getting married fast means the situation with the heirs has changed. Can't have been her kids since they won't get anything now."

He shook his head. "They'll get half. A spouse only gets it all if all the deceased kids are his and hers. If the widow or widower has step-kids from the marriage, those kids get half the estate."

"Oh really?" Not that it changed the murder, but Taylor sure thought Fawn would be glad to hear that her years of working for a pittance wouldn't have gone entirely to waste.

"So, who would kill Reynette for half her fortune? Husband or kids?"

Taylor crinkled her nose. "No one. Everyone loved her."

"I bet your first instinct is right and it's not murder at all. She probably had a bad back from all that quilting and didn't want to admit it."

Her heart fluttered a little. She liked a man who agreed with her. Especially if it got her off the hook for solving a murder.

The food was as rich and comforting as Taylor had hoped. She could sort of tell what was steak and what was kidney, but she wouldn't let herself think about it too much. "Is the upstairs a hotel?"

John grinned again. "This is a classic public house in all senses. Want to see the rooms?"

"Totally."

He blushed slightly. "Good. I got us a one."

"Oh! I mean..." She put her fork down. "John, I can't. I've got to get back. Can't leave Grandpa Ernie...but you know that."

A shadow crossed his eyes. "No, I know. Right. I know that. And it's a Monday night which would be weird because we both work tomorrow. And I only invited you to dinner, anyway. Sorry. We can still go check it out. You know, show off my little brother's place." He seemed to recover, his cheery smile back in place.

Taylor finished her meal feeling a bit sorry for herself. John

Hancock was her uncomplicated friend. The one she could hang out with and not worry about things getting serious. Right?

The suits.

The flowers.

The way he offered her his arm, held doors open, chatted with Grandpa Ernie.

He'd been doing those things for months. Months. He'd been holding her hand when they had to walk in the dark and giving her hugs when they parted. Hugs had become kisses on the cheek.

One time, just once, they had kissed in the real sense. And not that long ago. It had been one of the last warm days of fall, and they had walked the whole of Comfort, holding hands, talking about nothing and everything while Cooper Dorney grandpa-sat for her. They had stopped under the shadow of the grain elevator and laughed about something together, and then…they had just kissed.

She had liked it.

But not enough, if that made sense.

It hadn't moved her or made her think they were falling in love. It hadn't even made her feel awkward after. They had just laughed, and hugged, and kept walking.

He had called a few days later, but it was a couple of weeks after that before they got together again, and that was for a movie where they had held hands during the scary parts.

This was only their second date after the kiss.

After the waitress cleared their plates they went upstairs. He opened the door to room three, and casually took her hand as they walked inside.

The room was a perfect mix of old-fashioned walnut wood and velvet drapes and the cool, fresh feeling that contemporary furniture gives. It felt clean, and the bed looked perfect for dropping into after a full delicious meal. Except, of course, for the small sprinkle of red rose petals that dotted the white comforter.

Taylor gave his hand a squeeze, lifted it to her lips, and gave it a warm kiss. "Oh, John. I think we might not be on the same page."

He let go of her hand but wrapped his arm around her waist, so they were side by side, not making eye contact, but still intimate. "I think I figured that out downstairs. The thing is, I'm kind of slow. It's caused problems in the past, too, so I thought I needed to pick up the pace a little here. Let you know what I was really thinking."

"Slow is charming."

He chuckled, shaking his head. "Slow is confusing to beautiful women who want to be romanced. But I can't help it. Same thing that makes me recommend savings bonds to young people. Every time someone under sixty buys one from me, my boss calls me into his office for a lecture on compound interest."

Taylor laughed and leaned her head on his shoulder. "I really do like you."

"And I'd really like to see what kind of compound interest we could earn together."

She sighed. She didn't want to build compound interest with John Hancock. She wanted to keep him securely in the friend zone.

Though they had known each other a while now, she wasn't sure how fragile his ego was, so she kept that thought to herself. Instead, she said, "They say after a loss you do need to be slow. To be cautious. It seems to me that your natural inclination and my needs are well suited right now."

He turned and looked at her with sad eyes.

She gave him what she knew was a goodbye kiss.

He'd figure it out eventually.

He lingered, his head resting on her forehead. "Nice room though, right?"

"It's a very nice room."

They left and discussed whether it was crazier to try and run a restaurant in a small town or a hobby shop like hers on the way home. As always, he walked her to the door. He looked like he wasn't sure if he should kiss her good night, so Taylor gave him a quick peck on the cheek.

The house was chilly after the warmth of the little luxury car, and only a dim light from a side table glowed. Grandpa had fallen asleep in his chair.

It took a moment for her to realize they weren't alone.

CHAPTER SIXTEEN

A girl stretched across the sofa had Belle's second favorite quilt—the Easter basket pattern their mom had made—draped over her lap. Taylor had been out just over three hours, but the visitor was sound asleep.

She didn't know her well, but Taylor recognized her immediately as Aviva Reuben, Cooper's friend and the waitress who was counting on her to solve the murder.

Taylor went into the kitchen as quietly as she could and made a pot of coffee. She couldn't guess why the young lady had come, but she knew she'd need to be able to focus.

She nudged Grandpa Ernie awake as quietly as she could. "Grandpa Ernie," Taylor whispered, "won't you be comfier in bed?"

"What, huh?" He shook himself awake with small grunts. "Yes. Bed. But see, that girl came by to see you and I couldn't leave her alone out here, could I?"

"Of course not. Thanks for being a good host."

He harrumphed as Taylor helped him out of his recliner, then made his own way to his bedroom. It was almost eleven. Early enough in theory, but pretty late for him.

"Aviva," Taylor nudged her shoulder gently. "Aviva, I'm back. What's going on?"

Aviva sat up, rubbing her eyes.

"Has something happened?"

She yawned. "I'm sorry for falling asleep. I've been up since four this morning baking at the diner."

"Don't worry. I just want to know how I can help." Taylor yawned also. It had been a long day for her as well.

"I was DMing Cooper while I had dinner and he told me that you guys went to see Art, but the next thing that happened was Art was in the hospital."

"Yeah, it's been a crazy day." The warm, homey aroma of coffee brewing began to fill the room. Taylor wasn't sure even that would keep her up.

"And I got to thinking about that morning again. Reynette Woods, Sissy and Cooper were all there for breakfast."

"Go on." Taylor sat on the floor next to the couch, resting her head against the slip-covered arm.

"And that's when Reynette got sick and died."

"Yes."

"And you guys went to the coast and Art got hurt."

"Yes, help me out though. I don't follow."

"The only person in both places was Sissy."

Taylor rubbed her tired eyes. "Sissy isn't my favorite person in the world, but she absolutely didn't murder her best friend."

"Are you sure? Sissy had the kind of access you'd need to poison her. It doesn't take all that much aspirin. Just more than ten a day for a few days. Sissy could have done it. And then there's Art."

"We went to Neskowin to see Art. We talked to him when we got there, but when we went back to pick him up, we couldn't find him. I was with her the whole time."

"So, she established an alibi. What if she did that on purpose to draw attention away from herself? Same as hiring you to help her find who killed her aunt. She could have done that, I know it."

"First, it's not like I'm being paid. I haven't been 'hired' for anything." Taylor yawned deeply. "You didn't say any of this to Cooper, did you?"

"Never. He's the worst about his mom. Practically oedipal. You can't say a word against the woman."

"Good. Keep it to yourself."

"But you'll look into it, won't you? You'll keep your eye on her?"

"I'll do my best. Are your parents worried about where you are?"

"Nah, I told them I was staying with Cooper."

The Dorney house seemed to be a teen hostel with the way kids casually told their parents they were sleeping over. Ten years ago, when Taylor had been in high school there was no way her mom would have let her spend the night at a boy's house, even if they were just friends.

"You're completely exhausted," Taylor told her, "but if you want to talk more, I made some coffee and we can talk more. If you don't want to, you can sleep up in Belle's room."

"I think we need to talk more." She pulled the quilt up around her shoulders.

"That's fine." Taylor went to the kitchen and poured them both half cups.

"What else has Cooper shared with you?" If Taylor had to be up still, she could at least get an outsider's point of view on the family.

"His cousin Fawn is supposed to be working at the big house, but she goes to Sissy's every day."

"Isn't Cooper in school?"

"Yes, but she's there when he gets home. Usually eating something."

So Fawn won't eat at Art's house. Is she afraid of the food

there or does she know something about it? "What else does she do while she's there?"

"He thinks she just hangs out and watches TV. But why doesn't she go back to work?"

"Give her some grace. Her mother just passed away."

Aviva frowned, her mouth pursing like a child.

"Anyway, I presume the thrift shop has employees. Is Monty hanging around the Dorney house too?"

"No, I think he goes to work. Long commute, but whatever."

"Maybe it feels good to him to have something practical to do. Men are like that."

"Why would he leave Fawn alone? Shouldn't he take her with him to make sure she's okay? Not like, going to hurt herself because she's so sad?"

How sad for this generation of kids that their first thought at the idea of overwhelming grief was self-harm.

"They've been married a while. He probably knows her really well. She might have told him she needs alone time."

"But shouldn't he be afraid the killer will be after Fawn next? I mean first Reynette, then Art…"

"Then Fawn? But why? We don't know what happened to Art, and we don't know that Reynette was murdered."

"I'd be scared. I'd want my husband near me if I thought a killer was out there."

"Art was just injured today. Maybe Monty will stick around now."

Aviva agreed through yawns.

Taylor sent her up to bed.

If Reynette's death was murder, and Art's accident was attempted murder then Fawn, Sissy, and Monty might not be safe.

Taylor wouldn't allow herself to consider that Una, Art's young daughter, might be in danger. And even if she was, she had two loving parents to look after her.

TAYLOR OWED Roxy more days off than she'd like to admit, so she didn't dare ask her to cover for her the next day. She had to suck it up and run her shop like the businesswoman she always claimed to be. They weren't busy in the middle of the week, so close to Thanksgiving, so Taylor spent the morning Googling easy side dishes she could make to bring to the Kirby house. And making pages of notes about each of the main players in the death of Reynette. The thing that stood out at the end of that exercise was that it was no wonder it took a long time to catch a murderer.

How was Taylor supposed to tell who was lying?

The outsider's point of view from Aviva hadn't been very useful, but Taylor was alone in the shop with Hannah, and she had barely begun to plumb the depths of Hannah's knowledge. "So, Hannah. Have you ever tried quilting?"

"No, my grandma and my aunt do though. They've even been here before. My Aunt Jennifer was really excited to hear I was working here."

"That's nice. Tell her I said hi."

Hannah smiled and nodded, her calm, cool self still calm and cool.

"Your mom doesn't quilt?"

"No, she's the rebel. She makes beaded jewelry."

"Do you have any? I'd love to see it."

Hannah lifted her arm and shook her wrist. She wore a pretty band of glimmering green and white seed beads in a somewhat Celtic design. It had tiny bells hanging off what might be the clasp. "This is her newest thing. It's easier to wear when working than some of her other styles."

"Does she sell it or just make it as a hobby?" Taylor was still seated at the worktable with her laptop. She hadn't come across the perfect Thanksgiving side dish that was both absolutely basic and wildly impressive at the same time.

"Sometimes she sells them at craft shows for charity, but never for herself."

"If she changes her mind, we can probably find room for a little display by the register."

Hannah looked up from her work, her eyebrows pulled together critically. "It's not really a quilt product."

"Quilters wear jewelry." Taylor waved at the current impulse display by the register—scissor charms so you could tell your Ginghers from your neighbor's when quilting in groups. "Have you heard anything about the real funeral for your old boss yet?" Taylor changed the subject. "The memorial at the college was nice, but it wasn't a funeral."

"I haven't heard."

"Would someone call? I'd like to go, if so."

"I don't know that anyone would call me. I haven't heard from them. I expect you'll hear from your friends first."

"Probably so." Getting words out of Hannah was like pulling teeth. Not that she had ever been voluble, but this felt like she was hiding something.

"Have you been able to deal with the pending online orders?"

"No. As I said, no one has contacted me."

"Do you want me to talk to Reynette's niece Sissy about it? It doesn't seem right that they are leaving you hanging."

Hannah's face softened. "Would you? That would help. I've been getting some angry messages. Even though I immediately stopped all future orders, there are folks still waiting for items I don't have access to. I've offered money back, but this kind of stuff is hard to find, and they actually want it."

"But isn't it just like the nicer of the thrift store donations?"

"I can't explain trends. Things come and go. Right now, it's fanny packs. I have a Fendi fanny pack from the late 80s that someone paid, well, a lot for. She refuses to take her money back and emails three times a day for it. And another lady won't stop about a Dooney and Burke briefcase, that frankly, I didn't even think was back on trend."

"And a thrift store really gets those kinds of name brand, big dollar donations?"

"Not every day. And you have to know what you are looking for. I mentioned earlier, I think on trend, knock offs are still worth selling online instead of in the store. The folks who are happy with a less expensive knock off aren't as obnoxious as the name brand only folks."

"Please forgive me, but I have to ask...Ever come across something someone might kill for?"

"In vintage fashion? No. We sold a fur once, but it wasn't worth the negative feedback we got for having a fur for sale in the first place. The anti-fur crowd wanted to kill our business over it, but they didn't want to kill us."

"I know Reynette's quilts were going for a whole lot of money."

Hannah gave her a questioning look again.

"I learned about it while putting the memorial together. Did you ever sell anything vintage that made as much as one of the quilts?"

"Now and again. When we auction something, the price can get pretty high." She didn't volunteer what that price might have been or what the item was.

"Monty and Fawn didn't mind the revenue going to a side business instead of them, huh? The online sales didn't directly benefit the food bank, did they?"

"I sold the items. Reynette did the rest. Did Fawn and Monty wish they were doing what I was doing? Who wouldn't? It's quite a lot easier than running a whole store. But over the course of a whole year the sales of the vintage items don't make as much as the store does."

"Sure, sure. But that money could have gone into the store, right? For more employees or upgrades or whatever?"

"That was up to Reynette and Monty. Not me."

"Makes sense. Roxy has a lot of sway around here, but in the end the decisions are mine and mine alone."

"Exactly." Hannah glanced at her watch. "Do you mind if I take a lunch?"

"Go for it."

AFTER THEY CLOSED UP SHOP, Taylor called Gracie. She wanted to check in on how Art was doing before she headed home. She'd been neglecting Grandpa Ernie and wanted to focus on his company tonight, but she still wanted to know what the news was.

Gracie answered on the first ring. "Good of you to call." She sounded alert—perky even. Maybe a day of nothing to do around a shop in the winter didn't aggravate her the way it did Taylor.

"I'll make this quick," Taylor said. "How's Art? Is he improving? Does he remember anything?"

"He remembers a little, but his head is still hurting, and they're keeping him in for another day or two. It seems excessive, but I don't know. Age makes all things a little worse."

"He's not that old, is he?"

"He's seventy. Things do start taking longer to heal after a certain age."

Seventy.

Was that old?

Taylor wasn't yet thirty, and a lifetime spent with quilters had taught her that if you were under thirty you were an infant. You weren't a teenager till you were at least forty, and you probably had nothing worth saying till you were fifty. So, from her perspective, seventy wasn't old. And yet he was closer in age to her Grandpa Ernie than he was to his ex-wife, and Grandpa Ernie was definitely old.

"Taylor? Was there something else?" Gracie brought her back to the moment.

"Not really. I was just worried about him. And wondering of course if his accident was related to his wife's death."

"He doesn't know. He says he remembers packing his bag because you were coming to pick him up, but then not wanting to wait around the house, so he went for a walk on the beach."

"But he didn't leave a note for us."

"I guess he thought he'd come back in time."

"I don't remember seeing his bag at the house." Taylor closed her eyes and pictured the scene.

"He said he carried it to the beach. He doesn't know what happened to it."

"But he doesn't remember falling huh?"

"No. And since the crack to his skull is at the back, the assumption is that he was assaulted—hit from behind."

"I'm just really sorry this is happening to your family and friends."

"Thank you. We're worried about the impact on Una. She's at such a tender age of development."

"How old is she?"

"She's about to turn twelve. You know how adolescence is."

"Yeah, that is hard. I was the same age when I lost my father."

"Then you understand how much she is worrying. We're going to take her away for Thanksgiving. Give her a distraction."

"That is very nice of you, but won't she want to be near her dad?"

Gracie sighed, the perk going out of her a bit. "You know how it is. He's more like an uncle than a father. She's worried about him, but not the way one might expect."

"Where will you be going?"

"We have a little place down in Belize. It's nothing much, but it's an escape. And it'll be a little bit warmer anyway."

"That's quite a trip for a short stay."

"Don't I know it. But even three or four days away from this will help, we think."

"Of course, enjoy yourself." Taylor ended the call and immediately called the sherrif's office. Sissy, Gracie and Taylor had looked for Art. But Taylor had no idea where Guy had been while they were looking, or Una for that matter. And now Gracie, Guy, and Una were leaving the country. That seemed like something worth calling in.

The deputy who took her message sounded like she cared, but who knows with professionals.

CHAPTER SEVENTEEN

*T*aylor and Belle were in the car driving to Portland for Thanksgiving when Sissy finally called again. The long break from detective work had been invaluable for getting ready for Black Friday sales.

All of the Comfort Quilt Shops had decided to do a "Spooky Good" sale featuring the Halloween and Halloween-adjacent prints they hadn't been able to unload during the summer. It sounded crazy on paper, but not to quilters. Crafting takes time —when you're in the mood to be surrounded by a certain season's fabrics, it's too late to sell it to people who need to make their projects.

The play on black in Black Friday, combined with black cats and bats and witches' hats and general spookiness was a fun new idea they had all liked. Taylor had shelled out some money on radio ads in the local area, and really hoped it would work. Shara insisted on Facebook ads, but Taylor didn't put her faith in them. She promised to poll her customers. They'd see if anyone admitted to coming to town because of something they saw on their Facebook feed.

They were well on their way, headed North on Highway 99 when Sissy called. Taylor had her phone on Bluetooth so it would use the car speakers, but she didn't like it. Not with Grandpa Ernie in the car. He'd have too many questions about the murder. Taylor answered it anyway. "Happy Thanksgiving, Sissy."

"Thank you. It's just awful, of course. I didn't know if you had plans, so I wanted to let you know you'd all be welcome over here."

Taylor's heart gave a little twist. Sissy was the last person she wanted to spend the holiday with, but it was such a nice offer. And Taylor hadn't even thought of checking on what Sissy might have needed during the sad holiday.

"It's the first Thanksgiving without your mom, after all," Sissy added.

The twist in Taylor's heart turned into a little sob.

"We're headed up to Portland to spend the day with the Kirbys. You know, Belle's...." Ug. Taylor still couldn't really say it out loud.

"Ah, yes. Colleen and Dave. That's really nice of you. Very generous."

Sissy was right. It was kind and generous. Even though all Taylor was bringing was a cherry gelatin and fruit salad she'd picked up at the grocery store after work the night before. "Is everyone coming to your place? Like, Fawn and Monty and..."

"As you know, Gracie, Guy and Una all left the country. Like you, I find that terribly suspicious. Art is out of the hospital, but still sore. He'll be with Gilly and Jason. But yes, Fawn and Monty are here with me. I thought they might go off to his parents, but he said Fawn wanted to stick around. I don't blame her. His folks are a bit iffy. Always have been. It's not that they're poor, God knows we've all been poor. It's just they are such heavy drinkers and they seem to wallow in their poverty. I can't take it much. I knew them when Fawn and Monty met, and hoped they wouldn't stick, but what can you do? Love is blind."

"I hear you. There's poverty and then there's..." Taylor had words for it, but they felt cruel.

"Foolishness," Grandpa Ernie supplied.

"Hi Ernie," Sissy hollered. "You're right. Lots of folks are poor, but they don't have to be fools too. Dayton and family are going to eat with us even though there's half a million Reubens in this town they could eat with, but that's okay because Dayna Reuben makes the best zwieback. Have you had that? You should. I think they serve it at Reuben's during holiday season."

"Sissy, is everything okay?" Taylor wasn't used to her rambling like this. She wasn't quiet by any means, but usually if she was saying a lot, it was because she had a lot that needed to be said.

"No. I am not okay. I was really looking forward to having my best friend live in town after all these years. I just...honestly Taylor, I'm just real broken up about this."

Taylor was silent for a moment as she navigated early morning holiday traffic in McMinnville. "I know. I'm sad today too."

"If you need a break you can call me anytime today, okay? Don't know how it will be at the Kirby house, but you might need to step away from it for a minute and have a listening ear."

"Thanks Sissy. And...same goes for you. I'm just a phone call away." They ended the call.

Sissy...that bossy bully of a woman...she wasn't all bad.

Belle was in the backseat, AirPods in her ears. Her hair wasn't black anymore. She had cut that off sometime between September and this weekend. The roots were just long enough to be a perky pixie cut. But it wasn't the golden blonde it used to be. It was sort of dishwater blonde now. Neither brown nor gold. An indifferent color Taylor couldn't blame Belle for wanting to change. Her head was leaned back, and her eyes were closed. She might or might not have been listening to anything. The AirPods, an absurd expense in Taylor's opinion, had been called a "school expense" and her trust had paid for them. Taylor had wanted to say no, but Grandma Quinny cautioned Taylor to pick her battles very carefully, and it was a fact that headphones were a necessary tool on a university campus. Taylor agreed with that, of course, and bit her tongue rather than suggesting the generic earbuds from the dollar store.

❀

THE KIRBY HOUSE was decorated to the nines. Colleen had stacked haybales under her porch roof, and scarecrows in her foyer. She had silk maple leave garland around the windows and wreathes that matched hanging on every wall. The table was set with a golden tablecloth and the dishes were cream, decorated with gold filigree. Her young sons were playing video games in the front room, probably to keep them around instead of losing them in the hidden depths of the house where they had a fully stocked rich-kid playroom.

Taylor took a deep breath, inhaling the heavenly aroma of garlic, basil, tomatoes and that special sausage from the Italian deli in town. She couldn't get enough, but it didn't smell a thing like Thanksgiving.

Dave's daughter Ashleigh was on the couch drinking coffee from a large maroon mug. "Don't fight it," Ashleigh said. "Grandma Kirby was Italian. All our holiday meals feature a first course of lasagna. But, don't panic either. There is a turkey in the oven."

Taylor laughed and felt her shoulders fall, not realizing they had been tense. Ashleigh and Taylor had met twice before, but Taylor still struggled with feelings of envy.

Ashleigh seemed to relate to Belle as a stepsister so easily. She was only a little younger than Taylor and that was awkward as well. Taylor was the big sister, and Belle was the little sister. With Ashleigh right between them, it disrupted the natural order.

And yet, Ashleigh was all right.

Colleen brought Taylor her own maroon mug of coffee.

Just the right amount of cream.

Colleen was so eager to please, she never failed to make Taylor nervous.

Belle gave Colleen a quick hug. "Happy Thanksgiving."

"I'm so glad you could all come. Ernie, can I get you a seat?"

"I've been sitting for two hours. I want to stand." He stood, a bit shaking, and leaning on his cane, but Colleen didn't push him.

"Coffee, then? You take yours black?"

He nodded, his frown turning up at the corners. "That's right."

"Ernie!" Dave Kirby, the man with the Italian mother, came into the room, arms open. "Colleen made the lasagna like my mother makes it, and meatballs too. And pumpkin ravioli—the kids love it. And even better, Colleen let me make sausage and mozzarella stuffing."

Grandpa Ernie frowned again, but this time it was comically exaggerated. "This is worse than you bringing spaghetti to the Fourth of July."

"You love it, Ernesto! You love it."

Grandpa laughed.

"Come with me to the garage, Ernie. I have a problem that you could fix for me."

Grandpa Ernie had been a dab hand at machine repair, and Dave was a dab hand at making guests feel comfortable. They walked slowly together to the garage where something waited to be fixed. Taylor wondered if Dave had broken it on purpose just to make Grandpa Ernie feel needed.

"Can I help with anything?" Taylor went into the kitchen with her sad little plastic container of Jell-O salad.

"Ooh, the boys love this!" Colleen accepted the tub from her with a smile and put it in the fridge. "With all that gooey Jell-O and whip cream, they don't even notice they're eating fruit."

Colleen had offered her a place in the family, fitting in as one of her flock since Taylor was her child's sister, but Taylor still had a hard time thinking of the little boys as any kind of relation.

173

They were just...kids. Small. And boys. She didn't know about boy children one way or the other. All the babysitting Taylor had ever done had been for her own sister.

"I heard there was another tragedy in Comfort." Colleen was tossing a salad.

"Yeah, there was. Kind of sad. Do you know Sissy Dorney?"

"The name's familiar but it's been a while." Colleen had left town in her late teens and lived rough for many years. She had been clean for a decade—slightly over now—but much of her old life was a blur.

"Sissy is a family friend. You've heard Belle talk about Cooper—Sissy is his mom."

She shook her head. "I've heard of Levi, the boy at the college, but not Cooper. I met Dayton, are they all friends?"

Taylor tilted her head a little. Belle hadn't told Colleen about her long-time best friend? That seemed sad. There had been a time Taylor would have been giddy to know stuff Colleen didn't. But sitting in this kitchen overflowing with food she had prepared to show them she loved them made it just seem sad. "Yeah," Taylor said. "They're all friends. Well, anyway. Sissy's aunt had remarried just a week before she died. They had moved to town for a job at Comfort College of Art and Craft..." Taylor told Colleen a short version of the story.

"Poor Sissy. I can't imagine what she must be feeling right now."

"She thinks trying to prove Reynette's death was a murder will make her feel better."

Colleen set the bowl of salad aside and nodded, her face serious. "It might. I think it really helped Belle."

"Please let me help with something."

"Oh! I'm sorry. I just...I get nervous, you know? And I try to keep busy. There isn't really anything to do right now. Maybe, um..." She pulled out a loaf of Italian bread. "If you slice that open and butter the two halves, we can toast it later."

"Garlic salt, too?" Taylor was appalled at the idea of garlic bread with Thanksgiving dinner, but at the same time it would be an improvement over the canned dinner rolls her mom had always made.

"Well, actually," her words were apologetic. "Dave only likes to use his garlic butter for this. Here." She passed her a little dish that was butter and fresh garlic mixed.

Taylor followed directions as Colleen fussed around the kitchen. She seemed to be moving things from here to there for no reason. "Colleen go sit with Belle. I'll be fine in here. When I'm done, I'll top off my coffee and join you." Taylor was going extra slow on purpose. It really didn't take any time to slice a loaf of bread in half and butter it. There were two loaves though and Taylor did them both.

Ashleigh joined her in the kitchen and topped off her own cup. "We won't eat till almost four. You'll starve if you don't have something." She pulled a box of donuts out of a cupboard and passed them over. "I begged Belle to eat but she refused."

"She hates food in the morning." Taylor took a nice big maple bar. "Thanks."

"Blending families is awkward at first, but you'll get used to it."

"Probably so."

"Come, sit with me."

Taylor followed Ashleigh to a little dining area off the kitchen —a breakfast room but quite a bit bigger than the average one. Considering the house also had a table in the kitchen and the formal dining room done up in gold, Taylor was again impressed by the sheer size of the place.

"The hardest part of combining families is the weirdness of traditions, don't you think? Didn't you and Clay find that?"

"I guess Belle told you about him?"

"Yup. She did."

"It was a little weird when we first moved in together, but we got used to each other."

"But what about when you got together with each other's

families? That's when it gets hard. Like the Italian food at every holiday. That was a big deal to Colleen at first, but she'd never admit it. She is way too eager to be loved."

"There are worse things to be eager for…"

"Yeah, I know. She only relaxes around the boys. Not even around Dad. But anyway. You get it."

"To be honest, my life in retail management meant I didn't really do holidays with Clay's family. I almost always had to work. And the years that I didn't, I ran home to see Belle and Mom."

"Ah." Ashleigh said it like it explained something to her. "Then I guess this is your first taste. I'm just saying…it's hard at first, but that's normal. Everyone feels this way. Like everything going on around you is somehow wrong."

"Was it like that for you when Colleen married your dad?"

"Oh my gosh yes. First off, she couldn't cook at all. Back then grandma was still around so she'd do all the cooking for us. She taught Colleen, praise the Lord. But also, Colleen's sober. She's awesome about it, but having a sober person around an Italian family during the holidays? I was used to red wine flowing like water, but once Dad remarried, that stopped.

"But you were a kid, you didn't drink it."

"You don't know Italians. Not that I had full glasses or anything. But it was different after they got married. Grandpa and Grandma would fill their glasses quietly in the kitchen and bring them to the table when they used to make a big fuss about it."

"Did they like Colleen?"

"Did my elderly ex-military grandfather and traditional first generation-Italian-American grandmother like my dad's ex-junky of a new wife?"

"I see."

She nodded. "But we all like her now."

"Because your grandparents are dead?"

Ashleigh laughed. "That would be it exactly. Colleen could

never have won them over, but you can't help but love someone who is always putting so much energy into being lovable."

"Wait, didn't you just say she was too eager to be loved?"

"Yeah, I think it must be awful to be her. Nervous all the time, terrified that you're going to do it wrong. I feel for her. But it's certainly easy to love someone who is constantly putting that much energy into being lovable."

Taylor wondered how true that was. She found herself resenting it. But maybe that would change with time. That said, she also wondered about Reynette. She'd been loved by one and all, even her new husband's ex-wife. Was that because she had been a...a try-hard like Colleen? Had she been exerting so much energy into being lovable at all times that she just snapped one day and ended it all? To Taylor, that seemed as likely as getting herself killed in such an improbable manner.

The car was quiet driving home. Belle had accepted the offer to stay the night and go Black Friday shopping with Colleen and Ashleigh the next day. After all, Taylor would just be working so she wouldn't miss her sister, right? Ashleigh would bring her back on Saturday. That was the plan. They all agreed. Taylor hated it.

CHAPTER EIGHTEEN

*T*he skies broke clear and blue. The sun shone and the day warmed up to sixty. They couldn't have ordered a better day for their Black Friday sale. The advertising efforts were rewarded with hordes of people, Halloween stock selling out, and shelves of other fabric disappearing by the bolt full. As agreed, all four stores closed at seven that night and met at the bar in town for celebratory drinks.

Loggers, the bar in town was cute. There was no better word for it. It had all the fixings of a biker bar on the edge of a small town, but somehow it still felt like a place farmers went to talk about the weather, or where quilt shop owners went to discuss big sales.

"So, Shara, what's the word? Facebook or Radio?"

Shara waved a paper napkin in surrender. "I was too busy to ask!"

"You're sorry you poo-pooed the idea of Halloween marketing, aren't you?" Carly from Bible Creek Quilt and Gift teased.

"Very much so. I made lots and lots of filthy lucre today." Shara seemed almost giddy, and not at all ready to dig Taylor's eyes out over selling the same line of fabrics. Taylor liked that.

She didn't like Shara, but she liked that Shara wasn't angry with her. Taylor held her glass up in salute. "To advertising like crazy!"

"To Black Friday!"

They all huzzahed and drank their drinks and enjoyed being off their feet. It was funny, this sense of community with folks who were also her competition. Taylor hadn't put much effort into getting to know them through the last months, but she wanted to. Now, after their successful day, more than ever. Black Friday was not traditionally a great day for sales at stores like theirs. They tried to make up for it with Small Business Saturday sales and things like that, but man, had this worked. And Taylor needed something to have worked.

Taylor was just sipping her second celebratory g and t when she spotted a familiar face in the corner of the bar. Maybe it was because she was now just a bit tipsy—none of them had had lunch after all—but she wanted to see a smile on that sad face. "Clay, get over here." She waved her arms at him. "We're celebrating a successful sale."

He shook his head.

"Then I'm coming to you. Excuse me, ladies." Taylor was not drunk, not after the one drink, but she was punch drunk. She went to the far back of the bar where her ex-boyfriend seemed to be hiding. "What are you doing back here?" He had one empty pint in front of him, and the remains of a burger and fries.

"Just eating dinner and contemplating my life choices."

"Part of that seems like a good idea." Taylor helped herself to a cold fry. He had been here awhile.

"If I had just come down here with you, I could have been a part of this life, this community."

"It's a pretty great place."

"I miss you, Taylor. Don't you miss me even a little bit?" His blue eyes were round and shadowed and sad.

"You don't miss me." Taylor leaned forward into his personal space. "I called you out on that already, don't you remember? You just miss having somebody."

"I didn't correct you. That doesn't mean you were right."

"You want me to call Lila and ask her? I'd bet all the money I made today that you tried to sleep with her, and she rejected you."

"You're half right."

She curled her lip. "You did sleep with her then?"

"Yeah." He dragged his hands through his hair. "But people make mistakes, don't they? Everything I did after your mom passed was a mistake."

"Yes, it was, but it wasn't an accident and I think you confuse the two. If I forget to carry the one when doing math, it's both a mistake and an accident." Taylor was suddenly very, very sober, and most of the fun had drained away. "What you did was a mistake. But it was very much on purpose."

"And you never make mistakes?" He scowled.

"Go home, Clay."

"I've got one more week of vacation, and I'm spending it here, praying you forgive me."

The bar wasn't full enough to hide the scene Clay was creating.

Taylor got up, ready to leave him but found herself surrounded by her Guild of Quilt Shop owners. "Is this young man bothering you?" June from Comfort Cozies asked.

"No, not anymore."

"Yes." Clay stood. "I am bothering her, and I'm going to keep bothering her till she forgives me.

From the corner of her eye, Taylor noticed someone stand. And walk over with firm steps, and broad shoulders. He put his hand on the small of her back.

Hudson.

"Wanna dance?"

She melted. He hated dancing and there wasn't any music

playing. And he hadn't jumped in and threatened Clay or punched Clay or had a fight with Clay. He had just...walked over and asked if she wanted something, leaving the escape up to her.

"I'd love to." She took his hand, led him outside, and kissed him, quite a bit more than she usually did in public.

"As much as I love that..." He smiled down at her from his very nice height but drew his brows together and kissed her again. Then, "Never mind. I love that."

"I don't think I've been fair to you." Taylor stroked his thumb with hers.

"You never said we were anything other than what we are."

"I know, but I've been leaving you on the hook for so long."

He cleared his throat, an embarrassed sound. "I've been dating other people too, you know."

"Oh." Taylor was the embarrassed one now. Somehow, she had taken his words to mean he had been waiting for her alone.

He gave her hand a squeeze. "Want to run away entirely or maybe go pay your tab first?"

"I think I'll go enjoy the party a little more. The quilt guild had a very good Black Friday."

They returned together, but he disappeared as she joined her quilt friends. Taylor had liked the idea of Hudson waiting patiently for her. She didn't like the idea that he might find someone he liked better.

But now was far from the best time to try and figure out her own heart.

ROXY AND TAYLOR put off filming the YouTube show till after the whole shopping weekend—Black Friday, Small Business Saturday, Cyber Monday. They did their best and made a solid profit. Tuesday Taylor was exhausted, but ready to film bright and early.

She hung one of her favorite quilts as a backdrop and set up a worktable in the apartment for filming this time. Changing up the setting like that wasn't supposed to be best practices for their type of YouTube video, but she didn't want to be bothered by customers rattling the doors before they opened.

"We're doing the homemade bias tape today, right?" Roxy was peering at the back of the phone as she adjusted it on the tripod.

"Yeah, but mom did one too. We should watch it and make sure I have something unique to say."

The first video was how to cut and press the bias tape. The second was binding a small project and the third was rebinding an old project.

The thing Taylor was sure of at the end of their review was that she had nothing to add to the conversation.

"Maybe you don't need to add anything new to it." Roxy stood at the ironing board pressing a length of forty-five-inch quilting cotton.

"I can't help but want to. Why fill up airspace with something that has already been done a hundred times before?" Taylor shifted the measured cutting board to an angle. She had been taught to write at a slight angle and it affected everything including how she cut with her rotary cutter.

"Maybe you saying the thing is enough," Roxy mused. "I've heard that you have to receive a message seven times before you become convinced to accept it."

"Working with that old sales acorn, I've got to make six videos about making your own bias tape to convince someone to do it," Taylor chuckled.

"It is content…" Roxy frowned at the fabric. "I like this one. It's gentle." She referred to the subtle waves of dark tan on the cream background she had selected from back stock. It wouldn't look like much on video except it had a distinct front and back as well as a horizontal pattern that might illustrate bias work nicely.

Taylor went back in the last video to the eleventh minute where her mom was musing on mixing old fabric and new when replacing binding on a worn quilt. "It's like this..." she was saying, "if the fabric is weak, nothing will hold it together. But if what you have is strong, if it's only the binding that has worn out, you can save the quilt. I've seen folks reinforce a quilt front and rebind it afterward. It can be done, but it is so hard. You have to really believe the piece is worth saving. It has to be like family to do that. Sometimes inch by inch unstitching the quilting and tying it off again just to make the patchwork stronger..." Taylor pressed pause. Her mom didn't make an analogy out of this moment. Didn't try and tie it to some life lesson, but Taylor wanted to include it in the compilation of advice anyway, because it was true. You could save almost anything if you went inch by inch making repairs, strengthening weak spots, unstitching what had gone bad so you could remake it better.

Taylor took a deep breath and squared her shoulders. "I'll never be invited to give a Ted Talk based on my videos, but we might as well keep going. I may not be saying anything new, but I might be saying it to someone for the seventh time."

"That's my girl."

They spent the next two hours filming, hoping they got enough quality footage to make the four fifteen-minute videos they had planned. At one point, Taylor found herself riffing on her mother's thoughts, on working to save something you love even though the work is hard.

When they were done, Roxy was dabbing at her eyes. "That's you, Taylor. You and this shop and the show and your family. Inch by inch you are binding it up, saving the beautiful quilt your mom patched together through her life."

Roxy wrapped Taylor in her thin arms, a hug Taylor needed though she hadn't been looking for it.

At the end of filming Taylor left Roxy and Hannah to run the store.

Taylor had taken the rest of the day off so she could focus on the death of Reynette Woods.

She found Sissy at her home. They needed to find out if Art and Reynette had been willing to do that careful foundation building work that their lives would need if they were really going to bind their two families together.

Sissy was in the middle of her kitchen, swathed in a faded hand-sewn apron made from Flour Sax's fabrics, but faded with time and use. The granite counters overflowed with loaves of bread in various stages of baked.

"What on earth are you doing?" Taylor hadn't really thought about Sissy's day to day life before, but there she was in the middle of a Tuesday surrounded by loaves of bread and batches of dough proofing.

"Just..." She shook her head. "Panic baking. Okay? You caught me. I took a few days off from the salon, but it turns out I can't just sit here on my hands."

"I don't bake." Taylor inhaled deeply, the warm, wholesome, and unmatched aroma of fresh bread taking her back to visits to friends' houses—friends whose mothers stayed at home to bake because their fathers weren't dead.

She snorted. She could turn any moment into self-pity if she tried.

Sissy looked at her as though the snort was a personal insult. "What?"

"Nothing. Sorry. Just laughing at myself for being jealous of all of this bread."

"Then take some home. Half my family is eating Keto and we'll never get through all of this."

"Are you stuck here all day now?" Taylor grabbed a seat at the kitchen island.

Sissy rubbed her chin and looked around her kitchen, assessing the state of baking. "I can slow the rise on those there by sticking them in the fridge, but I've got to wait another ten minutes for the loaves in the oven to come out. Those loaves," she waved a hand embroidered kitchen towel at her table, "were an overnight rise recipe. So are the ones in the oven. Those," she waved the towel at a tray of bread rolled into cute little dinner rolls, "aren't. But they can sit in the fridge, like I said. What are you thinking? Did you have a detectivey a-ha moment?"

"Maybe. A lot of things have been flying around my brain the last few days. They all relate to blending families and how it's hard."

"You're telling me. My hubby Phil's daughter Tansy just barely puts up with me. Now that her mom moved to Atlanta, she sees the value of having a spare grandma around, but after all these years you could say I'm not motivated to run at her beck and call."

"That's sort of exactly what I mean. It's hard work. Long work. Patient work. Art and Reynette eloped pretty suddenly. Do you think they were willing to do the kind of work it takes to make a blended family function?"

"Reynette would have. She'd longed to be married ever since her ex left her."

"Her ex...have we considered him as someone who could be behind the murder?"

Sissy gave a short, derisive laugh. "No. Not him. He died five years after he left her. She had to pay for the funeral and bury him and everything."

"Did she stay in touch with anyone from his family?"

"No, they were all from down in California." She said it with the disdain only a born and bred Oregonian can say the word.

"It's not just the married couple who has to do the work." Taylor stared at the perfect golden round top of a loaf of white bread.

Sissy sliced a piece, still warm from the oven and passed it over.

Taylor slathered it with butter. "Everyone has to be willing to work hard. Kids, adult kids, siblings. Who was least willing in this new marriage?"

"I don't know that anyone was willing, except Art and Reynette. Fawn is biddable, but that doesn't mean she liked it. Monty has always been an outsider, if you ask me. Not invested in the family. Jason? That guy is a snob."

"Guy and Gracie, as adult representatives of Una seem more committed than anyone else. I suppose they'd have to be, given she was the one that introduced them. Do you believe her when she says it was because of her daughter? That she wanted a good stepmother for Una?"

"I don't know exactly what to make of Gracie, but I don't trust her. She seems like the type to say one thing but mean another entirely."

"What does she get from this marriage?"

"If she's as close to Fawn as she claims she gets a whole lotta control over Art's life, don't you think? If she's being honest and Una is Art's kid, she has every reason to want to keep him on a short tether."

"You were the one that got Reynette the job at the college."

"I connected the two, yeah, but she got the job herself based on her talent." Sissy's defensive tone didn't quail Taylor.

"True, I know. Didn't mean to sound like I didn't. It just seems pretty great for Gracie. Art would be a lot closer to Neskowin than he used to be. How did you find out about the job at the college?"

"Pastor Beiste over at Bible Creek Chapel told me about it. She likes Reynette's work."

"Hmmm…" Taylor savored the bread. "Did you ever hear Jason's opinion about it?"

"I don't talk to him if I can help it."

A timer went off and Sissy removed two stoneware baking trays with crusty round loaves of bread on them.

"Today, you can't help it. We're headed to Jason's to bring flowers and sympathy to Art and to talk to them both a little bit about the complications of blending families."

"You don't look like you have flowers." Sissy looked at

Taylor like she was no better than she ought to be. "You know a florist in this town?"

"A card then. We'll run to Bible Creek Quilt and Gift. They're open today."

CHAPTER NINETEEN

*I*t was only as they stood knocking on the door of Jason's place that Taylor realized he might actually be off working somewhere. When Gilly answered the door with a look of disappointment at seeing them, Taylor figured she was right. She held up a card and a small pot of silk mums from the gift shop. "Is Art up for company?"

Gilly opened the door wider. "Yes, come in."

Jason's modest 1960s ranch home was full of mid-century modern furniture complete with patina and original upholstery. The nubby wools in dark avocado and rust looked surprisingly chic in his space. A wall of square shelves like Ikea, but probably much more expensive, held a collection of glass that complimented the color palate of the late seventies. Gilly had likely contributed these pieces to their shared home. "He's resting, let me get him."

Sissy and Taylor waited in the museum-like living room.

Art came out head bandaged, shoulders stooped, and feet shuffling across the wooden floor. He had a black eye, and the hand that held the velvet robe shut was thin, knobby and shaking. He couldn't have lost noticeable weight in his few days in the hospital, but his edges were sharper and the shadows deeper.

Gilly led him to a low-slung chair with a wooden frame and he sat slowly. "Can I get you a cup of coffee?" She was not talking to Sissy or Taylor.

"I don't know what happened." Art sat back. The chair wasn't high enough for him to rest his head, and lacking that crutch, he seemed taller and stronger. He would collapse if someone offered him the opportunity, but he could stand strong if needed. "I packed my bag and walked to the beach. That's all I know."

"It sounds like it was awful." Taylor sat across from him in a matching chair. Sissy stood at the shelf investigating the glass sculptures. "Are you still in a lot of pain?"

"Some. It comes and goes."

"It's nice that Gilly is here with you."

"She's a nice girl."

Gilly seemed older than Art's ex-wife in both manner and looks, but Taylor supposed she could seem like a "girl" to him. "Is there anything we can do for you?"

"The funeral home keeps calling about Reynette." He coughed into his fist, then winced like it hurt his head to cough. "I need to make the arrangements, but Gilly won't even let me get dressed."

"Will they not help you over the phone?" Sissy turned to Art.

"There are papers to sign and checks to write."

"But I'm sure they can wait till you're stronger." She crossed her arms and gave Art one of those assessing-looks as though she were his gym teacher.

"I'm not going to be stronger. Maybe in less pain, eventually, but not stronger."

"That's so bleak, Art, surely..." Taylor murmured.

"What is it they say you have?" Sissy quizzed him.

"ALS. Lou Gehrig's. It's coming on fast."

Taylor clasped her hands in surprise. She'd seen someone

pass from this before. One of her department heads at Joann's. It had taken less than a year for the dreadful disease to end her old coworker's life, though the disease had variations. "Is this why you eloped the way you did?"

He nodded. "I didn't want Reynette to have to be my caregiver, so it was hard to agree to marry her. But when she promised to hire nurses as soon as I needed them, I wanted to marry right away. To let her have some of my healthy life. To make sure she would inherit from me, so I could take care of her after I was gone."

"She didn't seem to need money," Taylor said.

"No, she didn't. But she was signing on for maybe a full year of unpaid labor as I die in front of her, whether we married or not. As my spouse she was entitled to half of everything we owned after my death. As my companion, or even fiancé, she would get nothing after suffering so much."

Taylor opened her mouth to speak but couldn't. The pieces seemed to fall into place. Art looking so much frailer than his age. The way he was keeping his distance from a daughter he wouldn't see grow up. His ex-wife's concern for him. Her concern that her daughter have a nice stepmom...

"Half of my estate would have been plenty for Jason. I've been giving him his mother's money for the last ten years to protect it from any claims Gracie might make for Una."

"Money," Sissy grunted. "The root of all evil."

"The love of money," Art corrected. "Gracie loves it. Una does too. But she's young and if I could have raised her myself, she might have grown out of it."

"Even if she's not your biological daughter?"

"I don't think greed is a genetic trait," he mused. "Though it could be. A case could be made."

"Do Reynette's kids know you're sick?"

"No. Reynette was firm that we not tell them. She felt..." He sighed. "She didn't have the highest regard for her daughter's understanding and felt that Fawn would make a problem about our marriage if she knew."

"Otherwise Fawn was happy with the relationship?"

"As happy as anyone ever is in these circumstances." Art straightened the thick black velvet robe over his knees.

"What about Jason?"

Gilly entered the room with a mug of coffee for Art. It was a travel mug with a handle and a lid. She set it on the side table and then stood, arms crossed, watching him.

"What do you say, Gilly? Did Jason approve of Reynette?"

"No." Her mouth was pinched and sour, but her gray eyes were sad.

"Did you?" Sissy's demeanor was defensive, and Taylor understood. They were discussing the woman who was both family and best friend to Sissy.

"I was withholding judgement until I could know her better." Her face was anything but sincere.

"Why didn't Jason like her?" Taylor nudged her question in before Sissy could take another jab.

Gilly sat on the arm of Art's chair. "Art, you and I go way back, correct?"

"Yes, Ma'am." His face creased into a little smile.

"Jason and I met when we were in college. We were friends for many years." Her serious face twitched as though she was trying to suppress a sense of humor. "Art is a lady's man. That's the only way to say this. After he lost his wife, Jason's mother, he became the most eligible man on campus. Handsome, smart, wealthy. First, he worked his way through the adjunct faculty, then he started in on the students. When Gracie landed him, we were all shocked."

Taylor was as well. Art didn't have the kind of magnetic personality she thought a lady's man needed.

"You exaggerate." Art smiled.

"Gracie left him for a younger man, it's true, but I contend she left him for a faithful man. What say you to those charges, sir?"

"Guilty. Gracie was a firefly, beautiful in the wild and exactly the thing someone wants to catch. But once you have a firefly in the hand, the charm is gone. They don't do anything but shine."

Gilly rolled her eyes. "He took up with older, smarter women while married to her and stuck with them after. With that in mind, I can assume Reynette was a smart woman."

His face brightened, then drooped again. "She was brilliant. A diamond in the rough."

Sissy snarled.

Taylor cringed. Though Reynette was around the same age as Art and clearly not a bright young thing, he still wanted her as something he could form or shape or mold. Men like Art grossed her out. "And that was why Jason didn't like her? Because she was brilliant?"

"He disagrees that she was brilliant." Gilly stopped to consider the red, seething face of Sissy Dorney. "No offense. He's highly prejudiced in favor of formal education. He didn't think she was brilliant and saw no reason for his father to marry someone he assumed was just the next woman of many."

"Did he not know you were sick?" It dawned on Taylor that Art was the most honest person in the room, despite his unfaithfulness. When he said he had married Reynette as a means of paying her for taking care of him as he died, he meant it. He likely loved her no more nor less than any of the women in his long string of ladies, but at the end of their time together he would owe her more.

"Jason is aware of the diagnosis. But many men, for example Steven Hawking, live very long and even productive lives with the disease. It depends entirely on the type. Jason still hopes mine is actually the slow progressing type, despite what doctors have said."

"It's hard losing a parent." Taylor looked away to the wall of delicate, brightly colored shapes of glass.

"But you did love her." Sissy's statement was firm, like a demand or a decree.

"She delighted me utterly," Art said. "She had wisdom and talent and comfort and her face, that smile and those dimples and the way her eyes lit up when she was pleased or excited or happy. That face was what I wanted to look at every night over dinner. I loved her very much."

Sissy relaxed, just a bit.

Gilly patted his shoulder. "Art doesn't go in for conquests," she said. "He falls in love entirely. Very romantic."

"Until he falls out again," Sissy said.

"She was my last. My final love. The last woman I would ever be with. She was worth the long wait to find her." His eyes were soft and moony.

"And yet," Taylor said, "your health is currently strong. You might meet someone else."

Gilly nodded with a bit of a smirk. "You see the situation clearly, I think."

Sissy inhaled sharply, and loudly. "So, Jason didn't want you to marry my aunt. Did he not want it badly enough to see her die first?"

"Jason is an intellectual," Gilly said.

"Jason is a cold fish. Tell them how long you had to wait for him to fall for you," Art said.

"I didn't wait. I had a nice life with my first husband."

"Widowed?" Sissy asked

"Divorced. It was nice until it wasn't. And then Jason and I, old friends, fell in love."

"She fell in love. Jason can't drum up enough passion to love or hate. Murder, especially premeditated, would have taken him considering someone else and how their lives intersected with his. He wouldn't have bothered." Art spoke like Jason was a character in a novel, rather than his own flesh and blood. Art might be able to drum up passion for women, but he seemed as clinical as he claimed Jason was otherwise.

"Art isn't wrong. Jason is wonderful at what he is wonderful at. Passion is not one of those things. But, as a second act in my life, he is just right." Gilly patted Art's shoulder and stood again. She walked first to the shelf of sculptures, then turned again to face Taylor and Sissy. It felt like a show, like she was performing for a class of art students.

"You found blending your family with his was worth the effort though?" Taylor asked.

Gilly considered for a moment. "I have a daughter. She's in college herself now. She likes Jason, but at the same time, I don't live here. We're not blended so much as running in parallel."

Taylor pictured two quilts carefully folded, set next to each other on a shelf, rather than a front and a back, bound together, or new cloth added to an old quilt to restore what time and life had tried to destroy. It was a cold picture, but she suspected Gilly would agree it was accurate.

"Gilly is a good girl," Art said. "And Jason is okay too. They are happy the way things are, and so am I."

"Who is going to care for you now that Reynette is gone?" Taylor asked.

"We'll make sure he's cared for." Gilly's voice was warm, almost sad. Maybe she had more heart than Taylor was giving her credit for. "He doesn't need to find himself a wife to make sure he's not alone."

He sighed, dreamily. "I will miss Reynette every day for the rest of my life."

He meant it, too, as he had the days of his life numbered.

"It's easy to say a man doesn't have the energy to murder." Sissy drove them in her minivan, hitting the corners like she was a race car driver. "But there are a lot of cold-hearted psychos out there. Jason had every reason to want to see Reynette dead."

"Even so, would he have had the access he needed to poison

her slowly?" Taylor watched the little ranch houses speed by as they drove toward the center of Comfort.

"Why wouldn't he have? He's in town and that's his father's house."

"Can we go there today?"

Sissy pulled the wheel and they took a sharp left. "Sure."

"If Fawn is there, let's talk to her about how much time Jason spent with his dad at the house. If she's not, let's look through everything that could have been poisoned. We've been focused on motive, but maybe we need to spend more time on the means."

They were at the house in seconds. "If we knew why, then we'd know who." Sissy yanked the e-brake though they were parked on flat road. "But we can't figure that out, so you're right. It's time to think about how."

The historic home was set back from the road but had no driveway. Instead there was an alley between the house and an old barn. Fawn's car wasn't in the alley or parked at the curb. "They sure have a lot to maintain here. You say they were just staying six months?"

"They had it on a six-month lease, but Reynette said she was hoping they could talk the owner into selling it. If they did a good job getting it into shape—nothing major, just cleaned up and maintained, then the owner might consider it."

"Who owns the place?"

"Reynette dealt with a property management company. I don't know who inherited it after old Harrison passed." Sissy let them in with a key. The back door opened to a screened porch that acted as a mud room. They went through it into the kitchen.

The kitchen felt like something Joanna Gaines could only dream of. White cupboards original to the 1930 addition flanked two walls of the huge square room and a large butcher block topped old farm table stood in the center as a sort of kitchen island. The appliances were nothing to write home about, but half the counters were marble—old marble that had lost its polish over time—and the other half were stainless steel. A large window over the sink flanked by soft bleached cheese cloth curtains allowed the weak winter sun to peak in.

Sissy went straight to the farthest cupboard and flung open the door.

Taylor started in on the carton next to the counter. It was full of spices. She opened one and sniffed. Mild American paprika. "Not the cartons." Taylor spoke to herself mostly. "This is the food they hadn't been eating. Hey Sissy, how long had they been living in this house?"

"Two weeks."

"And this is the most they'd unpacked?"

"Honeymooners." Sissy slammed a door shut and opened the next. "They ate all of their dinners out, often at Berry Noir. Reynette wasn't much on lunch but liked a nice breakfast."

Taylor tugged open the old fridge door. It had been more than a week since Reynette's death—almost two. She didn't want to smell the milk in the paper carton. "Eggs. Milk. Bacon. Cheese." She slid open the vegetable crisper. The veggies weren't so crisp anymore. "Of all of this food, I guess someone could have poisoned the milk." Taylor squared her shoulders, opened it, and smelled. It was sour, but not poisonously so.

"Aspirin doesn't smell." Sissy slammed another door shut.

"Then how do we check….?" Again, the question was for herself. Taylor longed for a fancy little wand she could dip in the milk to test it, like a sort of pregnancy test but for aspirin.

She moved an orange juice container. It was empty. "The OJ is gone. I wonder. If she really liked that."

"She hated orange juice. That had to be Art's."

"Oh." Behind the orange juice was a lidded glass jar full of what looked like fuzzy iced tea, but Taylor had her doubts. She took it out, unscrewed the lid and took a sniff. It had a musky, beer like sent. "Kombucha."

"Yes, she brewed her own."

"That would be easy to poison..." Taylor put the lid back on and set it on the counter.

Sissy slammed another door and held out a jar of jelly. "So, would this. Homemade. Gooseberry. I bet she had it on her toast. Mostly gone."

"Do you think we can convince the police to test these?"

"Can't hurt to try." Sissy opened another door just to slam it.

"I'll go up to the bathroom and look in there," Taylor offered.

"I'll call the cops."

Taylor took the steps two at a time. Surely because of the attack on Art, the cops would be willing to check this out.

They looked through everything in the house at least twice more and left messages with the sheriff's office. While the person who took Sissy's message was polite, she made no promises. Sissy stormed around the house as rain poured outside.

"All we can do is wait." Taylor sat on a Rubbermade bin by the front door.

"We can take the evidence with us." Sissy strutted into the kitchen.

Taylor tipped off the box with care. She was tired, worn out from a long day of getting nowhere fast. "You can't take any of that." She put a restraining hand on Sissy's shoulder. "Not if it's murder evidence. We have to leave it here for the police."

Sissy let out a string of invective that made Taylor blush.

"We need to get out of here. Let me take you out for a drink."

Sissy leaned on the counter, her eye on the fridge. "Whoever did this to Reynette is going to get away with it."

"No. No way. We'll never let them." Taylor found it easy to lie when the lie might be comforting, but Sissy saw through her.

She glared at Taylor. "I think you tried harder for your mom."

Taylor bit her lip to keep herself from repeating some of the things Sissy had just said. Then she squared her shoulders and left. Rain or no rain, she needed to get as far away from Sissy as she could.

CHAPTER TWENTY

*T*aylor buried herself in work the next day, first hitting McMinnville to restock her office supplies. There was a sale, so she loaded the family Audi with at least a year's worth of printer paper. And folders and sticky notes and boxes of pencils left over from back to school. So many pencils. Maybe she could get the store name printed on them. She didn't know. She didn't care. As she slid the company card into the card reader a weight lifted from her shoulders. She was prepared now for any pencil situation that could arise at her shop. Ever.

She had deliberately ignored all of the links Grandma Quinny had sent her over Facebook that had to do with counseling or grief after she clicked one that suggested over-shopping was an unhealthy way of numbing yourself to your feelings. Sometimes numb felt amazing.

It had been another dark and dreary end of November day, with few shoppers. As closing time approached, storm clouds rolled in that were darker, wetter, colder.

Taylor was just wishing she could shut the shop for the night when a rain-soaked child slunk in. The happy ring of the bells was at odds with her bedraggled appearance.

She was long and thin, taller than she looked old, with

stooped, rounded shoulders. Her head was covered with the hood of a wet sweatshirt, but Taylor caught a glimpse of profile —broad cheekbones and an upturned nose.

"Good evening," Taylor called to her from her perch at the register.

The girl looked up, startled.

Taylor had never seen the girl before in her life, but there was no mistaking that face. Una Woods was the spitting image of her mother and, if her tall, slender build and stooped shoulders told her anything, it was that Art was truly her dad.

Taylor could see what they meant when they said she also looked like Guy, but Guy and Gracie were almost brother and sister in their looks, as married couples sometimes were. But neither of them were built on that long lean scale Una was.

"Can I help you find something?" Taylor asked, hoping she was hiding her excitement. She assumed a lot, in naming this girl Una, but she would have bet money it was her.

"Is Hannah Warner here?" Una's wide eyes and youthful face spoke of fear.

Taylor wanted to grab a quilt off the wall and wrap her in it and tell her everything was going to be okay. "She's not, I'm sorry. Is there something I can do for you?"

The girl chewed on her bottom lip. "I was um, I was wanting to talk to Hannah."

"Do you need her number?" Fingers crossed that was an okay thing to do. Taylor remembered the moment that had cost her closeness with her childhood bestie Maddie last year. How making assumptions on what was safe behavior with kids had caused problems between Maddie, Taylor, and even Hudson.

Una's brow folded.

"Why don't I call her and see if she can come in. Would that be better?"

The girl nodded.

"Can I tell her who's asking for her?"

She nodded again. "Una. We only met a couple of times before."

Taylor picked up her office phone, the sturdy old-fashioned land line kind. "Are you sure she's the person you need?"

Una was looking at a wall of quilt block patterns, but she nodded.

Taylor dialed Hannah's number, but there was no answer. Not even voicemail. This time her face wrinkled in confusion. She hated it when people didn't have their voicemail set up. She switched to her personal cell phone and sent a text instead. "No answer, I'm so sorry. Do you want to hang up your coat?" Taylor waved at the coat rack.

Una shivered.

"You'll be warmer without that wet jacket on. And we have hot water for coco or tea if you want."

Una unzipped her sweatshirt and hung it up, but still shivered.

While waiting for a response from Hannah, Taylor made the child a cup of cocoa, only spilling a little as she stirred the full paper cup. "Hannah is usually pretty good at answering messages. Do you want to get comfy and wait around?" Taylor waved toward the armchair covered in linen with French words in scribbled text, the one that sat in front of her mom's quilting show playing on a loop.

Una accepted the cup and sat, watching the videos.

It felt good leaving her in her mom's care. Safer.

Taylor sent another text, this time to Sissy. "*Una is in the shop. She wants Hannah. How did she get here? What should I do?*"

Sissy responded immediately. "*I'll be right there.*" She was almost literally right there, bursting through the front door, shaking rain from her jacket. "Ooh, Taylor! This day has been the worst! Can I grab a cup of tea while I shop? You aren't closing up, are you?"

"Sure, yes, tea! Let me get it. And no, we're staying open a little later today..." Taylor raised an cyebrow.

Sissy nodded. "I've got to get going on this graduation present for Dayton. I can't believe we're losing another one of the old gang.

"Cooper has another year after this doesn't he?" Taylor asked.

"Yes, yes, but Dayton skipped a grade in middle school. I could have killed the Reubens for doing that. But then when your sister left school even earlier, I had to just give up, didn't I?"

Taylor poured hot water from the water cooler into another paper cup and grabbed a bag of Tetley.

Despite the ruckus Sissy was making, Una hadn't looked up. In fact, she had sunk into the chair a little more, one arm wrapped around herself, the other holding her cocoa up like she wanted to hide behind it.

Sissy spotted her. "I need a new walking foot for my Husqvarna. You have those somewhere?"

Taylor led her to the wall of notions that was behind the video. "We have all sorts of machine accessories right here.

Sissy froze, a big smile on her face. "Why Una Woods! What are you doing out here?"

Una looked up, wide-eyed with confusion. She shivered again and her little cup of cocoa shook spilling cocoa on her jeans.

"Sorry for startling you. Don't you remember me? I'm Reynette's niece Sissy. We met at the barbecue. Your mom was very welcoming to all of us crazies from Reynette's family."

Una sighed with her whole body and looked relieved. "Hi Mrs..."

"I'm just Sissy to you, okay? Even though Reynette's gone, we're family." Sissy dragged another armchair over and sat down. "I need to get off my feet. It's been a long day. Isn't this show good? I've always loved Laura Quinn's quilt advice. Taylor's isn't bad either."

Taylor wanted to join them, but Una looked fragile and if

Sissy didn't crush her with the weight of her personality, the two of them together might.

"Is your mom here?" Sissy asked. "I don't see her." She made a show of looking all around the store.

"No," Una said. "I came to see Hannah. She said I could if I ever needed anything."

"Hannah from Reynette's shop? Now why would she do that?"

Una shrugged.

"Listen, Hannah's a sweet girl and I'm sure she meant well, but she's not family. What can she do anyway? I'm here. Can I help?"

Una nodded. Then she took a deep breath. "We just came home from three days in Belize, but Mom and Guy want to go back. They want me to stay with Grandma and Grandpa Sauvage this time, but I don't like it there."

"Where do they live?"

"In the hills. All alone in the forest. It's not far from our cabin, but I don't want to stay. It's creepy."

"Guy's parents are creepy?" Sissy leaned forward, like a protective hen.

"No, I like Grandma and Grandpa, but I don't like to be up in the woods, especially at night."

"But why did you want Hannah?"

"She said she'd help me if I ever needed anything. I took the bus here and I want to stay with her."

"You don't want to stay with Hannah. What does she know about kids? She's practically a kid herself. You come home with me, all right?"

Una swallowed.

"I hope I don't scare you. You don't have to come home with me. Why don't you go stay with your brother?"

Una frowned.

"With Jason."

She shook her head a little. "Oh yeah. I forget he's my

brother. He's so old. My friend Freya asked if he was my grandpa."

Taylor did the quick math. In his mid to late 40s...he was too young to be her grandpa, but she could see why kids would wonder.

"Would you rather stay with Jason?" Sissy repeated.

Una scrunched her mouth. "I could stay with Gilly. I like her."

"Why don't you call her?"

It was strategic of Sissy not to make Una call Gracie, especially since sending her to Gilly and Jason was technically sending her to her dad. Nonetheless, Taylor texted Gracie.

"Were your Grandparents expecting you?" Sissy asked.

"Not yet. Mom and Guy are still home." She looked up and then down quickly.

"Do you need Gilly's number? We can probably find it for you. And let me get you more cocoa." She held her hand out for the cup.

Una passed it over.

Sissy carried the cup to Taylor. "Call Cooper and tell him to get here with my Breadyn. Breadyn and Una are about the same age. I suspect Una will be willing to come home with me if there are people her own age around." Her whisper didn't carry. Taylor was impressed.

As directed, she texted Cooper to come to Flour Sax with his little sister.

A few minutes later, while Sissy and Una watched the quilt show and warmed up, Fawn and Breadyn showed up.

"Hey Sissy." Fawn dragged Breadyn over to the chair. "Cooper said you wanted us."

Taylor dropped her head into her hand. Leave it to a teen boy to screw this up.

"Oh good! Yes. Thank you. Hey Breadyn-Butter." Sissy scooped her daughter into a side hug and gave her a kiss. "I needed your opinion on some fabric for Dayton's quilt."

Breadyn's face brightened. Taylor was impressed. The kid must like fabric, which was remarkable in a town like this. Most kids resented it at best.

Sissy led Breadyn to the line of fabric that made Shara of Dutch Hex so angry.

"I don't think Dayton will like that," Breadyn said. "It's for babies."

Fawn stared at Una for a minute. "Una?"

Una looked up, her face transformed by relief. "Fawn!" She jumped and ran to her, giving her a big hug. Una was almost as tall as the soft faced young woman, but made out of a tenth of the material.

"What on Earth are you doing here?" Fawn asked.

Una looked around the room. "This is my sister," she said with pride. "When Dad and Reynette got married, I finally got a sister."

Fawn laughed. "I had to wait longer than you."

"It's going to be okay now," Una said. "I'll stay with her."

"You're welcome to stay with me, of course, but where did you come from?" Fawn kept one arm around Una as she talked.

Una told her the story of the scary house in the woods and her parents shipping her off. This retelling was more dramatic.

Sissy watched from across the room, her face pinched in disappointment.

"You can stay with me tonight, Una, but only if you call your mom and tell her where you are. She is going to be worried sick. That bus ride over the mountains takes forever." Fawn clucked.

"It does, and I got super car sick. I puked, but I didn't tell the bus driver." She looked embarrassed but also laughed.

"The best part about us being sisters," Fawn spoke to Una, "is that I've known her since she was born. She doesn't remember because I didn't see Gracie all that much, but you know, Gracie was one of my best college friends."

"That's right." Taylor was relieved. She liked this much better than her running away to someone who was practically a stranger.

Sissy had wanted to use this surprise visit to advance their investigation, but Taylor's first want was for Una to be safe and comfortable.

"Hey, Una, your dad is at Jason's. After we call your mom, we'll go see him." Fawn pulled a phone out of her coat pocket. "Then we'll get something to eat and go home. I'm staying at the big house right now. I hope that's not as scary as the woods."

"I'm fine, but don't call Mom, please. She'll drive down here and get me, and I'll be in so much trouble."

"That's why you wanted Hannah, huh? Because she wouldn't have made you call your mom?"

Una grinned ruefully. "Hannah is cool. She isn't the kind of person to call a mom, I'm sure of it."

Fawn laughed. "I'll call Gracie and we'll hit the road. Sissy, you got Breadyn? I need to take care of something."

Fawn was a different woman with this child to care for. Strong, confident, warm. Taylor's heart dropped. As far as she knew, Fawn didn't have any kids of her own. Not that a woman needed kids. Who knew if Taylor would ever settle down and have a family of her own? But the difference in Fawn was stark. Fawn had so much untapped potential.

Fawn greeted Gracie on her phone, but she took the call outside.

A few minutes later she came back in.

"Una, you are in serious trouble. You know that, right?" Fawn frowned sadly at the young girl.

Una straightened her back, firming herself, but her face looked young.

"Good thing your mom hates driving over those hills in the rain, my friend. She said you can stay the night with me, but she's coming here tomorrow."

Una nodded, chin up. "Then we have time to figure out how to convince her I can stay with you while they're gone."

Fawn shook her head, laughing. "Good thing Monty likes you. Otherwise he'd drive you home himself."

Una rolled her eyes. "Monty. He's hilarious."

Una grabbed her jacket. "Thanks. If Hannah calls back, tell her never mind."

"Una," Fawn was asking as they left. "Why didn't you just ask your mom if you could stay with me? She knows I'd say yes."

Taylor didn't hear Una's answer. The door swung shut and the ringing bells drowned her out.

Sissy sidled up to Taylor. "I could throttle Cooper. How dare he send Fawn? Now how will we get Una to tell us all about her family life?"

"We could always bring donuts over tomorrow, before Gracie gets there."

Breadyn was right behind her mom. "Donuts sound good to me."

Taylor had forgotten the old adage that "little pitchers have big ears."

"Come on, Breadyn-Butter," Sissy said. "I don't really want fabric. I was just hoping we could drag Una home with us if you were with me."

Breadyn grimaced. "Could you please stop calling me Breadyn-Butter in public?"

CHAPTER TWENTY-ONE

*T*he next morning Sissy had grabbed donuts from the little grocery store on the edge of town and picked Taylor up before she called Roxy to tell her they weren't filming. She sent her best employee a quick text as she grabbed her coat and hopped into Sissy's van.

As they drove the few blocks to the gorgeous old house across town, they came up with their game plan.

"First, we fill her with donuts. Then we just chat a bit, casually about how Thanksgiving was. What she likes or doesn't like about their little vacation place in Belize."

"Is it me, or is that kind of impressive for a surf shop owner?" Taylor stroked the top of the donut box that Sissy had trusted her with.

"Maybe Una knows how they can afford it. Kids often say things they don't realize they aren't supposed to say."

"Think she'd accidentally out her stepfather as a murderer by saying he's in terrible debt and needed an increase in child support from Art?" The sugary aroma of the hot-from-the-fryer donuts was overwhelming. Taylor hoped Una would leave her some.

Sissy pulled the e-brake viciously as they parked. "No,

because I don't think Guy did it. But surely with enough sugar Una will tell us something that we need to know.

"Wait. Real fast. Whatever happened with the samples for the police?"

Sissy scrunched her mouth in extreme displeasure. "Nothing. They didn't care. In fact, they implied I was nuts." She exited the car, slamming the door shut.

Taylor wasn't sure Sissy was in the right mood to cajole a preteen. She dearly hoped Una liked donuts.

Also, Taylor wondered what kid around that age would be up on a random morning at 7:30.

"Sissy..." Taylor nudged her when they got to the door. "Why isn't Una in school?"

"That's a question only she can answer, I think."

Fawn greeted them at the second round of knocks. She had bags under her eyes, but otherwise looked happy and put together. She was snuggled in a perfect winter morning outfit of yoga pants and slouchy wide necked sweatshirt.

Sissy held out the box of donuts. "Didn't want you to have to do all the work for Una." Fawn accepted the box and let them in. "It's hardly any work." They walked to the formal

dining room. As always it was full of unopened boxes, but the table and chairs were out, and Una was sitting at one. She was dressed in jeans and a T, probably the same as last night, and completely enthralled with something on an iPad.

"Hey Una, heads up." Fawn set the box on the table and pushed it across the smooth surface to the kid.

"Umm. Thanks." Una grinned. "Give me five more minutes and I'll be done."

"Una is finishing up her day's schoolwork. She's ahead right now with the online program and could take some time off till January, but her goal is to be all done for the year in May." Fawn beamed.

"Nice." Taylor watched the kid whiz through some screens online and wondered what she could be learning that fast, but at least their question about why she wasn't in school had been answered.

"Why don't you join me in the kitchen for some coffee?" Fawn asked.

They followed her, Sissy with longing glances at the studious Una.

"How did visiting Art go last night?" Taylor asked.

"But first how did the call to Gracie go?" Sissy interrupted.

"Gracie was beyond pissed." Fawn answered Sissy's question first. "And I can't blame her. I tried to frame it as her daughter was safe and sound, etc., but she had been freaking out lookin everywhere for her. Una caught that bus at six forty-five in the morning. It took her almost twelve hours to get here. Gracie hadn't heard from or seen her child in all that time."

"But it's only a forty-five-minute drive…" This bus trip was impossible for Taylor to fathom.

"Sure. Cars don't drive down to Lincoln City first and stop a million times on the way."

"Una must have been terrified." Taylor sipped the coffee Fawn had brought her. It was strong and black. She wanted to ask for cream, but remembered what state the fridge was in.

"Una claims she was only car sick, but I bet that was at least in part because she was scared." Fawn poured herself a cup of coffee too.

"When did Gracie realize she was gone?" Taylor sipped coffee again. She still wished it had cream.

"Una is almost twelve. Guy has always worked the shop and Gracie homeschooled, but Gracie goes in to work more now that Una is older. Sometimes Una goes to the shop to do her school-work, but sometimes she gets to stay home alone. On days she stays home she sometimes goes to the library…" Fawn sounded like she was trying to clear Gracie's name in family court.

"Why didn't Gracie just send Una to school when she decided to go back to work?" Taylor was confused by this sched-ule. An 'almost' twelve-year-old home alone all day seemed like a terrible idea. "Or why go back to work if you still wanted to homeschool? It doesn't make sense."

Fawn narrowed her eyes. "Gracie is brilliant. That's part of why Art fell in love with her. She won't let on, but she really is. She's a better teacher for someone as smart as Una. And right now, Una doesn't need her around every day."

Taylor held her hands up in surrender. She was no genius and she wasn't a parent. What did she know? "So she must have been at the library the day Art had his accident."

"I think so." Fawn agreed.

"But if Una caught the bus that early, how did they not notice?" Sissy demanded. She didn't look like she wanted to give this parent a pass on the neglect. Sissy was the kind of woman who would at least claim to always know where her kids were at all times. And half the other kids in Comfort, Oregon as well.

"I didn't ask for specific details. Gracie just said that she had left for work really early yesterday. They had some kind of construction going on. She kissed Una's forehead at like five and left."

"And then Una caught the bus at six forty-five. What time did they notice she was gone?" Taylor paced the kitchen, hands wrapped around that hot, bitter mug of coffee. She didn't want to drink it, but she didn't want to let go either. She felt safer, holding it.

"Gracie came home at three in the afternoon. It was a super long day and she brought a pizza. When she got there, Una wasn't in, but Gracie figured she was at the library. She messaged her and got no answer.

"Una got to our place at five-thirty," Taylor mused.

"And Gracie was in a complete panic by six when I called her. Three hours of not being able to find your eleven-year old is a lifetime. She had already called the sheriff."

"Three hours of panic…" It was a terrifying idea. Taylor's gut dropped at just the idea of her baby sister disappearing.

"It's a good thing you got in touch," Sissy said. "Gracie should be kissing your feet."

"I'd like to agree, but man, she was weeping for a solid twenty minutes before she was calm enough to want to lock her child in a tower."

"Letting Una stay here would be rewarding her behavior. She can't do that," Sissy spoke sadly.

"Nope. She can't, but she should rethink sending Una to her Grandparents. I've been to Guy's folk's house before. It's isolated as heck. Plus they have a bunch of empty old outbuildings. Fun in the summer, with other kids around. Dreadful in December all alone."

"I can imagine." Taylor shivered. There was something about the primordial rainy forest of the Oregon Coast range mountains. Dark, dripping woods even in the summer.

"And done!" an excited voice called from the dining room. Una joined them with the box of donuts. She set it on the counter next to an empty mug. "Can I have some coffee?"

Fawn laughed. "No. You're eleven."

The long lean eleven-year-old was almost as tall as Taylor. She considered how they used to say coffee would stunt your growth and wondered why Una couldn't have any.

"How about a glass of milk to go with the donuts?" Una's smile was charming—the kind of smile that could twist a step-dad, who wanted to be the "cool parent" and a bio-dad who felt guilt about the divorce, around a little finger.

"Sounds good." Fawn pulled a new half-gallon of milk from the fridge. "Your mom will be here by noon. Have you figured out how you'll apologize? I think bending the knee and begging forgiveness is the only right answer."

Una accepted the glass of milk and sipped it. "I'm trying to figure out how to make her let me stay."

"How can they go to Belize if they're in the middle of a construction project?" Taylor asked. So many pieces of this story didn't fit together.

"Grandpa will supervise," Una said. "He's good at it. He's a retired contractor. They're just finishing the upstairs anyway. They can turn it into rental if they get it right."

"That's a big conversion." From reinforcing support beams to adding plumbing, turning an attic into an apartment wasn't something most people would plan and then skip town.

"They are only going to Belize for a couple of weeks." Una spoke with a mouth full of maple bar.

"Una, why aren't you going with them?" Sissy asked.

Una's face fell a little. "They just need time away together. They get like that sometimes."

"Did you see your dad last night?" Taylor asked.

"Yup. Went over there. You were right," she turned to Fawn. "Gilly said there was no way on earth I could stay with her."

"What about staying with Art and Jason?" Sissy asked.

Una scrunched her face. "It's so boring there. I'd rather stay here or with Hannah."

"You don't even know Hannah." Fawn swatted Una with a towel. "But I'll beg your mom to let you stay with me. It can't hurt."

Someone thundered down the stairs and it echoed through the whole box-filled house. A bathrobe-clad man trotted into the kitchen and kissed Fawn on the cheek. "Morning."

"Hey Monty. Sissy brought donuts." Fawn's voice lost the warmth and strength that it had while talking about Una.

"Cool." He poured himself a cup of coffee before looking around the room. "What are you all doing in here?" He yawned. "I've got to clean this place out today. Go somewhere else." He stood in front of the fridge, next to Fawn. "I've got to get ready for Art to come back."

They all shuffled out of the kitchen.

Taylor winced at the thought of him cleaning the place out. Surely the poison was still there somewhere.

Sissy, Fawn, and Una all sat on the table.

Taylor sat, but her legs were shaking. What was he going to

ruin with his cleaning? What would he destroy? She popped back up and hustled into the kitchen.

Monty was fiddling with a radio.

"I have the morning off." This was true as the store didn't even open till eleven. "Do you need any help?" Her words were too loud, too rushed. But she had to protect evidence, whatever it might be.

He turned. "You're the detective, right?"

"Friend of the family. Just helping out."

He shrugged. "Sure. Why not?" He found a news station on the radio and left it there. "Art won't want my interference in his stuff and Fawn and Hannah are supposed to take care of Reynette's business. But I gotta do something, you know? So, I'm going to clean this mess up. Fawn went to the grocery store, but all the old food has to go. And all those boxes need to be emptied into cupboards."

"Let me do that." Taylor picked up a medium sized cardboard box and set it on the table. The weight of it was good, it felt firm. But as soon as she set it down, she was shaking again. She had to find a way to protect the food. "I can fill a cupboard with the best of them."

"Thanks." He gave her a half smile, pulled out a hefty bag, and opened the fridge.

Every item he dumped in that bag was like a punch in the gut.

When he pulled the jar out of the back, the kombucha, she almost cried out.

"Ooh, is that home brewed?" Taylor asked, her voice rising. "I mean it's kombucha, right?"

"Yeah."

"Don't toss it. I'll take it home. I love that stuff but don't have a..." Taylor scrambled for the word. Brewing your own kombucha was popular in Portland and half her staff at Joann's did it. "Mother." Taylor almost shouted when she thought of it. "I don't have a mother and would love some."

He screwed the lid off, sniffed deeply, and then made a ridiculously dramatic face. "No way.'" He immediately poured it into the sink. "That stuff has gone bad. Real bad. But Fawn has some back at our place. We'll get you a mother."

The brown liquid slowly drained away. Monty rinsed the jar out and left it in the sink.

If only she had let Sissy take it home with her.

Kombucha never goes bad.

Kombucha *never goes bad.*

Taylor's gut was twisting, and shivers of fear raced up and down her spine.

She was standing in the room with a murderer.

She had to be.

If they brewed kombucha at home, then he knew it never went bad. And he only said that to keep her from drinking it.

And he'd only want to keep her from drinking it if he'd poisoned it.

It had to be Monty.

But why Monty?

She was staring, she knew it, so she looked down fast at the ground and rubbed the toe of her sensible shoe on the linoleum. This looked just as guilty. He couldn't know what she was thinking. She had to hide it. She coughed into her fist. He looked up and frowned.

Why Monty?

Money?

The store?

Maybe he didn't want to split half of it all with Art?

Maybe he thought Art would make her shut the store down?

Maybe he was doing something illegal in the store, like selling drugs or prostitution and he didn't need Art sniffing into his business.

But if so, why kill Reynette?

She coughed again, which was stupid. She needed him not to look at her.

But they'd eloped.

He didn't know they were getting married.

He was trying to kill her before…

A million maybes fought for her attention, but how on earth would she ever prove any of them?

How could she convince this tight knit family that the doting son-in-law had killed the beloved Reynette?

His saying kombucha had gone bad would never be enough.

Taylor was breathing shallow and fast now, and her hands that held a white ceramic plate were shaking. "What's your favorite?" The words came out stiff and funny and quiet. "Favorite kind?"

"Of that stuff? I hate it all. Disgusting. Drink a beer for God's sake." He laughed. "Tastes the same, anyway. Hoppy. But it won't get you drunk. And don't tell me it's a miracle cure for what ails you because Reynette still had ulcers after drinking it for a whole year. Every day that woman drank that stuff."

"You say Fawn drank it too?" Taylor's teeth chattered, but she forced herself to pick plates out of the box and stack them in the cupboard.

"Yeah, but I wouldn't let her drink her mom's stuff. I swear it was always contaminated. I never smelled anything like what she always had going. Strong. It's probably what killed her."

Taylor never agreed with anyone more. "Did she, um…add stuff to it? Like…oils, essential oils or anything?"

"I never asked. But maybe that's why it was bad. Ask Fawn. She and her mom were crazy for that stuff."

He knotted his trash bag and hefted it over his shoulder. "I feel like a messed-up Santa." He chuckled and headed out with the garbage.

Taylor stared at the sink where the evidence had been rinsed away.

But the lid was still there, and maybe, just maybe, it had residue on it. She shoved it in her purse and hoped it wouldn't get contaminated. "Hey Sissy, I need to run. You okay?"

"What?" A chair scraped the floor in the other room and Sissy joined her. "What do you mean you have to leave?"

Taylor pointed at her purse. "Emergency text." Then she mouthed "I'll text you."

Sissy shook her head but didn't try to stop Taylor. The morning was less dark, and the clouds seemed to be clearing out. Not that it mattered to her as she hustled across their small town to get to her car so she could drive to the police station in the county seat and beg them to consider the lid as evidence of murder.

CHAPTER TWENTY-TWO

*T*aylor came up with a terrible but effective plan as she drove to McMinnville. It was ridiculously easy to execute.

She entered the sheriff's office shaking with adrenaline. She swallowed a few times, squared her shoulders and approached the desk. The receptionist was not the one she'd met before.

She leaned forward, her face very close to the plexiglass screen and began in her loudest speaking voice. "I need to speak to a detective. A real detective." Taylor used the 'I want to speak to the manager' tone that she had heard many times at work over the last ten years.

"Calm down, how can we help you?" The receptionist gave her a smile she recognized as one she had given upset customers many times.

"Unless you're a detective, you cannot help me. I'm here about a murder. A murder, do you understand?" Taylor spoke even louder, bending so her face could be a little closer to the pass-through hole of the plexiglass.

"I said calm down." The receptionist's smile waned.

"I will not calm down! I refuse to calm down. I need justice. We called and begged you to get murder evidence, but you ignored us, and it got washed up. I have a tiny scrap left and I need an expert to analyze it. I *need* this." Taylor didn't have to fake the crack in her voice. She was every bit as overexcited as she had decided to be. She was scared. She was emotional. She was really freaking out. Faking a freak out to get police attention was a terrible idea and she couldn't believe she'd gone through with it. Big fat tears rolled down her cheeks.

The receptionist picked up the phone and spoke softly into it.

Seconds later an armed deputy was at Taylor's side. "You need to come with me."

A sigh that resembled a shaking sob escaped and Taylor followed him to a room she recognized from when she had begged them to help her with her mother's murder.

Now that she had someone willing to listen to her, her plan was to calm down, but she found herself overwhelmed with memories of losing her mom.

The phone call from home saying there had been an accident.

The moment Belle said their mom had been killed to get custody.

The time she was in this room, telling the sheriff's deputy it had been murder.

The way the murderer attacked her in her own kitchen...

Taylor's breath was suddenly shallow, her head was spinning, and the room was spinning. She gripped the table. She opened her mouth to apologize but it didn't come out.

"Hey, you okay?" The deputy's voice was familiar, but Taylor didn't know him. Had never seen him before. He wasn't an old friend made in a similar circumstance who would give her attention not usually given to the average citizen.

He was a guy who could lock her up for the act she'd just pulled.

"In my purse." Each word was a shallow breath. "A lid. My purse. Can you get it?"

He stared at Taylor, his bushy eyebrows drawn in a straight line over deep black eyes. "You're hyperventilating. Hold your hands over your mouth like this." He cupped his hands and held them over his mouth. "Exhale a long time. Then breathe in."

Taylor followed his directions. It took many breaths, but soon she could focus a little and the air she did inhale seemed to find its proper place. "I think I found evidence of a murder and it is in my purse and I feel like you should get it out for me, so you don't think anything bad." The words and breaths were coming out fast again.

"Do the thing with your hand, or I'll get you a paper bag. I'll get in your purse if you want me to."

Taylor was wearing the purse over her shoulder and let it slide to the floor. Then she put her hands over her mouth and breathed. Slowly.

The death of Reynette was not her problem.

Why had she made it her problem? Why had she let Sissy talk her into this?

How had Taylor found herself in that kitchen watching someone named Monty pour poisoned kombucha down a farm-house sink?

The deputy picked up Taylor's purse, opened it and spilled its contents on the table that stood between them.

"That." Taylor pointed at the lid from the mason jar. "Reynette Woods died a few weeks ago of, of, of…" She shook her head. She couldn't remember the word for the stuff in aspirin. She could barely remember Reynette's name. "Of aspirin overdose. But she didn't even have any, anywhere. She never took it. I think her kombucha was poisoned, but a guy, he poured it out and that…" The breaths…

The deputy cupped his hands over his mouth again.

Taylor mirrored his action.

"Hold tight, okay?" He excused himself and came back very quickly, this time with an evidence bag and a paper lunch sack that Taylor breathed into with relief.

As he put the lid in the evidence bag, he began to ask slow careful questions.

Who had died?

Taylor told him.

Why did Taylor think it was murder?

She repeated the thing about Reynette never taking aspirin.

Where did Taylor get the lid?

She told him that too.

He sat down. "Feeling better?"

Taylor nodded.

"I don't know that there's much we can do about this."

"I know. But we know the cause of death. And I think the murderer was the guy who cleaned out the fridge, her son-in-law."

"Why would he want her dead?" The deputy was being so nice, Taylor couldn't help but relax. She noted his name tag said 'Craig.' She'd only ever known good Craigs in her life.

"It has to be money. She had a lot of businesses and quite a bit of money from what I could tell. So, he'd want the inheritance."

"He would have been smarter to kill her before she got married."

Taylor nodded. "What if that was what he was trying to do? He was poisoning her, but real slow. I think the goal was for her to die before she could go through with the wedding, but she eloped. He didn't have enough time."

"That's pretty dark."

"I know." She slumped in her seat. Murder was the darkest thing in the world.

Another deputy filled the open doorway. He also looked familiar, but at this point, dressed in uniform the way they were, Taylor supposed they all would.

"Taylor...Quinn, right?" the deputy asked.

"Um....yes?" Taylor couldn't help answering like it was a question. Maybe this was the person she had worked with regarding her mom's murder. Maybe it wasn't. Her brain was mush.

"Reg. Reg Franklin. It's been a very long time." He reached out to shake her hand. Taylor let him, but his name wasn't helping her out.

"Craig, this lady helped me solve my first murder like… what…ten years ago?"

Taylor gaped, recognition coming slowly. Ten years ago, she had helped solve a little problem. Not murder… "But that was a dog!"

"Yeah, technically an animal cruelty case, but you and I know it was murder. How is your friend…let me see. Hold on…Isaiah. I'm gifted with names. How has he been?"

"You are. He's okay." Breathing finally felt normal. Reg….Reg! It had been so long, those ten years. She had forgotten this man existed at all. And ten years ago, when she had been a teen freshly instituted at college, the deputy she had worked with had seemed older than Reg did now. Now they seemed about the same age.

"Did he ever get a new dog?"

Taylor hated that she didn't know the answer.

"I hear you helped solve a murder earlier this year too."

Craig stared at the bag with the lid in it. "Are you saying she makes a habit of this?"

"Wait. It's true though." Taylor waved her hand at the bag. "I'm not attention-seeking, I swear."

Reg laughed. "You were attention seeking the first time, but it worked in my favor. Hey, you know what, speaking of favors, I owe you one. Is there something I can help with here?"

Reg sat.

Craig filled him in.

Reg frowned at the bag. "That's not much to go on, and to be honest, if the kombucha had been poisoned with salicylates I doubt there'd be enough in the residue on the lid to prove anything. But don't toss it out. Let me think about this and I'll call you as soon as I have something we can work with, okay?"

Taylor nodded.

"And hey, why didn't you ask for me about your mom? I would have helped you in a heartbeat."

Taylor looked at her hands and shook her head. She could never admit she'd forgotten he existed. "I guess...I just didn't really think of it. I had a lot on my mind."

He gritted his teeth, then nodded. "I can understand. Finding out who killed a friend's dog is a very different thing than what you dealt with when you lost your mom. Craig, did you get her number?"

"She's about to write a statement for me." He pushed a paper and pen across the table. "Are you good to do that?"

Taylor nodded and began to write.

"Add your phone number when you sign it," Reg said. "And I'll call. Probably later tonight."

TAYLOR WENT to the shop and found Roxy and Hannah going through the motions of opening. It wasn't ten yet, they still had an hour, but it felt like it might as well be midnight. Taylor's mind was spinning with ways she could catch the killer. It was desperately searching for tricks to snatch a confession from him so she wouldn't need evidence. She paced the floor, ignoring her employees and their not so subtle looks of confusion.

Eventually Roxy couldn't take it anymore. "Taylor, may we speak privately?"

"What?" Taylor stopped in place, her gaze fixed somewhere in another dimension. "No, not right now. Sorry."

"Please? It's sort of an emergency. Can we go upstairs?" Roxy tugged her sleeve.

"Roxy, I'm just, I'm preoccupied."

Roxy cleared her throat and leaned in to speak more quietly. "Yes, that's what we need to talk about."

"Fine." Taylor led the way upstairs.

Roxy shut the door with a click. "What's the matter?"

"I know who killed Reynette, and my friend Reg who's a deputy is going to help me catch him, but I don't know how."

"Sit down." Roxy opened one of the folding chairs.

"No, I can't. I have to get to the bottom of this."

Roxy opened a second chair and sat. "Please?"

Taylor sat, but the heels of her feet drummed the wood floor.

"Anniversaries are hard. Especially the first year."

"Roxy, I really don't have time for this."

"The holiday season is especially hard as well." Roxy smoothed the wooly cuffs of her sweater with her slim fingers. "You've just had your first Thanksgiving without your mother, and I don't think you've really processed that yet."

"I have. Sort of. I mean, I did a little bit on Thanksgiving Day, with Dave Kirby's daughter."

"That's wonderful." Roxy smiled, but her eyes were sad. "But hon, you've lost more than just your mom."

"It feels like it, right? But I didn't even know Reynette. I never said one word to her, but after these few weeks it really does feel like a loss." Taylor pictured driving to the big house while Monty was throwing out family heirlooms and poking him verbally with taunts about Reynette, getting him to talk about how bad she was.

"Being around Sissy so much must be hard. Her grief rubs off on you, but I'm thinking of Clay. He's been here. He's been bothering you. For the first time since your mom died, you're really facing up to the divorce."

"We weren't married."

"I know. But you lived together for four years. That's basically a marriage, but without the gifts. The pain of the breakup is the same."

"But it's not a divorce. I'm not divorced, I'm just single. That's what the census will say next year."

"Your brain says that's true, but it's not. Wedding ceremonies are very special, but those years living together, that's what marriage is, and yours broke up because your partner wasn't willing to go through a hard time with you."

"This isn't helping me catch a murderer." Taylor stood and began to pace again, her feet moving almost against her will, like they wanted to walk away from what Roxy was saying. Maybe Taylor could take Monty out drinking tonight and, when he was sloshed, he'd admit how much he hated Reynette, or how much he wanted her money. The money was the only logical motive anyway. It's all about the money.

That's why it didn't make sense for Clay not to come to Comfort with her last year. There's so much more money in owning a successful shop than in managing someone else's store. "Why wouldn't he come with me?" Taylor stopped and stared at Roxy. Her face seemed to break into a million pieces, collapsing as angry tears spilled from her eyes. She lifted a hand to smooth her face back into place, but her fingertips found the hot tears. They were there, but they weren't real. They couldn't be. None of this was. Not the half empty apartment, not the sister in college, not the dead mom, not the murder investigation. It had to be one very long exhausting nightmare that was getting closer to its one-year anniversary.

"Christmas, New Years, Valentine's Day, birthdays, yours, your mom's and Clay's will all be really painful for a while. Some for a long while. I know you've been dating and I'm glad you get out, but please don't rush yourself into anything. Let yourself feel your pain and grieve."

"Rushing is the last thing I'm doing." The private rose-petal strewn room upstairs at John Hancock's brother's pub flashed through her mind, the fragment of an embarrassing memory.

"And don't take Clay back."

"He's long gone." She wanted to pace again, to walk, to stop talking, but her feet felt sewn to the floor. To pick them up would rip something, tear something, break something she didn't want broken.

"I saw him this morning at Cuppa Joe's coffee shop."

"It's been weeks. Way longer than he said he'd stay. He must have quit his job."

"Don't let him stay with you. He has family in the city. He can go to them." Roxy's voice was firm and motherly.

"That's what I told him."

Roxy nodded approval. "Taylor, you're a wreck. I don't know what happened or why you couldn't come in this morning, but I thought it might have had something to do with Clay. For most of this year you've worked twelve hours a day six days a week, and a solid six hours on Sunday. And then, he gets here, and suddenly your schedule is erratic."

"It's all been to help Sissy."

"Are you sure? Are you sure it hasn't just been to distract you from the pain of him being around?"

"Oh…" She sat, letting her feet come away from the floor, wanting it to hurt, but it didn't. Because she'd just been standing and now she was sitting and all the boiling raging feelings inside her had nothing to do with the room, or the apartment, or even Reynette Wood's death.

"Take today off. Go home. Rest. Cry. Call a counselor and set up some appointments. Do whatever you need. But…let your heart feel what you're feeling. Please."

"You're right, Roxy." Taylor looked at the seated figure of her petite employee. A woman with her own tragic backstory of loss. Then she bolted down the stairs and rushed home.

It would be much easier to figure out a way to trap Monty if she wasn't distracted by the store.

CHAPTER TWENTY-THREE

*T*aylor didn't go home.

That's not exactly true. She went home. And then she kept going. The college was only a mile down the road. She kept going till she was at the office where her friend Isaiah sat at the front desk immersed in a literary looking magazine.

"Good morning, Taylor." He closed the magazine with care. "How can I help you?"

"Did you ever get another dog?" She was panting from her run, but she took a moment to center herself and slow her breathing down. Now was not the time for another panic attack.

First Isaiah's face was sad, possibly reflecting on a loss he hadn't been thinking about at that moment. Then it lightened. "Yes, indeed. A beautiful golden lab. But she passed away this summer. Old age comes so very quickly for larger breed dogs."

"I'm so sorry." Taylor stood at the desk not sure what to ask next, and yet feeling so strongly that the answers lay here, in this school. The place where she had first stumbled on a crime, and the place where Reynette Woods had been about to launch yet another facet of her varied career.

"Was there something else you needed?"

Taylor scratched her head and thought for a moment longer.

"You wouldn't know if Gilly from the glass department is in, would you?"

"Oh yes, she's here constantly. A very faithful employee." His face wasn't warmed by the thought. Almost like being a faithful employee was the best thing he had to say about her personally.

"She's down in her little outbuilding?"

"Yes."

"Thanks Isaiah. Let's, um, let's do coffee sometime, okay?"

"I'd like that." He opened his magazine again.

Taylor attempted to look like a model alumni as she went back to the space where the artists created sculptures from glass. Glass seemed like such an unforgiving material.

There were several people in the studio, and Gilly was at her desk on the phone. Taylor waited till she hung up, then approached her.

"Yes?" Gilly showed every sign of recognizing Taylor, though she didn't seem glad to see her.

"I'm still trying to figure out just what happened to Reynette. Do you have a minute to talk?"

"Fine, but only for Art's sake."

"I'm glad. See, whoever attacked Art must have killed his wife."

They went outside but stood by the door so Gilly would have a view of her students.

"Has Jason ever met Reynette's son-in-law, Monty?" Taylor asked.

"Once or twice. We really didn't have much opportunity to associate with the family before she died." Gilly faced her studio, but her eyes held a glazed and distant expression.

"What's his general impression?" Taylor needed to get Gilly invested in the conversation, ease her into it.

Gilly didn't move a muscle. "I'd say he wasn't impressed."

"How much time was Monty spending at Art and Reynette's place after they moved in?"

"They hadn't moved in. Not really. They'd come to town,

found the place, delivered their belongings, and then went away. Fawn stayed at their place to run the shop and Monty was here doing repairs."

"But Reynette wasn't there with him?"

"Let me think for a moment. I wasn't really paying much attention to what they were doing. Neither was Jason, to be honest."

"Understandable, I suppose." Taylor did her best to imitate Gilly's cool, distant tones.

"After Art and Reynette arrived with their van of belongings, they immediately went to Catalina for a weekend. Then they came back and did a bit of work for her online shop, I believe." Gilly turned to face Taylor. "Then they went to the coast to spend some time with Gracie and Una. Then back home. It went on like that, back and forth, for about two weeks. The day Reynette died I think they were headed out again. Something about a quilt fair in British Columbia."

"That sounds exhausting."

"Yes, very much, but Reynette was a healthy woman. I know it didn't look like it. Some metabolisms are just like that. But she'd been devoted to eating organic, to her essential oils, and kombucha. She'd swing back by the house and load up on everything before they travelled."

"They let her fly with a jar of kombucha?"

"I think she packed it in her checked luggage, but yes, she was able to take it with her. And the oils."

Taylor didn't care about the oils. She only cared that Reynette refused to travel without her own kombucha. Kombucha Monty had access to all the time Reynette was away. "She had some in the fridge still. I wonder if she had some more brewing somewhere."

"Likely in the summer kitchen. Once while Jason and I were over, she said she was looking forward to making sauerkraut, pickles, kimchee, kombucha, etc. in the summer kitchen."

Taylor had to force herself to keep breathing normally. If

Reynette had already started brewing in the summer kitchen, and Monty had poisoned that...No. He'd have to have poured it all out by now. Right? If he was smart.

Was he smart? "Gilly, you've been a true help. Thank you."

"Hmmm." That was her version of "Don't come back," but Taylor pretended it was a "you're welcome," gave her a bright smile, and left.

When Taylor was half-way home, she stopped and texted Sissy. *"Are you still at Art's?"*

"Yes"

"Get to the summer kitchen, find the kombucha and sneak it to your car."

Sissy responded with a thumbs up.

"First take pics of it in place please. And try not to get fingerprints on it or wipe it off." As she wrote she realized she ought to have just called.

"Why don't I lock the summer kitchen instead?"

"How?"

"I've got Cooper's gym lock in the van."

Taylor sent a thumbs up this time. At some point Reg was going to call her and she was going to have his evidence.

Up the street she could see her driveway and the red rag top parked there. A light mist was falling, but she was protected by her rain jacket. What wasn't protected was her heart, and it was mad.

Maybe Clay was asleep in the car, chilly and hoping she'd come by and invite him in. Maybe he was already in, trying to make Grandpa Ernie fall in love with his boyish charm.

She hustled past the house and the car.

Clay wanted to win this relationship battle he had embarked on.

Taylor wanted to catch a killer.

Supposing Sissy had managed to lock up the summer kitchen, Taylor stood a decent chance of having access to the poisoned kombucha. And that kombucha might have Monty's fingerprints on it.

As she rounded the corner that would take her to the house where the action was, she paused. Was it enough?

Monty had been given access to the house. A case could be made that he helped his mother-in-law with her home-brew. If so, then of course his fingerprints would be on the jars. She needed something that would tie him to the aspirin too. Taylor sent another text to Sissy. *"got it done?"*

Sissy sent another thumbs up.

"Meet me"… Taylor paused the text. Where could they talk? The house was out. Public was a bad idea. Maybe upstairs at Flour Sax?

No. She didn't need Sissy. She needed someone with a different set of skills.

She found Cooper's number and sent him a text. *"Meet me upstairs at Flour Sax as soon as schools out."*

Then she sent a text to Belle. *"how soon can you be at Flour Sax?"*

Belle replied quickly. *"About an hour, why?"*

Taylor checked her watch. *"Can you hack?"*

"Hack what?"

"computers." Taylor stared at her phone willing her to be an expert.

"You want Dayton"

"OK."

Mercifully, Belle didn't ask for an explanation, but did send Dayton's number. Taylor sent the same text she had sent to Cooper, then hustled back to Flour Sax. It was already 2:20, they'd be out of school any minute.

When the teens arrived, Roxy ushered them upstairs. Taylor was beyond anxious and it felt like hours, though her phone said only twenty minutes had passed.

They stood in the doorway, watching her with suspicion.

"Come in. Sit. I'm in desperate need for your help."

"About Reynette?" Cooper asked.

"Yes."

He sat and poked around on his phone a bit. "Aviva's on her way. Don't want to leave her out."

Dayton wandered over to the window and looked out. "She's headed over. I see her."

"Is she any good with computers?" Taylor asked

Dayton shrugged.

"Belle says you could probably help me out with some, um, hacking." Taylor felt like an idiot. She knew that computer hacking was a thing, but she didn't know if that was what kids this age called it.

"Sure, probably." Dayton sat in the other folding chair Taylor had waiting.

"I think I know who killed your great Aunt." Taylor swallowed, nervously. She didn't know what Cooper thought of his cousin-in-law Monty. She didn't want to have to prove her case to him, but she didn't feel like she had time to explain, so she plunged ahead. "I need you to get Monty's computer for me. Whatever means necessary. And I need Dayton to find evidence that he's been ordering aspirin, or whatever else might have salicylates in it, online."

"That shouldn't be too hard." Dayton shrugged and checked the window again.

The door to the apartment opened and Aviva rushed in. "What's up, what's wrong? Have you cleared my name yet?"

"Sit," Dayton ordered.

Cooper stood and offered Aviva his chair. He ran his hand through her ponytail as she sat. So that's what's what with the kids this month. Taylor glanced at Dayton but saw no shifting of emotion. Dayton and Aviva were cousins. If there was a rivalry for Coopers affection, Taylor couldn't tell.

"I'm sure I know who's responsible for Reynette's death, and I'm positive I know how. I just need the evidence. Sissy has some of it under lock and key. The rest has got to be on Monty's computer."

"What computer though?" Cooper asked. "He doesn't run around with a laptop in a messenger bag or anything. And they use an iPad and a Square as a cash register at the thrift store."

"Just get his phone." Dayton sounded unimpressed. "I'll get what you need from it."

"I'm a great pickpocket." Nervous anxiety made Aviva shake in her seat.

"Where is he?" Cooper asked.

Taylor held her breath, then texted Sissy. "*Is Monty around?*"

"*He just got here. He's watching TV with Fawn and Una.*"

"He's at the house. Go together. Do whatever you have to." Taylor wanted to go with them but was afraid he'd think something was up. Especially if he went outside and saw the summer kitchen was locked up. "And hurry."

"Just bring it back here," Dayton said. "I'll be waiting."

Taylor patted Dayton's thin shoulder. "Thanks."

Aviva and Cooper left, him holding the door for her, then grabbing her hand as she passed.

"Don't worry about me," Dayton said. "Go back to business as usual and I'll wait here. We'll get what you need."

"Can I get you anything? A Coke, popcorn, whatever?"

"Why not?" Dayton smiled softly. It was a pretty smile, and it made Taylor wonder why Cooper ever thought he loved anyone else. Maybe the Dayton-Cooper saga was one that would play out over the many years and find them at a wedding long after they had given up hope, like Jason and Gilly. Or maybe Taylor was making too much of this, and like so many kids raised together in a small town, these two probably felt more like siblings than anything else.

Taylor ran downstairs, threw some popcorn in the microwave and grabbed a generic Coke from the mini fridge. She slowed down to breathe while she waited. She had to quit running, quit panicking. She knew her actions were being spurred by the primal fear that comes from traumatic past experiences. She knew that, but she didn't know what to do about it.

Maybe catching this killer would sooth the overfiring amygdala in her brain. But maybe it wouldn't.

When the microwave beeped, Taylor jumped.

She desperately needed to unwind.

"Hey, hey, Tay." The voice from her past hit her like a slap.

"Damn it, Clay. What's your problem?"

"I'm wet, cold, lonely, full of regret, and desperate to be absolved."

Taylor grabbed the popcorn and Coke and went upstairs.

He had the nerve to follow her.

She flung the door open, shoved the snacks at the teenager who was about to make a major dent in the unofficial investigation, then turned to Clay, seething. "I don't know how many ways there are to say this but let me try one more time: Go home. I don't want you here."

"But you need me?" He spoke in an almost baby voice, eyebrows raised slightly, corners of mouth upturned.

Taylor had never wanted to hit anyone more in her life.

Cooper and Aviva rushed in. "Seconds!" Cooper shouted. "It took her literally seconds. We drove there, so that was just like half a minute. Monty and everyone were just hanging out in the back room with the TV, I could hear it, but his coat was on a hook. She grabbed it and we ran again." He was moony over the girl.

It was hardly pickpocketing to take something from a coat on a hanger.

Cooper tossed the phone to Dayton who went straight to work.

Aviva shoved passed Clay who stood a couple of feet in front of the door. She draped herself over Dayton's shoulder, to watch the action;

"Aviva, I need to talk to you." Taylor called the girl over.

Taylor took Aviva to the side of the room with the kitchen

wall. "So, you got the phone, did you notice anything else while you were in there?"

Aviva bit her bottom lip, then looked up and to the left, a sign Taylor had once heard that meant someone was about to lie.

From the other side of the small room, Cooper answered for Aviva. "Nothing. There was nothing to notice. We were too fast. I tell you, she's good."

Aviva blushed and smiled at Cooper.

A hand brushed Taylor's elbow. "Let's talk downstairs." Clay's voice was in her ear. His breath sent uncomfortable shivers down her neck.

"Back off." Taylor stepped away from him.

He stepped with her.

"The lady said back off!" Cooper shoved Clay.

Cooper was a solid twelve years younger than Clay Seldon. And taller. And fitter. But that didn't seem to impress Clay. He squared his shoulders, cocked his elbow and punched Cooper in the face.

"What the—?" Aviva seemed to act without thinking, and kicked Clay in the balls, hard, landing in a defensive pose. "Black belt. Classic Karate."

Clay was doubled over, hands on his crotch, his face red, and his forehead sweaty.

"She said back off," Aviva repeated.

"What the hell, Taylor?"

"I said back off." Taylor shrugged

"Got it," Dayton's exclamation was quiet, clearly not for attention.

Taylor looked over and spotted that soft smile.

"A standing order at Amazon for willow bark extract delivered to the thrift store. Willow bark is the salicylate that makes Aspirin work. He's been getting it weekly for two months."

"About the same time Reynette and Art started to get serious." Taylor's heart was racing again, and her mind spinning—a tornado of murder, Clay's advances, and the sudden outbreak of violence.

"Exactly." Dayton held the phone out. "Too bad it wouldn't be admissible in court."

"I'm working on that." Taylor began to pace and wondered how badly Reg the cop wanted to pay her back for her help in the crime against Isaiah's dog, ten years ago. She couldn't think it was enough to accept illegally acquired evidence.

"We'll have to get him to confess." Aviva remained in her defensive stance, though her hands were lowered.

Cooper was washing his face at the kitchen sink, though it seemed his nose was still bleeding.

"He'll have to do it in front of witnesses." Dayton stood. "And we're a lot of witnesses. Let's go."

Cooper turned off the sink and followed his friend. Aviva was torn, watching them head out the door, but unwilling to leave her post.

"Come, on, we have bigger fish to fry." Taylor sounded like her grandfather.

Clay caught Taylor's eye and gave her the most pathetic puppy dog look she'd ever seen.

She snorted. "You, too. You're not hanging out up here."

He gathered himself up and followed her out.

CHAPTER TWENTY-FOUR

They paused in the parking area behind the shop, sheltered by the dumpsters. Taylor stared at her motley and young crew. "I don't have a plan, but anyone who is underage needs to do their very best to avoid an assault charge, and also avoid making a murderer angry with you. Got it?"

Cooper had his head tilted back to stop the dripping of his nose.

"You'll choke." Taylor tipped his head forward. "Why don't you and Clay, um…" She was going to suggest staying put, but she didn't like that. Too much like inviting Clay to stick around. "Why don't you lead the way, looking for your mom. Tell her about the assault and see what kind of distraction you can create."

"Hey now!" Clay said.

"Suck it up. You punched a kid. Go. We'll be right behind."

Cooper stormed off. If he wasn't thrilled to be cast as tattle-tell, he didn't complain. As he had only just turned seventeen, a small part of him might actually value seeking his mother at this moment. Clay gave Taylor one last appeal, with those big eyes of his, but followed.

"We'll come right behind them." Taylor directed this to Dayton. "We have to turn the conversation to Reynette."

"Easy," Aviva interrupted. "I just jump in and say I kicked Clay because I'm still traumatized by what happened to her right in front of me. And I kind of talk a lot anyway so I can just go off on how I knew Reynette was poisoned and what kind of idiot would do that...if I get some solid burns in, he's bound to confess. A murderer who's proud of his work will have to correct me."

It sounded iffy to Taylor, but at least it would get the conversation started.

"No," Dayton said. "No to the second part. The first part is good though. After that, I think we all rush around Sissy and ask how she's doing, the trauma and all that."

"Does she need a warning in advance?" Aviva asked.

Taylor shook her head. "No, she'll catch on. Listen though, Una is there, and maybe Breadyn. They're just kids. We can't do anything that puts them in danger. I feel rotten enough involving you all."

"I'll take them outside," Dayton said. "I'm the least connected here. Aviva, you get really wild, crying or something. No insults though. I still think that's the wrong tact to take."

"But you're the one who found the evidence." Taylor felt bad leaving Dayton out of the good part.

Dayton tossed Taylor the phone. "I just opened an app he was logged into. It was nothing."

"Take the girls out back." Taylor wanted someone between Monty and the physical evidence in that summer kitchen. But at the same time, she didn't want the kids in danger. "No, take them down the block to the park. I'll call my friend Reg and see if he can't come down and be handy for the confession."

"But how will we get the confession? I still think we badger him."

"We might," Taylor nodded as she spoke, to affirm Aviva, who was definitely going to be a player in their final show down. "But let's read the situation and improv as needed, okay?"

"I'll try my best."

Cooper and Clay had a good head start, so Taylor led the way to Art's house.

She ran the layout of the house through her mind as they walked, ticking off each thing she knew as means of calming her racing thoughts.

The TV room that Cooper had mentioned must have been the back parlor, or the second formal room, or whatever it used to be called.

Fawn must have set the TV up just because Una was with them.

It would be fastest to get to that room via the mudroom off the kitchen, if the door was unlocked and Taylor was letting herself in, but perhaps it was more normal to go the front door, since she wasn't with Sissy or Cooper or anyone who had a family tie.

And with a murderer in the house, she wanted to seem as normal as possible.

Taylor didn't want to rely on these young adults, these people who were really just children, to lead her. Fight or flight was driving her brain, but she had to focus, had to harness the energy and make rational decisions. If she was trying to exorcize the demon fear, she had to grasp hold of her decisions and drive this action.

The house loomed before them, standing on its large piece of land, surrounded by similar historic homes. Quiet. Stern even, with its faded gray exterior and trees, gnarled with time and naked for the winter. "Front door."

The kids followed.

Taylor knocked, then opened it with a friendly but loud, "Hey, Sissy?"

"Back here!" Sissy's voice carried like always.

Taylor pushed the door open with a shaking hand. She held

her breath as she crossed the threshold. Then, looking back to see that Aviva and Dayton were in reach in case she needed to throw herself on them, she pushed herself to the back of the house.

The TV was turned off. Una and Breadyn sat on an old gingham covered bench looking at their phones.

Clay sat in a recliner with a bag of frozen peas on his lap.

Cooper had a matching bag on his nose, but stood in the kitchen doorway, effectively blocking Monty from easy access to the back yard.

Monty and Fawn were on a love seat, his arm over the back of the couch. He looked amused, but she looked tired.

Sissy stood in the middle of it all with her arms crossed, her face red. Taylor knew she'd play along, but she had forgotten Sissy might be legitimately pissed off at Clay for punching Cooper.

Taylor nudged Aviva forward; this was her show now.

Aviva looked at Monty, and all of the color drained from her face.

She wavered—her thin body like a baby tree on a windy day.

Taylor put a hand on Aviva's back.

Aviva slipped under Taylor's touch in one smooth, fluid motion.

Taylor grabbed for her, but was slow, and Aviva landed on the wood floor with a thud that shook the room.

Taylor dropped to the floor and fanned Aviva's pale face.

Dayton stood, mouth agape.

Breadyn laughed.

Monty laughed. "What's wrong with her?"

"Low blood sugar," Sissy snapped. "Stupid kids. What have you been doing? Don't you know she's hypoglycemic? You've had her running around all day, stressing her out, haven't you?" Sissy glared at her son.

"No, I swear."

"And you—" She turned to Clay. "Do you have any idea the kind of stress you put her under making her kick you like that?

She had to quit karate because it was too hard on her physically."

"Hey now, I didn't tell her to kick me."

"Dumb ass." Monty laughed again. "Was this really the guy you were living with?" The scorn in his voice was too much for Taylor. She wanted Aviva to rise up from her faint and kick him in the balls too.

"Watch your language," Sissy snapped. "We have kids in the room."

Monty laughed again.

Fawn patted his knee. "Come on, please?" Her voice had lost the strength and energy she'd had taking care of Una.

Taylor hated Monty for whatever it was he had done to that nice lady, and also for being a murderer.

"We all make mistakes with men, don't we Fawn?" Taylor replied.

Fawn went pale.

"What's that supposed to mean?" Monty leaned forward.

"It just means we fall in love for superficial reasons and stick with them because it seems better than being alone, no matter how much just being anywhere near them ruins us as people."

"Come on Tay," Clay said. "I never ruined you."

"No, and you didn't kill my mother either. We can't all be so lucky." Taylor spoke with her eyes locked on Monty.

Cooper cleared his throat.

Aviva shivered on the floor where she lay, then lifted her head a little. She opened her eyes, shook her head slightly, then lay back down. Taylor could hardly blame her.

"Hey, girls, why don't we um get out of here?" Dayton held out a hand for the two younger girls.

They showed no inclination to leave.

"Taylor, maybe you should sit." Fawn's voice was a whisper.

"Or maybe you should stand. I think the time has come."

Monty laughed. "Fawn's never needed to stand. Not with Reynette around to do everything for her."

"Then she'd better learn, huh? Because her mom's dead and you're going to prison."

"You need to watch your ugly mouth." Monty's face contorted in anger.

"Taylor is a lot of things, but she's far from ugly." This was Clay's attempt to knock the tension out with humor. In his discomfort with all things conflict-like, he had forgotten that creating a scene and driving Monty to a confession was the whole goal.

"Let me get you all a drink." Fawn did stand, one hand angled toward Monty as though asking him to stay seated. "Something to take the edge off."

Taylor realized, as she stood there, that she hadn't invited Reg over. She shivered in fear and reached for a wall. They might get Monty to confess, but then what? If he had a gun, it was over for all of them. "You know what I could use? A nice, cold kombucha. Got any?" The words were shaky and full of fear. Taylor stepped one foot forward in an imitation of Aviva's karate pose to compensate.

Monty smirked.

"Mom has some. Let me just go outside." Fawn walked to the door Cooper was blocking with faltering steps.

"Let her pass, Coop," Taylor said.

"I know what you're doing," Monty said. "And I think you're an idiot."

"I've been called worse."

"Here's the deal," Clay spoke up again. "I may have just been knocked down by a teenage girl, but if I hear you say one more nasty thing about the smartest, most beautiful, caring and good woman who ever walked this Earth, I will come over there and beat the ever living shit out of you."

"Language!" Sissy hollered. "We are not one of those families that screams profanity till the neighbors call the cops."

Taylor took a deep breath.

She closed her eyes and gave herself to the count of three. It could work.

That could work.

She opened her mouth and yelled every profanity she could think of.

All of them.

Dayton, the only other person in the room who was thinking clearly, joined her.

Cooper was a bit slower, but smart enough to open a window. Then he went outside. Taylor hoped he had his phone on him to call the cops about the domestic disturbance.

Taylor stopped for a breath, but that was okay because somewhere in the middle of insulting Monty's mother, and his mother's mother, Monty had joined in the screaming.

It was no confession of murder, but it was loud.

He jumped from his seat and kicked over a stack of cartons. He called Taylor names she hadn't heard since middle school.

He picked up a small glass sculpture and threw it at the wall. It hit with a thud and slid down, not shattering. His fists flexed and he grabbed a small box, throwing it at Sissy.

"Please stop, please stop. Oh, please stop." Tears streamed down Fawn's face.

Guilt gripped Taylor's gut. She hated compounding Fawn's trauma, hated knowing that the end of this terrible scene was going to be even worse for her.

"That's enough." Sissy grabbed Monty by the collar and glared down at his weasely face. She spun him, hooking his arm behind his back. "Aviva isn't the only one who took karate."

"What's your problem?" He twisted in her grip but couldn't manage to free himself.

"My problem is that my best friend is dead. My problem is that I think you killed her. My problem is you have her child under your thumb like a bully and it took Taylor Quinn pointing it out for me to notice." The slightly disgusted way Sissy said

Taylor Quinn made Taylor wonder, yet again, why she had gotten herself tangled up in this mess.

Fortunately, the door opened and Cooper walked in with two uniformed officers of the law. "This is where the domestic disturbance is."

It was now or never. If the deputies started arresting them, they'd never get a confession out of Monty.

Taylor kicked Aviva.

It was her turn.

Aviva sat up slowly, head in her hands. "It hurts so bad," she murmured.

"What's going on?" One of the deputies, a motherly though well-armed woman, knelt by Aviva on the ground.

"I fainted. I, see, I was there when she died, and so when I got here, I just. It was too much for me."

"When who, died sweetie?" the cop asked.

Monty twisted hard, almost knocking Sissy over.

"Hold on there." The other deputy was the boy-Taylor— Taylor Green, who had graduated with her from Comfort High. "Why don't you let me take care of him?" Taylor Green asked Sissy.

"You gonna cuff him?" Sissy asked.

"Depends, what did he do?" Taylor Green had the same kind of affable smile Clay had, but he was huge—a bulky six-one and not to be messed with.

Aviva sat up slowly, bent her knees and wrapped her arms around them for stability. "Reynette Woods died at my restaurant. Well, she got sick there. It's not my restaurant, it's my uncle's, but I was there that day and the ambulance came and Reynette died later and they said it was poisoning, but it wasn't us. I swear we didn't do it. We couldn't have." Aviva rested her head on her knees.

Aviva was actually hurting, and Taylor was the one doing this to her. She was sick with guilt—like find the bathroom and be sick, sick. But she held herself together by force of will. She had gotten them into this, she'd get them out. "Hold on, kiddo, it's okay."

Aviva took a deep breath. "We didn't do it, I swear because this kind of poison, the aspirin kind, it's either a big fast overdose or it builds up slowly over time and she hadn't eaten anything yet. Just like a sip of coffee and there was no way there could have been enough in the coffee. Right? And everyone wants to know who did it, but only one person could have, don't you think? The only person close enough to her to sneak poison in her food over and over and over again would have been…"

"Not my father!" Una shouted. "My father didn't kill her! I swear it forever. He loved her so much. I loved her too! She was like a real sweet aunty or grandma. Please don't arrest my father. He's really sick and he didn't do it and I just…I'm not supposed to know." Una stood, shaking, her tall, thin, young frame looking ready to collapse.

"Oh, honey!" Taylor reached for her, but there were just too many people in the way.

Breadyn put an arm around her friend. "No one thinks your dad did it." Perhaps Breadyn thought she was being quiet, but her voice was like her mom's and carried through the room. "We all know Monty did it, but we're afraid to say it."

Taylor stared at the child.

"Monty couldn't have done it," Aviva said. "He's not smart enough. It had to be someone really smart."

"No, no. You don't have to be that smart." Breadyn was ingenuous. She didn't know this was a trap, she was just being… honest in the way only a kid can be, because they don't know enough to lie about it. "He used to bring these packages with him all the time to the house and I saw him putting this stuff from little brown bottles into that big gross kombucha jar out back, in the shed you have locked. I know it was him."

"Couldn't be." Aviva's weak voice argued. "He's much too stupid."

The motherly well-armed deputy shushed Aviva.

"What do you think you saw, kid?" Monty seethed.

"What were you doing here?" Sissy twisted Monty's arm harder but addressed her daughter.

"Aunty Reynette said I could play here sometimes, in the shed out back, like, playhouse I think, but I'm too old for that. But I did come anyway, because it's a cool old house and I liked to sit out there and read and stuff." She scratched at her knee. "And I saw him putting stuff in her drink, and one time when we were all here, he told me not to drink any. And he did again that time you were here." She looked at me. "Remember he told them not to drink the kombucha because it was bad?"

"I remember," Una said.

"As do I." Fawn sat down. "I remember he said that, but it didn't make sense because it doesn't go bad. I just thought...I thought he didn't really understand."

"You thought I was stupid?" Monty spit the word out.

Fawn nodded.

"I'm the smartest one of you all. How were we going to keep running our business once Art got his fingers in it? We had to be able to keep it going. Ask Hannah."

"Why don't you let go now?" Deputy Taylor Green said to Sissy.

Sissy dropped Monty's arm.

Monty shook his arm and glared at Sissy. "Everyone kept calling Reynette a genius, but only an idiot would think she could make the kind of money she was making by selling used clothes online. You think I'm stupid? Art thought I was stupid, but I showed him. He never even saw me coming. He was an idiot. You're all born idiots. If you wanted the good life, babe, we had to get the business all to ourselves so Hannah and I could do what needed to be done."

"And what was that?" Taylor Green asked.

Monty stared at him and seemed to realize the man was with the law. He clammed up.

"Why don't you come down to the station with us." Taylor

Green took Monty's arm as Sissy had done. He took the other as well and cuffed him. Then he looked around the room. "Quinn, you and that guy." He pointed at Clay. "And Sissy and...you." The last was for Fawn. Why don't you all come down to the station." He looked at Breadyn for a moment. "Sissy, bring your daughter."

CHAPTER TWENTY-FIVE

*C*hristmas break at Oregon State University where Belle went to school, would begin tomorrow. Taylor would have three short but sweet weeks with her baby sister.

Some of their plans were tougher than others.

The summons to appear at the trial for the woman who had murdered their mother was stuck to the fridge with a Flour Sax Quilt Shop magnet. Taylor was due there on December 21.

Sleep wasn't easy to come by as the date approached. At the moment, Taylor sat in the kitchen with her friend Reg.

"It takes time." Reg, it turned out, was full of both concern and clichés. He also had a business card for her. A counselor whose expertise was in grief and trauma. "But it takes a lot longer if you try to go it alone."

Taylor took the card. "Thanks."

"I have a feeling you think you don't have time for it."

Taylor shook her head. "Who has any time?"

"Life doesn't get less busy or less complicated as time passes. You might have noticed."

She had. Here she sat across the table from a man anyone would be willing to call cute. Though they had met just after her high school graduation, while he was a working man, he was still only a couple of years older than her.

He was single and had expressed his interest.

That was why he was at the house.

They were about to go to Portland together to have some dinner and see a band they both loved.

Grandpa Ernie was in the living room with Ellery, who'd spend the night here with him, since they wouldn't be back till well after midnight.

On the fridge next to her summons was her grocery list. Belle's bio family was coming to their house for boxing day to exchange gifts and celebrate a little.

And Clay was upstairs.

Yes.

She knew.

But he didn't have anywhere else to go, and she felt like she owed him one.

Monty Dipple was in prison, being held for the murder of his mother-in-law Reynette Woods and for selling drugs, though the actual charges had something to do with mail fraud as well. A lot of pot went from Oregon to states where it wasn't legal, via the US mail.

Hannah Warner was out on bail for the same charges.

Taylor was out what she had thought was a great new employee, but Clay had stepped in. He knew holidays in a retail environment.

Once Belle got back to claim her bedroom, Clay would move into the apartment above the shop. It wasn't a permanent move. Taylor promised herself that.

She flicked the card between her fingers a few times. She needed to see this counselor.

The real reason Clay was living in the second upstairs bedroom of her house was because Taylor was still struggling with night terrors. She still pushed her dresser in front of her bedroom door a few nights a week.

She was just too scared to live alone.

This was also the reason she still hadn't called Bible Creek Care Home to find a space for Grandpa Ernie. But she knew this, and she acknowledged it, so maybe she didn't need a counselor. Right? She understood herself so what did she need from anyone else?

Taylor had a text from Hudson East on her phone that she hadn't responded to yet. He had seen the news of the arrest three days earlier and wanted her to know he was here for her.

She also had a message from John Hancock, the charming bank manager. He had tickets to the winter show at George Fox University and wanted to know if she was up for it, no strings attached.

No, nothing seemed to get less complicated with time.

The counselor was a good idea.

"Ready?" Reg asked.

"Sure."

They had a long drive up to the city to discuss the way the case had unfolded, or whatever else they wanted to talk about. Part of her longed to do whatever she needed to get him to tell her what was revealed when Monty and Hannah had been interviewed. Had they confessed all? Had they been planning this murder from the beginning? And had they planned on running away together? But though signals all implied that a carefully draped hand on the knee, or a whisper in his ear, or other womanly wiles might soften him up, she refrained.

What she already knew was good enough:

Based on Breadyn Dorney's statement the police were able to collect and test the kombucha from the summer kitchen as well as dig around in Monty's Amazon account. They found the salicylates in the drink and the regular order for willow bark extract.

From Monty's statements, both in their dramatic show down and to the police, they were able to pin the marijuana sales on Hannah and Monty alike.

Fawn was implicated as well. She knew exactly what was

being sold behind her mother's back and who was growing it, but she also explained the threat of physical violence she lived under and was willing to be evidence against her husband in exchange for a plea deal.

The surprise to Taylor was that the surfer with the handy out of country hideaway wasn't a part of the scheme, though it was early and there was still a chance that Guy Sauvage's name would turn up in the pot selling part of the affair. It still seemed impossible that Guy and Gracie could be as rich as they seemed from a little surf shop in a tiny town on a cold ocean.

"You seem a million miles away," Reg said as they drove in the thick, slow traffic of the I-5 corridor.

"Sorry." Taylor dropped her hand on his knee after all, but only because she liked him.

Just like she liked Hudson, and John Hancock.

She had loved Clay once upon a time.

She had a feeling it would be quite a while before she ever felt that way again.

"You're good at this crime thing, you know? Have you ever considered joining the force?"

"Sounds like a great use for that degree in fiber arts I've got."

He laughed. It was a good laugh, solid. "Maybe fiber arts are your past and crime fighting is your future."

"Nah. I've got quilt fabric in my blood. There's no way I'm giving up Flour Sax."

This was her first statement of absolute commitment, and it surprised her. Taylor had still been holding on to the maybe.

Maybe after Grandpa was settled in a home.

Maybe after Belle graduated college.

Maybe, maybe, maybe.

But firm felt great. "Nope, nope. It's Flour Sax for me, all the way." She sat up a little straighter, enjoying this confidence.

"So...you're not moving back to Portland?"

"No way. Comfort is home, and I'm back home for good."

He glanced at her for a sec, with a warm smile. "If you're

going to be around, you won't mind if I call for a little outside advice every now and then, right?"

Taylor laughed. "You don't need crime as an excuse to call." Nope. This guy could call whenever he wanted. As could Hudson, or John Hancock, or whoever. She wasn't going anywhere.

CUPS AND KILLERS: A TAYLOR QUINN QUILT SHOP MYSTERY

Friends keeps saying it's time to send Grandpa Ernie to an old folks home, but Taylor Quinn doesn't agree.

As Grandpa says, "Everyone who moves there dies."

And since the latest death at Bible Creek Care Home was the chaplain who was stabbed in the back during the annual resident tea party, Taylor is beginning to believe her grandpa.

One of the waitstaff thinks she saw the murderer and turns to the only person she knows can help: Taylor Quinn, Comfort, Oregon's favorite amateur detective.

While Taylor isn't sure she's the right one to solve every murder, she's ready to help. After all, Comfort is a small town, and townies take care of each other.

BUY Cups and Killers to cozy up with a great mystery today!

VISIT TESSROTHERY.COM TO learn more about the Taylor Quinn Quilt Shop Mysteries!

FLOUR SAX QUILT SHOP ROW
2015 "Sew the Seasons"

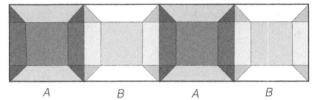

| A | B | A | B |

SEASONS UNSPOOLING

To give your row a sense
of the seasons passing,
make the first A block in dark
winter colors, the first B block
in light spring colors, the second
A block in bright summer colors
and the second B block
in light fall colors.

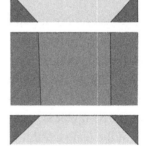

4 half square triangles (2x2 squares)

very dark for A blocks/ medium light for B blocks

4 half square triangles (2x2 squares)

medium light for A blocks/ very light for B blocks

2 5x2 strips

medium dark for blocks A/ light for blocks B

2 5x2 strips

medium light for blocks A/ very light for blocks B

5x5 squares

dark for blocks A/ medium light for blocks B

ABOUT THE AUTHOR

Tess Rothery is an avid quilter, knitter, writer, and publishing teacher. She lives with her cozy little family in Washington state where the rainy days are best spent with a dog by her side, a mug of hot coffee, and something mysterious to read.

Sign up for her newsletter at TessRothery.com so you won't miss the next book in the Taylor Quinn Quilt Shop Mystery Series.

Made in the USA
Coppell, TX
31 October 2020

40535135R10152